THE MUSEUM OF MODERN LOVE

By Heather Rose
The Museum of Modern Love
The River Wife
The Butterfly Man
White Heart

For young readers, aged 8–12, under the
pen name of Angelica Banks
Finding Serendipity
A Week Without Tuesday
Blueberry Pancakes Forever

The MUSEUM of MODERN LOVE

Heather Rose

Algonquin Books of Chapel Hill   2018

Published by
Algonquin Books of Chapel Hill
Post Office Box 2225
Chapel Hill, North Carolina 27515-2225

a division of
Workman Publishing
225 Varick Street
New York, New York 10014

Originally published in 2016 by Allen & Unwin, Sydney, Melbourne, Auckland, London.
Printed in the United States of America.
Published simultaneously in Canada by Thomas Allen & Son Limited.
Design by Sandy Cull, gogoGingko.

"Last Year's Man," words and music by Leonard Cohen. Copyright © 1971 Sony/ATV Music
Publishing LLC and Stranger Music Inc. Copyright Renewed. All Rights Administered by
Sony/ATV Music Publishing LLC, 424 Church Street, Suite 1200, Nashville, TN 37219.
Reprinted by Permission of Hal Leonard LLC.

"Hope There's Someone," written by Anohni. Copyright © 2005 Rebis Music LLC. Used by
permission. All rights reserved. International copyright secured.

This is a work of fiction. While, as in all fiction, the literary perceptions and insights are
based on experience, all names, characters, places, and incidents either are products of the
author's imagination or are used fictitiously.

LIBRARY OF CONGRESS CATALOGING-IN-PUBLICATION DATA

Names: Rose, Heather, [date]–author.
Title: The Museum of Modern Love / Heather Rose.
Description: First edition. | Chapel Hill, North Carolina : Algonquin Books of
    Chapel Hill, 2018. | "Originally published in Australia in 2016 by Allen & Unwin."
Identifiers: LCCN 2018014224 | ISBN 9781616208523 (trade pbk. : alk. paper)
Subjects: LCSH: Abramović, Marina—Exhibitions—Fiction. | Performance art—
    Fiction. | Film composers—Fiction. | Conduct of life—Fiction. | Man-woman
    relationships—Fiction. | New York (N.Y.)—Fiction.
Classification: LCC PR9619.3.R619 M87 2018 | DDC 823/.914—dc23
LC record available at https://lccn.loc.gov/2018014224

10 9 8 7 6 5 4 3 2 1

First Edition

For David &

for Marina

&

all people of art

THERE ARE SEVEN STEPS
IN EVERY PROJECT:

1. AWARENESS

2. RESISTANCE

3. SUBMISSION

4. WORK

5. REFLECTION

6. COURAGE

7. THE GIFT

MARINA ABRAMOVIĆ

THE MUSEUM OF MODERN LOVE

PART ONE

*Life beats down and crushes the soul,
and art reminds you that you have one.*
STELLA ADLER

1

HE WAS NOT MY FIRST musician, Arky Levin. Nor my least successful. Mostly by his age potential is squandered or realized. But this is not a story of potential. It is a story of convergence. Such things are rarer than you might think. Coincidence, I've heard, is God's way of being discreet. But convergence is more than that. It is something that, once set in motion, will have an unknown effect. It is a human condition to admire hindsight. I always thought foresight was so much more useful.

It is the spring of the year 2010 and one of my artists is busy in a gallery in New York City. Not the great Metropolitan, nor the Guggenheim, serene and twisted though she is. No, my artist's gallery is a white box. It's evident that within that box much is alive. And vibrating. But before we get to that, let me set the scene.

There is a river on either side of this great city and the sun rises over one and sets over the other. Where oak, hemlock, and fir once stood besides lakes and streams, avenues now run north–south. Cross streets mostly run east–west. The mountains have been leveled, the lakes have been filled. The buildings create the most familiar skyscape of the modern world.

The pavements convey people and dogs, the subway rumbles, and the yellow cabs honk day and night. As in previous decades, people are coming to terms with the folly of their investments and the ineptitude of their government. Wages are low, as are the waistbands of jeans. Thin is fashionable but fat is normal. Living is expensive, and being ill is the most costly business of all. There is a feeling that a chaos of climate, currency, creed, and cohabitation is looming in the world. On an individual basis, most people still want to look good and smell nice, have friends, be comfortable, make money, feel love, enjoy sex, and not die before their time.

And so we come to Arky Levin. He would like to think he stands apart from the riffraff of humanity, isolated by his fine musical mind. He believed, until recently, that he was anesthetized to commonplace suffering by years of eating well, drinking good wine, watching good movies, having good doctors, being loved by a good woman, having the luck of good genetics, and generally living a benign and blameless life.

It is April 1, but Levin, in his apartment on Washington Square, is oblivious to the date and its humorous connotations. If someone played a practical joke on him this morning, he would be confused—possibly for hours. The morning sun is spilling into the penthouse. Rigby, a gray rug of cat, lies sprawled on her back on the sofa with her paws stretched high above her head. In contrast, Levin is curled forward over a Model B Steinway, his fingers resting silently on the keyboard. He is so still he might be a puppet awaiting the first twitch of the string above. In fact, he is waiting for an idea. That is usually where I come in, but Levin has not been himself for many months. To write music he must hurdle over a morass of broken dreams. Every time he goes to leap, he comes up short.

Levin and I have known each other a very long time, and when he is like this he can be unreachable, so caught on the wheel of memory he forgets he has choices. What is he remembering now? Ah yes, the film dinner from the night before.

He had expected questions. It was why he'd avoided everyone, hadn't attended a function since December. It was still too raw. Too impossible. For the same reason he'd ignored emails, avoided phone calls, and finally unplugged the answering machine in February after one particularly upsetting message.

And then last night, in a living nightmare, three of them had gotten him at one end of the room and harangued him, berated him. Outrageous claims of abandonment and lack of responsibility.

"You don't seem to realize I had no choice in this," he had told them.

"You're her husband. If it was the other way around . . ."

"Her instructions are perfectly clear. This is what she wants. Do I have to send you a copy of the letter?"

"But, Arky, you've abandoned her."

"No, I haven't. If anyone has been abandoned . . ."

"Please tell me you are not suggesting, Arky, that you have the raw deal here?"

"You can't just leave her there."

"Well, what exactly did you have in mind?" he had asked. "That I bring her home?"

"Yes, for God's sake. Yes."

They had all seemed stunned at his reluctance.

"But she doesn't want that."

"Of course she does. You're being unbelievably blind if you think anything else."

He had excused himself, walked the twenty blocks in a rage, aware also that he was weeping and grateful for the handkerchief he never went anywhere without. The bitter taste of helplessness lingered on his tongue. He scratched at the rough patch on his hand that might be cancer. He thought of the night sweats too. Waking drenched at 3 a.m. Having to change his soaked pajamas and slide over to the other, empty side of the bed where the sheets were dry. He wondered if it was his heart. If he died in the apartment it could be days before anybody noticed. Except Rigby, who would possibly settle on his corpse until she realized he was not getting up to feed her. It would be Yolanda, their housekeeper, who would find him. Yolanda had been in their life for years. Ever since they were married. Lydia had thought it as normal to employ a maid as keeping milk in the fridge. She had stayed on, Yolanda, through the move to Washington Square. Levin never liked to be home when Yolanda came. Lydia was good at small talk with shop people and teachers and tradespeople. Levin was not.

Levin thought that if he died, the trees on the deck in their tall glazed pots would almost certainly die too for lack of water. He got up and made another pot of coffee, sliced an onion bagel, and lowered one round into the toaster. Within minutes it was smoking and blackened. With the second half he assumed complete vigilance, spearing the thing with a knife when he sensed it was ready, hoisting it up, and reinserting it in a slightly different position. Why had Lydia bought this particular toaster and not a version that didn't destroy his breakfast every morning? How was it possible they could invent drones to kill a single man somewhere in Pakistan, but not perfect the toaster?

Leaving his plate and cup in the sink, Levin washed his hands and dried them carefully before returning to the piano. On the music ledge was an illustration of a Japanese woman with long blue-black hair and vivid green eyes. He wanted to write something spellbinding for her. A flute would be good, he had decided a few days before. But everything he came up with reminded him of *The Mission*. He felt like a beginner again, searching through old melodies, attempting transitions that didn't work, harmonies that tempted and then became elusive.

And so for the next few hours Levin immersed himself in the process, moving from the Steinway in the living room, where so many of his ideas began, to his studio in the western end of the apartment with its Kurzweil keyboard, Bose speakers, and two iMacs giving him every variation of instrument at his fingertips. He took the ink drawing with him and put it back on the corkboard where storyboard sequences in the same distinctive style were pinned. There were also more illustrations of the same Japanese woman. In one she was bending over a pool of water, her dress the green and shimmer of fish scales. In another she was reaching out to touch the nose of a huge white bear. And in another she was walking with a child along a snow-laden path, red leaves the only touch of color.

Levin switched from flute to violin on the keyboard, hearing the same transitions from C to F to A minor. But violin wasn't right. It was too civilized for forest and river. I suggested the viola, but he dismissed me, thinking it too melancholy. But wasn't melancholy what he was looking for?

I had encouraged him to take this film score because solitude may be a form of contentment when you live in a fairy story, but not when you are an artist in New York who believes your best years are still ahead of you. Artists are stubborn. They have to be. Even when nothing is happening, the only way through is to work and work.

I drew Levin's attention to the day outside. He went to the window and saw sunlight dazzling the fountain in Washington Square. Purple tulips were blooming on the walkways. He looked again at the audio file on his screen. I reminded him of the previous evening, before the women had pinned him against the table. He had sat with his old mentor, Eliot, who had told him of the Tim Burton exhibition at MoMA. It was not the Burton I wanted him to see, but it was a way of getting him there. For all he wasn't listening to my musical suggestions, he was amenable to an interruption.

"You will have to wait," he said to the Japanese woman, but he might as well have been talking to me. In his bedroom he chose a favorite blue Ben Sherman jacket and his dark gray Timberland slip-ons.

He took the E train and got off at Fifth Avenue, crossed the street and walked into the Museum of Modern Art. With the membership Lydia bought them each year, he skipped the lengthy line for tickets. The narrow corridor to the Burton exhibition was jammed with people. Instantly he was surrounded by the warmth of bodies, the gabble of voices. Within a few minutes the illustrations of stitched blue women, their wide-eyed panic and long-limbed emptiness, mingled with the odor and proximity of warm bodies, began to make Levin nauseated. He saw with relief an exit sign. Pushing open the door, he found himself in an empty corridor. He stopped, leaned against the wall, and breathed.

He intended, at that moment, to go downstairs and sit in the sculpture garden to enjoy the sunshine. Then the murmur from the atrium drew him in.

2

IN THE ATRIUM OF MOMA, visitors were observing a woman in a long red dress sitting at a table. It was a blond wood table with blond wood chairs, as if it had come from IKEA. Opposite the woman in the red dress, a younger woman sat wearing a lightweight beige coat. The two women were gazing into each other's eyes.

Levin noticed white tape on the floor marking out a square. People rimmed this square. Some were standing, others were sitting cross-legged, and all of them were watching the two women at its center.

Levin heard a small girl ask, "Mom, is that lady plastic?"

"No, of course she's not," the mother replied in a hushed voice.

"What is she, then?" the girl asked. "Mom? Mom?"

The mother had no answer and her gaze did not leave the spectacle in front of her.

Levin could see the child's point. The woman in the red dress was like plastic. Her skin looked as if the floodlights had bleached her to alabaster.

Suddenly, without any cue, the young woman got up and left the table. The woman in the long dress closed her eyes and bowed her head, but remained seated. After some moments a man sat down in the empty chair. The woman now raised her head and opened her eyes to look directly at him.

The man had a crumpled face with untidy gray hair and a short hooked nose. He looked small opposite the woman. The two of them gazed into each other's eyes. More than gazing, Levin thought. Staring. The woman did not smile. She hardly even blinked. She was entirely still.

The man rearranged his feet and his hands twitched on his lap. But his head and eyes were very still as he looked back at the woman. He sat like that for maybe twenty minutes. Levin found himself absorbed by this spectacle, unwilling to leave. When the man finally left the chair, Levin watched him walk to the back of the atrium and lean his forehead against the wall. Levin wanted to go ask the man what had happened as he sat. How had it felt? But to do so, he realized, would be like asking a stranger what he prayed for.

By then another woman—middle-aged, broad-faced, tortoiseshell glasses—was sitting. Levin moved toward the black lettering on the wall that read: *The Artist Is Present—Marina Abramović.* The text beneath was obscured by the crowd entering and exiting the room.

A professional photographer appeared to be documenting everyone who came and went from the table through a long lens mounted on a tripod. Levin nodded to him and the young man smiled briefly. He wore black pants and a black turtleneck, a three-day growth on his perfect jawline. When you lived in the Village you could be forgiven for thinking that cantilevered cheekbones and sculptured bodies were taking over the world.

The middle-aged woman sitting opposite the person Levin assumed was Marina Abramović had never been beautiful. She left after only a few minutes and the crowd took the opportunity to dissipate. Levin heard comments as people made their way to the stairs.

"Is that all that happens? Does she just sit?"

"Don't you want to see the Picassos?"

"Do you think there's any chance we'll get a table? My feet are killing me."

"Do you really want to try to get to M&M's World today?"

"Have you seen the Tim Burton? It's so crowded."

"Is there a restroom on this floor?"

"What time was she meant to be here?"

Levin returned to the side of the square where he could see both people in profile once more. He sat down on the floor. A young man now sat opposite the woman. He was strikingly handsome with luminous eyes, a wide mouth, and shoulder-length curls, the face of an angel sent to visit dying children. Levin was interested to see if the woman would respond to this aesthetic but she didn't, as far as he could see. She maintained the exact same gaze she'd been giving everyone else. She gazed gently and intently. Her body didn't move. She sat very straight with her hands in her lap. From time to time her eyelids blinked but nothing else.

A hush descended on the atrium. It became evident that the young man was weeping. It wasn't a dramatic gesture. Tears were running down his face while his glistening angel eyes continued to gaze at the woman. After some time, the woman began to weep in the same silent passive way. The weeping went on as if they could both see they must settle for losing something. Levin looked about and realized the atrium had quietly filled again and everyone was staring at the two people.

Levin thought there ought to be music. The woman in red was surrounded by the crowd and she was alone. It was utterly public but intensely private. A woman beside Levin pulled out her handkerchief, wiped her eyes, and blew her nose. Catching his glance, she smiled self-consciously. Along the row of faces watching the performance, Levin saw that many eyes were wet with tears.

Time went by and the man at the table was no longer weeping. He was leaning in toward the woman. Everything between the man and the woman became microscopic. Levin felt that something was lifting right out of the man and creeping away. He didn't know if it was a good thing or a bad thing, but it was unfolding. The woman seemed to become enormous, as if she stretched out and touched the walls and stood as tall as all six floors of the atrium. Levin closed his eyes and breathed. His heart was racing. When he opened them again, she was once more a woman in a red dress, the right size, no longer young but full of virility and elegance. Something about her was as alluring as polished wood or light catching a sleeve of antique silk.

The afternoon passed. Levin didn't want to leave. The man on the chair stayed too and the gaze between him and the woman never wavered. People moved in and out of the room, their mingled voices rising and falling. At 5:15 p.m. an announcement over the loudspeaker informed them the gallery would be closing in fifteen minutes. The suddenness of it made Levin jump. People leaned away from walls and looked about. Men and women rose from the floor, stretching out knees and hips and calves. Gathering their belongings, they smiled at one another, lifting their eyebrows in looks of mutual curiosity. Others shook their heads almost imperceptibly, as if they had quite forgotten where they were and how late was the hour. Soon there was just a smattering of onlookers keen for the last moment.

The man and the woman remained motionless in the center of the room, their gazes still locked. At 5:25 a MoMA official walked across the square and spoke quietly to the man. He bowed his head to the woman and stood up. Some people clapped.

"The gallery is closed," another official said. "Please leave."

Levin stood and stretched. His knees ached and numbness became pain as he walked toward the stairs. The woman was alone at the table, her head bowed. Only the photographer remained. Levin looked for the man with the angel eyes in the emptying lobby, but he had disappeared.

Emerging onto West 53rd, he heard a woman remark to her female companion, "She must be dying for the restroom."

"What day is this?" the friend asked.

"Day twenty-three, I think," the woman replied. "She's got a long way to go."

"I expect she has one of those tubes," the companion offered. "You know, and a bag. I mean, who could wait all day?"

"You mean a catheter?" the first woman asked.

They disappeared into the subway entrance. Levin headed east to Fifth. He walked hearing nothing but the hush of the gallery crowd and the silence between the man and the woman. It was an oboe, he thought. An oboe that played off against a viola.

Once home he wished that Lydia was there. He wanted to tell her about the woman in the red dress and the crowd and the walk home. But the apartment was silent. He sat at the Steinway and, working up and down the keyboard, he teased out the melody he had glimpsed. He played as the city grew black and neon suffused the sky.

I watched him. There is nothing more beautiful than watching an artist at work. They are as waterfalls shot with sunshine.

Night crowds ebbed and flowed across Washington Square below. Levin's shoulders and hands grew weary. At last, in an act of utter tenderness, he let his hand drift across the black sheen of the piano before closing the lid over the keys.

In bed, he turned onto his right side, imagining that at any moment Lydia would slip in beside him and hold him, and darkness would wing them to sleep.

There I left him and went back to MoMA. I stood in the atrium and considered the two empty chairs and the simple table. Every hour of the day an artist falls to earth and we fall beside them. I fell a long time ago with Arky Levin. But I fell before that beside Marina Abramović.

3

JANE MILLER WAS NOT AN artist. She noted Levin's dark pants, white shirt and blue linen jacket, his wavy silver hair and round glasses, the slip-on shoes and manicured hands. She would have liked to speak to him but he seemed lost in thought and she did not want to interrupt. The lunchtime crowd about her was swelling along the boundaries of the square. A boy of maybe sixteen was sitting opposite Marina Abramović. Jane observed the great mop of brown hair above the boy's elfish face. The sweet turned-up nose. The oversized jacket the boy wore and his long feet. He slouched in the chair as if Abramović was a school principal about to lecture him on his behavior. But he did not take his eyes from hers.

Earlier that morning Jane had strolled through the lobby of her hotel and out onto Greenwich Street, catching sight of the silhouette of a man standing high on the edge of a nearby building. She had squinted, puzzled, ready to be alarmed. But then with a thrill she recognized it as one of the Antony Gormley sculptures dotting New York's skyline through spring. On rooftops uptown and down, the city was being visited by watchful beings who appeared to speak not to the mortals moving on the pavements below, but to the space beyond the building. Take one step and fall twenty, thirty, fifty storeys down.

What was the space beyond? Jane wondered. What did the rush of air between life and death taste of? Did crashing to the ground at velocity move you deeper, faster into death than simply dying in your sleep? And if you were under the influence of morphine did you go whole or did you depart in pieces, leaving fragments of yourself floating about in the room? She had wondered a lot about that after Karl's death. How could she ensure all his best parts went with him? Little bits of him seemed to remain. In her head she said his name over and over, as if making up for the fact that she rarely said it aloud anymore. She missed him achingly, gapingly, excruciatingly. Her body hadn't regulated itself to solitude. She'd needed extra blankets all winter. Now that she was in New York, she wanted to talk to him more than ever. She hadn't realized traveling alone could be such a quiet experience. Other than the hellos she exchanged with the staff at reception, or the short conversations with a waiter, there was no one to tell about the things she was seeing for the very first time. *I'm here!* she wanted to tell everyone. *I'm here in New York!*

Perhaps it was really Karl on the tops of all those buildings; not thirty-one sculptures in cast iron and fiberglass, but her husband watching out for her as she moved across the city. Impulsively, she had waved up at the sculpture and smiled.

She had taken the E train from Canal to 53rd, liking how it had become familiar in the past three days. Passing the Dunkin' Donuts store wafting hot baked goods, climbing the stairs. The pavement was patterned with years of discarded gum, which at first she had mistaken for confetti. The noise of traffic, the movement of people, it was all intense. But there was also the surprise of sea air blowing between buildings. This time she wasn't ferrying a bunch of students on an excursion. She wasn't trying to explain anything to Karl. She had only herself to consider, and it had been a long time since life was that. Better still, she had two more weeks in which to do whatever she liked.

Jane considered again the words stenciled on the wall of the atrium that she had now read several times:

The Artist Is Present distorts the line between everyday routine and ceremony. Positioned in the vast atrium within a square of light, the familiar configuration of a table and chairs has been elevated to another domain.

Visitors are encouraged to sit silently across from the artist for a duration of their choosing, becoming participants in the artwork rather than remaining spectators.

Though Abramović is silent, maintaining a nearly sculptural presence with a fixed pose and gaze, the performance is an invitation to engage in and complete a unique situation . . .

She frowned at the line: *distorts the line between everyday routine and ceremony.* Rather like Karl being dead, she thought. His death had distorted the everyday routine. He could not be called to supper or asked to please fix the broken lock on the back door. Yet she wanted so badly to believe he could still hear her, see her. She had spent every day for weeks saying, *Please, God, let him get better . . . please don't let him die.* And then, *Please, God, let him die. Please don't let him suffer anymore.* But God had proved useless other than being the person to whom she could direct such requests.

She had likewise begged the flowers in her garden, the oak tree at the start of the driveway, clouds above the greenhouse. Even the lilies in the Monet print on their bedroom wall. She had looked for any kind of power that might make the everyday something more than a battle of time and biology. But nothing had made a stick of difference. He had died, her Karl, and not pleasantly. Reluctant. Frustrated. Frightened. Desperately wanting there to be more life.

She kept a candle burning by his photograph on the hall table and, every time she left the house or returned, she said, *Hello, Karl.* She continued to set a place for him at dinner. She didn't serve him food—she wasn't mad—but she laid a knife, a fork, a plate, and a water glass and that felt entirely natural. She wasn't ready to let him go and she didn't think he was ready to go either.

Sometimes she was certain Karl was sitting in his chair. So they spent the evening like that, her reading, him just quiet. Sometimes she put a ball game on for him and he seemed to like that too. She was somewhere between everyday routine and ceremony. A ceremony for the letting-go of life. It was called mourning, but it was much more like the farm at night. Smell and sound were heightened, and other senses came into play. Texture, memory, scale. Mourning had its own intense, pungent intimacy.

A woman's voice behind Jane said, "If she was painted, she would be a Renoir."

"Without the dancing or the spring flowers," a man's voice replied.

"God, don't you think she must be bored?" the woman said.

Abramović was now sitting opposite a woman in a soft blue top. They were of an age and they looked into each other with an acute regard.

Then Jane heard the woman say, "Is it art, do you think, what she's doing?"

"How do you define art?" the man asked.

Jane glanced back and saw the man and woman wore matching trench coats. And the woman was possibly his third wife. At least twenty years younger.

"I don't want to argue with you," the woman said.

"But I'm not arguing," he said in a midwestern drawl. "What you have to understand is that art is irrelevant. If everything goes to crap, it won't be art that saves us. Art won't matter one iota. You can't write your way alive, or paint your way out of death. Sitting is not art, no matter how long you do it for."

"Then what is it?" the woman asked as she continued gazing at the two people in the center of the room.

"It's sitting," the man said. "Nothing changes that. Like running or eating."

"Maybe it's meditation," the woman said.

The man chuckled. "Who wants to see a Bosnian meditate?"

"Serbian."

"Still the last people in the world anyone should take advice from."

"But she's an artist."

"Double whammy," the man said. "Serbian artist."

"She's doing something, otherwise all these people, they wouldn't stay."

"Yeah, and Warhol painted tins of soup and sold them for millions. Rothko painted big red squares. And someone put a shark in formaldehyde. You put anything in a frame, call it art, get enough publicity, and people will think it has to be important."

"People are stupid, right?" the woman said.

"Most people," the man conceded.

"Except you?"

"Of course."

"Shall we go?" the woman asked.

"Okay. Let's go."

Jane wanted to follow the couple and argue with the man. She wanted to insist that he was wrong. Instead, she turned to the silver-haired man beside her and said, "I think art saves people all the time."

The man on her left was, of course, Arky Levin. He blinked and looked confused. Jane saw she had disturbed him.

"I know art has saved me on several occasions," she said. Quickly she reprised for him the conversation she had overheard, that she had assumed he too must have overheard. Levin offered her a slightly baffled smile.

"I'm so sorry," Jane said. "I interrupted your thoughts. It just alarmed me."

"Maybe he's right," said Levin. "Maybe what we do isn't that important."

Jane nodded, hearing the "we" and wondering what sort of artist he was. "But you only have to come here to see what pleasure art brings," she said.

"Yes," said Levin. "Excuse me." He got up and went to the bathroom. When he returned, Jane saw him choose a place farther along—no doubt, she thought, so he didn't have to talk to a complete stranger.

Jane watched as a black woman left the table and was replaced by a young Asian man. As time passed he slid sideways in the chair, but his gaze remained unwavering. She wanted to tell him to sit up straight.

Jane wondered how many times she had looked into Karl's eyes for more than a few seconds. In twenty-eight years of married life, what was the sum total of eye contact they had ever made? What might they have seen in each other, if they'd really looked? Her restlessness as she marked another batch of essays, folded another load of towels, did another round of dishes, planned another week of food? Had he been restless too? Might she have seen deep in his eyes some coastline he wanted to visit? Some little house overlooking a beach that required only the barest upkeep and no paddocks or fields? Sometimes he had talked about going big-game fishing in the Gulf, but they'd never been.

Once a year he'd taken five days off and gone hunting deer with old school friends.

In ten years I will be as old as Marina Abramović, Jane thought. In twenty-five years I'll be as old as my mother. Twenty-five years ago I was just twenty-nine. There's still time. Please let there still be time.

Earlier that morning she had pretended that in fact she lived here in New York. She had made the bed and smoothed the quilt. She ran her hand across the carved beading of the headboard and imagined spending Christmas here. She would walk in the snow in Central Park, see the Christmas tree at Rockefeller Center, choose gifts at Barneys. She would be a person with friends who had interesting pasts and they'd invite her to their favorite restaurants.

It was not the time to be making decisions. Everyone told her that. Three different people had given her copies of Joan Didion's *The Year of Magical Thinking* as if that would solve everything. She knew people meant well, but she hadn't been able to read it. She hadn't been able to concentrate on anything. She was too busy listening for Karl.

She imagined him lying on the bed reading the papers at the hotel, fully dressed for the day, his sagging boat shoes, his cable cardigan. He would be happy for her to be off trawling her galleries. He would spend the morning finding a diner where he could have a second breakfast and watch the world go by. He would be sure to find someone to talk to. That was Karl. It was one of the things they'd had in common. The way each of them would come home with conversations they'd had with complete strangers.

4

MUCH TO HIS SURPRISE LEVIN found himself going uptown to MoMA almost every day. He walked across the lower lobby and deposited his raincoat and umbrella at the members' end of the cloakroom, then checked himself through the electronic gates. The lobby was crowded today. Perhaps it was the blustery weather. The place looked like it was full of students.

He stared up at the big blue Tim Burton balloon. At the foot of the stairs, leaning against the white wall, he overheard a girl describe her sister's wedding cake and for a moment he was in Mexico with Lydia on their honeymoon. The sound of mariachis prowling for custom, the scent of the night and the dreadful sky.

His mother had bought him a telescope for his seventh birthday, but the abyss of the night had terrified him even then. He had worried about clinging to the earth by just his feet. It didn't seem enough. And all that matter, spiraling toward him, light and dark racing at him through millennia and so much of it utterly unknown. His father had died when he was four years old after only a few weeks of illness. "A headache, some vomiting, and then he was too sick to move," his mother had told him. The vagueness of this had haunted him all his life—that simply a headache and vomiting could lead to death.

His mother had taken him every year to see the little plaque in the white concrete wall where his father's ashes resided. But his father's spirit, she said, was out there, somewhere, indicating the sky above. There was nothing to be afraid of. Didn't he, like she, feel that other beings lived out there? This couldn't be the only habitable planet in the entire universe. They didn't have to be scary or blue or have strange powers. They wouldn't abduct him. There were forces at work, unseen forces that were there for good. They would look after him. Yes, these same forces had loved his father too, but maybe they had needed him back. Eventually everyone went back. It was nothing to worry about.

Nothing she said had ever reassured him. He was on a planet that had undergone cataclysmic events on a regular basis. Human life was a sort of genetic accident. The world was spinning in an inconceivable infinity, and life, every form of life, was a fragile experiment.

During his teenage years he was prescribed various anti-anxiety medications. None of them numbed or deluded him enough. When he was sixteen, his mother died. What do women who have drunk chamomile tea each night before bed, believed in invisible forces, and played Chopin études before breakfast die of? A falling tree in a storm.

He'd dispersed her ashes on the rose garden at the crematorium. Whatever those gritty remnants of bone and skin were, they were not what he remembered. Her music wasn't there. Her expectations of him. The things she disagreed with. The things they'd argued over.

His aloneness was confirmed. He went to live with his father's parents. It had all happened fast. They came to help him take what he needed before the house was sold. He had packed a bag with his clothes wrapped around every record he'd ever collected, said goodbye to the house, the winding road that led past his school, past the whole-food store where he'd worked stacking organic fruit and vegetables, bagging almonds, weighing granola.

They'd flown into LA and on the trip to Santa Barbara he'd found that the light of the city obliterated the void beyond. He resolved that wherever he ended up, it was going to have to be somewhere big. So when he moved to New York a few years later, and found the stars in their gaping darkness were nowhere to be seen, eclipsed by SoHo apartments and Midtown high-rises, Chinatown neons and flashy Fifth Avenue commercial buildings, by coal-consuming giants in the Financial District, stately old ladies on the park and brown-brick boxes on the East River, he felt he had won. That humanity had won. New York was brighter than the universe bearing down on them. For this alone he had decided that he could live here forever and entirely expected to.

He still wondered often about his health. An ageing body was an unreliable mechanism. What was happening to his cells? He knew everything was meant to renew every seven years, or every thirty days—he couldn't remember which. He never did get sick. He didn't get colds, he didn't get headaches, and he had only once had food poisoning. But he had regular medicals.

"As fit as a buffalo," his doctor liked to say to him. "Blood pressure one ten over seventy, pulse sixty-five, bloods are good. You're doing fine for a man your age, Arky. Just fine."

The buffalo nearly died out, Levin thought.

For a brief moment in the lobby, across the crowd, he caught the gaze of a woman leaning on the wall away from the stairs. She looked vaguely familiar. She held his gaze for a moment, gave him the briefest smile, and he realized she was the woman from a day or two ago. The one who had started talking to him about being saved. Nothing was going to save her from her shirt, he thought. She had the look of a tourist from the Deep South.

The kind who might tend her garden in a large hat. The crowd was swelling toward the stairs and he lost sight of her.

He wasn't sure why he needed to keep returning to the sidelines of this strange performance, but he kept finding himself taking the train, walking in the door, climbing the stairs, taking his place by the white line. The atrium was a magnet, or maybe it was Abramović. Something about this was important, but he couldn't say why.

5

JANE MILLER TRANSFERRED HER GAZE to the rather shabby lawyer she had met on her first day at MoMA. She knew that ever since the Abramović performance began back in March, the lawyer had come to the gallery almost every day at lunchtime to sit and watch. Matthew? Matthew, that's right; that was his name. She made her way over to him.

"Why, you're early today."

"I suddenly had the urge to see how it all starts," Matthew replied, looking a little awkward.

"Well, hold on to your hat," Jane said.

The guard standing on the stairs indicated to the crowd that there was one minute to go. She put a hand on Matthew's arm.

"There's no hurry. Unless you're planning to sit with her."

"No," he said. "Not today."

"Then let's let these eager bunnies hustle and bustle and we can just take our time, find a nice place on the side of the room, and be the observers that we are."

She didn't know why she'd begun to talk like someone from a Tennessee Williams play. She observed in a flash Matthew's dusty brown loafers, the suit that didn't match his shoes or work very well with his shirt. The plain tie and the blue kindness of his eyes. Karl was everywhere.

At 10:30 they watched as fifty, sixty people took flight up the stairs, running, stumbling, pushing each other, fleeing toward art. Racing to join a line to make eye contact with an artist.

No one will ever know I was here, Jane thought. There will be no picture of me taken by the photographer. Nothing recorded of my attendance in a book, no picture of me on the website. In fact, she thought, my whole life, but for the family photographs, will go unrecorded. A grove of olive trees that I've planted. The pullovers I've knitted, which will wear right out within a generation or two. Probably by then people will give up wearing anything that needs handwashing.

The farm was more than a hundred years old when she and Karl had moved back. The front garden had been the careful design of Karl's grandmother, and the vegetables and herbs the work of his mother. Jane had seen little she wanted to change. She had always liked certainty. It was one of the pleasures of being a teacher. There was a great deal of structure to rely on. A calendar, a curriculum, the types of students one had every year. She had a sudden sense, not entirely unpleasant, that uncertainty might have its appeal, going forward. But she put that thought away, like linen in a drawer, and thought instead of Gustav Metzger. Metzger liked to drape cloths over things. He had draped cloth over images of the Holocaust. He might drop a cloth right over Marina Abramović. Leave only her hands visible. Would people still sit in the chair opposite if she were draped in a cloth? Or was it her very real eyes and very real skin, her very real heart beating in her body, that drew them to her? Perhaps she was the most accessible person some of them had ever seen. Jane thought of her students, the snatched conversations in the first weeks as they flitted by her desk, until they knew her to have a sense of humor. Knew she would listen. And then how some of them had talked! What a thing, to be seen, Jane had surmised, early in her teaching career. For a child, it was everything.

She had worried irrationally, once the end was certain, that she had not spent enough time seeing Karl for all he was. She had rubbed his feet, trying to memorize the cloudy right big toenail, the slender middle toes, the way the two smallest toes on each foot curved inward like parentheses. She tried to take in the curve of his ears. She wasn't sure whether, if she'd been shown his hand in a police lineup of ten similar hands, she would have known it above all others. She wanted to think she would, but she couldn't lie to herself.

She had watched all the weight drop off him. Not that the years of peach cobblers and pecan pies, fried chicken and corn bread, bacon and waffles, had contributed much in the way of additional weight. He'd been six foot four and always well built. Still, all of it, in the end, every scrap of weight and muscle and even some of his height, fell away, leaving him a Giacometti man, all lean purpose against the wind of death.

He had told her so many things in the last weeks and days. How farming had run out his patience with God. He said all he really trusted were chemicals and good equipment because seed and weather were a problem marriage unless it was genetically modified, and that felt like a dance with the devil all its own, though he'd felt he had no choice. That's what the devil does, he'd said: gives you no choice. They weren't great thoughts to prepare a man for dying.

He said he wished they'd traveled like she'd wanted to when the children had grown. He wished he'd known this was coming. How they might have sold the farm, if he'd been brave enough, and gone and done those other things they'd planned before his parents had left him to carry on with everything. And he hadn't felt strong enough, not after all those Millers had worked so hard, generation after generation. The farm had survived the war, survived the weevils and, by God, it was going to survive him, that's what he said. It was what his father had said before him. That kind of teaching goes in hard. Still, they might have made other choices. Stayed in New Mexico where they'd met while he was passing through on a road trip that was taking him west to surf the beaches of California.

He wanted to know if he had made her happy. Yes, she had told him, she had been happy. Are you sure? he had asked her, following the lines in the counterpane with his fingers. Yes, she had said. Yes.

He worried a lot about heaven in those last days. He wanted to know, before the morphine shunt took him from her, where she would meet him. If there were steps, he'd be there. He'd be waiting. But where? If there was a cottonwood tree . . . an olive grove?

He said, his face so gaunt that only his eyes were familiar, that he would do what he could for the Falcons next season, if he had any say once he got to wherever he was going.

"What will you miss, Janey?" he asked her. "Tell me what you'll miss."

Your whistle when you come in the door, she had told him. Your shirts on the clothesline. The evenings when we watch fireflies dance under the harvest spotlights. Your heart. The things only you and I remember about the children. The way your skin is always warm. Your coffee mug half-empty on the veranda railing at 7 a.m.

She could have gone on but he was tired and it had been enough. The real answer to his question was everything. She would miss everything. What she didn't know, what she took for granted about living with Karl and being a wife, was far larger than the things she could name.

6

"HELLO THERE," SAID JANE MILLER to Levin. "I'm Jane. We spoke a few days ago."

Her pale brown hair was swept back in a simple knot. Her eyes, rather oversized for her face, were the color of a high blue sky and in some way made up for the lemon shirt and unfashionable jeans. She sat down neatly, like a child on the mat at school, her arms wrapped around her legs.

"I remember," said Levin. "You're a tourist?"

"Does it show so badly?" She laughed.

Levin observed her sensible, almost orthopedic shoes and thought it did.

"I'm from Georgia. And you? Are you from New York?" she asked him.

"I was born in Seattle, then moved to LA. But I've spent most of my life here."

"I came to this on my second day in town," she said, her voice sliding along in an accent that might have come from *Gone with the Wind*. "I know I could be off right now wandering the Metropolitan or spiraling the Guggenheim, or taking pictures from the Empire State or visiting Liberty Island, but this is one of the most curious things I have seen and I can't leave." She laughed. "Have you sat with her yet?"

"No," Levin said.

"But you will?"

Levin shook his head. "I'm not sure I want to."

"No," Jane said. "It doesn't seem my place either."

They both observed a man leave the chair opposite Marina Abramović; another man, slender and stooped in a green tweed jacket, took the chair. He left after only ten minutes and next came a young woman with a tiny pair of shoulders and long lank hair. Her dress was thin, as were her shins, and she appeared to be bowed under the weight of a short and exhausting life. At first the girl sat on the edge of the chair as if she might flee at any moment, but as the minutes passed she shifted back and her gaze became curious and focused. Abramović appeared to have roused herself from some deeper place and was returning the gaze with particular intensity.

Jane said, "Did you see the woman in the wheelchair sitting opposite Abramović yesterday?"

Levin nodded. He had seen that. A black woman. He had wondered how she got in and out of bed.

"It struck me how the person who couldn't leave was able to walk away, and the one who couldn't walk couldn't stay," Jane said. "People were saying how they thought that was the performance—a woman who was able to walk sitting opposite a woman who couldn't. But then when she left, people got confused."

"Ah," said Levin.

"I liked how they just took the chair away and wheeled her in," said Jane. "They didn't make her sit on the chair."

Levin hadn't noticed that.

"They did it for another man who was here too—the one

with the big bushy eyebrows and the slightly crossed eyes? I think he's an art critic. A friend of Marina's."

"How do you know all this?" Levin asked.

"Oh, I've been talking to people. There are quite a few who come regularly. Some of them are here every day. Marina fans. Some of them are studying her. Trying to be performance artists or actors. There are lots of students."

She indicated the young people about the square with their backpacks and scarves.

Behind them someone said, "Is it a staring competition?"

She smiled and Levin gave her a wry grin. He'd heard that comment at least once every day he'd come. Clearly Jane had too.

After a while Jane, her eyes not leaving the young girl sitting opposite Abramović, said quietly, "I do get annoyed that nearly everyone takes photographs although there are signs everywhere saying not to. The guards come and say, 'No photography,' and most people put the camera down, but quite a few, as soon as the guard turns his back, snap another one. It must be the teacher in me."

"What do you teach?" Levin asked, more from politeness than curiosity.

"Art. In middle school."

Ten minutes, twenty minutes, half an hour passed and the gaze between the two women didn't falter. On the shores of the square people shifted slowly, quietly.

Jane said softly, "I am sure that what Abramović is saying to that young girl is *grow, little butterfly, grow!* Don't you think she's definitely growing bigger? But you can see it's quite an effort, because inside she's still all slumped and she doesn't really want to be a butterfly, or whatever it is Abramović is suggesting."

Levin thought that Abramović was definitely encouraging the young woman in some way, using her gaze, and the young woman sat up. Her shoulders straightened. Her head lifted. Her complexion seemed to glow. It was as if the girl knew, wholly, without any artifice, for the first time in her life, that she was beautiful. And strangely, as he looked at her, he saw that she was. He looked about the square and saw people smiling, as if they too could see this transformation taking place right in front of their eyes. Yet when he squinted, there were just two ordinary people sitting on wooden chairs at an ordinary wooden table, gazing into each other's eyes.

"It's mighty curious," Jane murmured. "Do you know very much about her?"

"No, nothing. You?"

"A little. Have you been upstairs to the retrospective?"

"No."

"She's quite a collector. There are receipts, notes, letters. But all the art too. And the re-performers of course. People think we're old-fashioned in the South—but the fuss New York has been making about those nudes . . ." She laughed. "It's good. You must go up and see it."

He nodded.

"It gives this a different context. Her life's been a progression. It's led to this. It's no different from any other artist—Matisse or Kandinsky. But she's used her body. Pain seems to help her get where she wants to go. It's hard to believe she's sixty-three. Can you imagine how painful it must be to sit like that for a whole day, let alone day after day?"

"Where does she want to go?" Levin asked.

"I don't know," Jane said, almost whispering now. "But I do feel touched by something here. It's hard to say just what.

It makes me remember the sheep in the stained-glass windows when I was a child at church. They looked grateful to be sheep."

It was how he had felt when Lydia had agreed to marry him. Grateful. "It's good to hammer in your tent pegs, Levin," his grandfather had said. "Saves a lot of bother in life if you know who you're going to see at the end of every day, who you're going to make a family with. You need that. And she's a wonderful girl."

Levin saw Lydia lying very still and staring out the window. She wasn't reading or listening to music. She simply lay there.

"Not feeling well?" he had asked her.

"No," she had said in a quarter of her voice.

During those episodes when her illness claimed her, Lydia became someone else. Her face lost its animation, the light in her eyes dulled. Everything about her spoke of disappointment. He was certain he disappointed her; that she thought he ought to be a different man when she became ill. But his wasn't a nine-to-five job. If a score was due, it was eighteen-hour days and more. He had to travel too. There were studios and sessions booked, orchestras waiting, producers asking questions, an editor with a new cut.

If Lydia was having one of her episodes, she wanted to sleep alone and so he ended up in the guest bedroom. Then came the long weeks of recuperation that exhausted them both. She resumed her schedule and yet she was so tired each night.

"Do you know," said Jane, after a long silence, "that Brancusi, the sculptor, for thirty years or more, worked almost exclusively with two forms—the circle and the square. Every sculpture was a marriage of the egg and the cube."

"Okay," said Levin.

"They don't look like eggs and cubes," she said. "But when you know, you can see it."

He saw how her students must see her. This bird of a mind leaping from branch to branch.

"And once you know," Jane went on, "you can never not see it. I think Abramović probably has the same thing in mind. She's asking us to look at things differently. Maybe to feel something invisible. Mind you, I guess feelings are invisible. Funny how we don't teach that at school. You know, how things that are unseen are nevertheless real. Anyway, what I'm meaning is that when you see the retrospective you'll realize she's always been exploring either intense movement or utter stillness."

He nodded.

"Are you an artist?" Jane asked.

"Musician."

"Oh, goodness," she said when he told her the names of the films he'd written the scores for. "I wish I could say I'd seen them all, but I'm sorry. This is one of those New York moments. You're someone famous and—well . . ."

"I like to think that the best is yet to come," he said. He had solitude now. He didn't have to think about Tom or Lydia or Alice. He didn't have to think about anyone. He knew there was a tsunami of young composers building behind him, trying to overtake him, but he had years on them, experience, knowledge.

"Well, really, I'm honored," Jane was saying.

He noted her wedding ring. Maybe she was divorced, maybe her husband had found someone else. She didn't seem particularly married. But perhaps he didn't either.

In front of them, the young woman who had transformed into a butterfly had slumped back into her usual self, as if the effort of expansion was all too much. She left the chair, disappeared into the crowd, and reappeared by the two young women to Levin's left.

"You were amazing!" Levin heard one of her friends say. "What was it like?"

"It was scary," the young woman replied. "I was so nervous but she seemed really kind. Oh, God, I feel so silly because I cried."

Her friends embraced her.

Jane leaned toward the girls, her scarf falling on Levin's leg. "You looked like you were growing bigger," she said.

The three young women turned and looked at her and Levin.

"You looked as if you were growing right out of yourself, becoming this strong, courageous thing," Jane continued.

The girl stared at Jane and her eyes filled with tears. "Really?" she said. "That's exactly how it felt."

Her friends nodded, smiling at Jane, clasping the girl.

"I'm amazed you could see that," the girl said to Jane.

"Don't forget it," Jane said. "That's quite a thing. Thank you for sitting."

The girl wiped her eyes with a tissue, laughing at her own emotions. Jane turned back to Levin, gave him a brief level smile, and, without further comment, withdrew her scarf and returned her gaze to Abramović.

1

NOW, I DO NOT WANT YOU to expect a love story. That is not the sort of convergence I had in mind. This is not a story that begins with attraction and ends with a kiss. At least not between Levin and Jane.

It's hard to imagine a man more capable of living in his own cocoon than Levin. Art creates a certain familiarity with loneliness. And possibly with pain. Physical, mental, it doesn't really matter. It's all a catalyst. I don't like to admit that because it's depressing, but in truth pain is the stone that art sharpens itself on time after time.

It would be easier if humans lived longer. The span is brief. It takes so long even to begin to understand the job ahead. Art is really a sort of sport. To master the leap is essential. It is the game of the leap. Practice, practice, practice, then leap. The starting point may be different for each, but the goal is the same. Do something worthwhile before you die.

Every idea is invisible until it isn't. Love is invisible yet we can see it. Attraction is the same. Inspiration is invisible, though it sings and dances through every day.

In case you were wondering, I am one of many. We are here in the unseen, just as Levin's mother suspected. We are here to help. Remember that when you are feeling uncertain.

8

THERE IS ANOTHER PERSON WATCHING Marina Abramović
day after day. She has been dead for three years and she finds
death rather as she found life—an inconvenience. Her name is
Danica Abramović.

"Quite a dress," Danica was telling the man beside her. "What,
she thinks she's a queen? Orthodox red. Blood red. So she remembers. She has not forgotten."

Nobody can see Danica staring down at the square. Nor do
they hear her or smell her. Danica is observing the photographer,
Marco Anelli. She has watched him arrive every morning since the
show began. She has observed the way he unpacks his equipment.

"Pah, no soldier, that one. Italian," she said, lifting her chin.

She remembers a boy who sang her a love song in a sea cave
in Dubrovnik. He had been a Marco too, probably dead now.
Her daughter had this Marco in captivity for seventy-five days.
It was a long time for a handsome boy like that, she thought,
to be staring down his lens at Marina and the years in her face.
Still, for all the MoMA guards observing the crowd, it would be
Marco who would dive in front of her daughter to stop a blade
or bullet. She was sure of that. For that she almost forgave him
the Tom Ford sweater. She knew the lure of beautiful things.

Danica saw leaves burning the ground red and orange. Light running through trees like water. The fabric of her lungs was molten silver and her throat mother-of-pearl. No fear. No flag. No wind. Hadn't that been a Rumi poem? She saw ahead a man on a white horse and all the breath went out of her. He rode between trees, dancing between bullets. Vojo!

"They cannot kill me, Danica," he shouted to her. He was young with the eyes of a tiger, wild and full of light. "If you believe in something, you can never die."

She had nursed him on her lap. She had staunched the blood. She had rolled him over and saw that his back was riddled with bullet holes.

"Fill them with tobacco!" he said, laughing.

Her hands were big and clumsy as she plugged the wounds. She rolled him back and his tiger's eyes were undimmed.

"We are the dragons of the past," he said.

After the war they had married. She had borne him two children, first Marina and then her brother, Velimir. Vojo said to her, his voice raw with *šljivovica*, "The age of heroes is gone. Nobody believes anymore."

"Why would we die for our beliefs when we can live with our doubts?" she asked, because she wanted to see him smile. If only he still smiled at her.

"It was all theater, Dani. You know that. There is nothing left to believe in."

"Believe in me. Believe in our children. We have a daughter and a son and they will need everything we can give them."

He wasn't a hero then. Not President Tito's and not hers. He had given all his fight to the war.

She dreamed of him on his white horse, unmoving in a summer field, holding the white flag. The same way Marina had made it look in that photograph. How had she dared to steal her mother's dream?

"Dani!" Vojo called to her. "I surrender. I do surrender."

"No!" she cried. "Don't surrender. Never surrender! I could not love you . . ."

But it wasn't true. She had gone on loving him long after he'd left her for another woman, a younger, more agreeable, less attractive woman; still she had loved him and longed for him to come home.

She remembered Marina, just a girl, asking, "What if I can't be that brave? As brave as Tata?"

"Are you born of metal or of sand?" she had asked her daughter.

How deep she had buried her own stories of the war. Why did she never tell Marina when she had the chance? Why did Vojo never say to the children, "Look at your *majka*—you know what she did?"

Because she was a woman and men did not talk of women in that way after the war. It was as if it had been only a man's war. And Vojo knew the night sweats and the way she woke up reaching for people who were no longer there, beating at the bedclothes to stop the fire.

In the museum there were so many faces and sometimes when Danica looked at them, every face belonged to her Marina.

"Run because you can," she wished she had told her daughter. "Run because you are born of horses and bullets and fire burning the earth and war lighting up the sky. You are born of the people who won. Never forget that."

At night, while Marina slept, Danica ran as ghosts run, measuring her speed in trees and stars, crossing Central Park and back again.

Some nights she stood and watched her daughter wake to the soft peals of the alarm and drink from a glass beside her bed. Danica saw that Marina was starving for sunshine. For sleep. For days and weeks to rest through the night. But for now there was this hourly ritual to hydrate her body ready for the seven-hour day of sitting and not moving.

Being dead for three years, Danica understood the slow starvation of a life without laughter and friends and conversation.

The alarm sounded again, marking the next hour, and Danica saw Marina wake and untangle herself from her sheets. Danica does not know that Marina has been dreaming of the old apartment in Makedonska Street. She had been hiding in the cake tin until her mother found her and ate her. But Marina had realized that she was a snake, and she slid through her mother's body and wriggled away across the floor. And there was her father, General Vojo Abramović, on a white horse. Marina the snake had cried out, but her voice was made of air.

Danica can hear Marina urinating in the bathroom, then sees her return to bed.

From across the room, Danica says to her, "They cannot kill you. If you believe in something, you will never die."

Marina turns and stares straight at her ghost mother. Danica is thrilled. Marina had sensed her!

"Are you born of metal or of sand?" she asked, but her daughter was laying her head on the pillow and closing her eyes.

Danica stood sentinel by the bed and, later, when Marina took her seat at the table in the center of the atrium, Danica took her place on the balcony. She forgets nothing. She notices everything. When I go by I salute her, though she cannot see me.

Major Danica Rosic Abramović. Onetime director of the Museum of the Revolution, Belgrade, in the former Yugoslavia.

PART TWO

It is easier to resist at the beginning than at the end.

LEONARDO DA VINCI

9

LEVIN STARTED IN SURPRISE AT seeing the next woman walk across the square and take the empty seat. She was over six feet tall with polished ebony skin and long black tightly curled hair. She wore black jeans over impossibly long, slender legs, a red jacket, red nails, bare feet.

"Oh my goodness—she's incredible," Jane said.

"She is." Levin smiled.

"You know her?" Jane asked.

"That is Healayas Breen," he said. "She does *Art Review from New York* on NPR."

He did not add that, until recently, Healayas had been one of his closest friends. Or that he'd played piano in Healayas's band at the Lime Club for the last ten years. Healayas had been Tom's girlfriend. Tom Washington had given Levin his first film score, the one that had started his career as a composer. Eight films over twenty-five years, theirs had been one of the enduring partnerships. And then Tom had found a younger composer.

"I just want to try this guy out," Tom had said. "I think he has something really unique he can bring to this project."

"We'll do another film next year," Tom had said at the last party he and Healayas gave together.

Shortly after that, Healayas moved from Los Angeles back to New York.

"He was a hard dog to keep on the porch—that's how you say it?" Healayas had asked Levin and Lydia in her accented English. How a man could ever cheat on Healayas Breen, how he wouldn't run after her to the ends of the earth, Levin didn't know.

And then Tom died in an avalanche coming home late one day on Ruthie's Run. "Familiarity is dangerous," the coroner said in the Aspen paper. "People think they can beat the conditions."

Levin hadn't quite forgiven Tom for the hole he'd left. Nor for dying in a stupid accident. He didn't know why he had to lose people that way. A falling tree for his mother, an avalanche for Tom. Since New Year, Levin had avoided Healayas as he'd avoided everyone else who would have an opinion on Lydia's situation. Her *situation*. It was inadequate but that's what it was. It wasn't normal. It wasn't remotely normal. But it was their *situation* and everyone had an opinion about it. No one yet had decided that it was okay for him to do what Lydia had instructed. Get on with his life, his music, and forget all about Lydia's *situation*. He was pretty sure where Healayas would stand, but he didn't want it confirmed. He knew she'd left messages. Sent texts. So had other people. At some point early on, he had turned off the message bank on his mobile. When emails came in, he deleted them unread.

When Marina Abramović raised her head and opened her eyes, he saw Healayas smile at her. Abramović's face did not change. But after a few minutes she leaned forward in her chair. Healayas, in mirror image, did the same. This was more than regard. Now it was a conversation that was happening entirely in the eyes.

"How wonderful for an art critic to feel this from the inside," Jane murmured. "It's got the art world jumping, this show. Chrissie Iles from the Whitney has come."

Healayas appeared quite at ease. Her height, the way she moved, you could have imagined her invulnerable. But you would be wrong. On regular occasions it had been Lydia who put her back together again. Lydia who fed her, talked with her—those long, serious, funny conversations women seemed to have together. It was Lydia who had made sure Healayas was invited for dinner, for Thanksgiving, for birthdays.

He wondered if Healayas had seen Lydia. Yes, he felt sure she had. Perhaps only yesterday. Last week. He did not want to think about how Lydia might look. He would not think about that. He got up and stretched his legs.

"I'll be back in a while," he said to Jane, as if she was his companion, not a stranger. He did not want to sit where Healayas could simply turn her head and see him. He moved back through the crowd to the wall, then stood and observed as people milled and dispersed about him. After a while it appeared Healayas would be there for some time, and his legs ached, so he returned to the space beside Jane. She gave him a brief smile of welcome then continued to watch the two women.

Love accounted for so many things. A series of biological and chemical interactions. A bout of responsibility. An invisible wave of normality that had been romanticized and externalized. A form of required connection to ensure procreation. A strategic response to prevent loneliness and maintain social structures.

He had exhibited all the signs of love. He had felt himself love Lydia over and over again. And there had been the bad patches. When she was sick. Unrecognizable. Not the Lydia he knew. The coroner had been right. Familiarity was dangerous.

He had spent most of Christmas Day, after he'd left the hospital, walking. He had walked to Brooklyn and on, and it was only when he realized that he couldn't feel his fingers and toes that he'd finally hailed a cab. He'd slept for almost a day. He didn't know where that fatigue had come from. But he knew that when she got sick, he got very tired. He remembered how the shampoo had run out. The cat was hungry. The milk had been past its use-by date but he'd used it anyway. He'd ignored the flashing messages on the phone. Lydia's friends and colleagues stretched far and wide, people who were useful anytime of the day and night. But not to him.

He remembered that he had been convinced that it was Lydia's electric toothbrush on the sink and he'd hunted high and low for his own and ended up using an airline one. Days later he realized it was actually his own toothbrush, but he only recognized it in relation to Lydia's. He had worried that this was somehow symbolic. Who was he without Lydia? Without her thoughts and clothes and food and friends? Her idea of time and entertainment? Who might he be if he was left to his own patterns and rhythms? How long would it take to become something beyond her? Who would that person be? He hadn't wanted to know. But he had no choice. If there was one thing he knew, it was that days kept coming at you, no matter if you were ready for them or not.

He started sleeping later. Not waking to Lydia's usual 5 a.m. start, he found his body inclining toward 7 a.m., then 8, until he was waking at 8:45 a.m. to the latest snowfall on the deck. He had, until then, been a hot-breakfast man. But he began to put on boots and coat and stroll across the square to Third Rail, where he'd order a long macchiato. Sometimes on the way home he'd pick up an onion bagel and toast it with a second coffee he'd make in the espresso machine around 11 a.m. Sometimes he bought blueberries. He tinkered in his studio, going over old material, considering his next album. He played all his vinyls at whatever hour he liked.

In March he moved Lydia's things into a lower drawer and arranged his bathroom items on the most convenient shelf. He stacked the dishwasher the way he liked and stopped hearing Lydia correcting him. He let Rigby sleep on the bed beside him. He watched James Horner and Hans Zimmer both lose out for Best Soundtrack at the Oscars. None of this made him happier. Quite the opposite. He worried that the world had become a little bit spongy. If he put his finger out and prodded it here or there, it might quiver. If life was unknowable, just a dance of unseen forces, then surely it didn't matter what happened between him and Lydia. But it did. He knew it did. And if this was a dream, then he wanted to know when it would end.

Maybe it would end if he went to see Lydia. But it was the one thing he was not allowed to do. Could not do. And all this he thought of as he gazed at Healayas sitting opposite Marina Abramović.

After almost an hour, Healayas left the chair. Levin rubbed his face, then let his hand linger over his eyes, breathed in that personal moment of privacy. He wanted her to see him, and he did not want her to see him. When he lifted his hand and looked around, she was gone.

10

ON THE THIRD AFTERNOON THEY spent together watching Marina Abramović, Levin offered to buy Jane a drink when the museum closed. She suggested the bar at her hotel.

"If that's not too forward. I'm just keen to sit there and it seems strange to do it on my own. And I do want you to know that I'm married. In fact, I'm a widow but only recently. I felt the need to tell you that."

"Nice hotel," he said, surprised she was staying there. "You know Robert De Niro owns it?"

Jane did, although she hadn't until she'd checked in. She didn't remember how she'd come to book it. Small decisions had become a mystery to her since Karl's death. It was as if there were parts of her brain going about life with no awareness on her part.

They took the subway to Canal and walked the few blocks toward the Hudson. Levin didn't ask any more about her personal circumstances, but now he could see the word *widow* was pinned to her like a conference badge. It might have been easier, he thought, if he had a simple descriptor too. *Turncoat. Coward. Bereaved. Abandoned. Abandoner.* Any explanation for his situation seemed to require a paragraph. A debate. A fugue. Sometimes followed by *silenzio.* Or *crescendo.*

The barman welcomed them, delivered iced water, a dish of warm olives.

"I hardly know what to order." Jane laughed.

The barman suggested a martini and she agreed. Levin ordered a Guinness. Away from the gallery, he felt as if they were devotees, two people drawn together by an obscure obsession. He realized they might have nothing else in common and suddenly felt awkward being with her.

"Do you get to meet the movie stars when you're the composer?" Jane asked.

He shook his head. "I work for the most part on my own. Then, when the director is happy with what he's hearing, I put together a team of musicians. It's very structured. I spend a lot of time consulting with the director, watching edits, but I'm a long way from the actors. When I was younger, I'd spend time on set. There's not much magic to it. It's all craft. Lighting. Acting. Editing. The music is just one of the elements to make the illusion seem real."

"What inspired you—you know, when you were younger?"

"Have you seen *The Good, the Bad and the Ugly*?"

Jane shook her head.

"It's an early Clint Eastwood," Levin said. "Ennio Morricone did the soundtrack. He did *The Mission* too. It's a remarkable score."

"We saw *The Mission*," Jane said. "It was terribly sad."

"Well, you'd know the soundtrack to *The Good, the Bad and the Ugly* too if you heard it."

Jane said, "I have to confess, we're not really filmgoers."

"You and your husband?" Levin asked.

"Yes," said Jane. "Karl only died in September last year, so it seems way too early to stop saying *we*. I'm not very good at this. Can we, you and I, just move on and pretend there's not a death on my shoulder?"

Levin nodded, instantly disliking the image. He felt certain that she was going to ask him if he was married. But she didn't.

She smiled and said, "So how did that happen? That you started making music for movies?"

"A friend of mine . . . a writer/director . . . We met at Julliard." He shrugged. "It often happens that way." There was no point in mentioning Tom. It was the death on his shoulder.

Jane said, "And you must have won awards?"

"There've been a few."

"Oscars?"

"Three nominations but no win. Still, that's nothing compared to Randy Newman. He's been nominated something like seventeen times and only won once."

"Sometimes," said Jane, "I think to be famous must be like having a disease. Everyone who meets you or sits next to you at a dinner, they all know you have it and I'm sure they change how they are because of it."

"That's kind of true," said Levin. "Unless they have more of it than you, and then you change. And in the film business it's very obvious who has more of it."

"Ah," she said. "Well, I shall promise to try to be entirely unimpressed by you."

"That would be terrible," said Levin. She was pretty when she smiled, he decided. He would have liked her to be his art teacher back in middle school.

"Shall we have dinner?" he asked. "We could walk over to the Meatpacking District. Although here is very good."

"Oh yes," she said. "I've eaten here and it's fabulous. I've done the Tribeca Grill too, and the Macao, which was wonderful, but it's hard on your own not to feel terribly conspicuous. And it seems such a shame to get room service when there's so much to see."

"Well, there's a little place that does a very good French fusion . . ."

"Are you sure your wife won't mind?" she asked, indicating the ring he wore. "You having drinks and dinner with a strange woman you met at MoMA?"

"No," said Levin. "She's . . . away. She travels a lot. She'd be pleased to know I . . ." *Wasn't lonely*, he thought. But instead he said, "That I was being hospitable."

"Can I have ten minutes? I'll go upstairs and freshen up. And we won't talk about my husband or your wife. Shall we agree on that?" She added, "And maybe not cotton farming."

"Cotton farming?"

"It's what my husband did, until he died. But that's enough about that."

When she returned she had swapped her jeans and sweater for a black skirt and a pale blue silk shirt. Her sturdy runners were now a pair of unassuming black flats and her hair was up. Suddenly she was an imperfect replica of Lydia, Levin realized, one from a fun mirror that had slightly distorted her, and he felt a wave of doubt sweep through him. What was he doing? He shrugged. She was a tourist. He was being hospitable.

Outside they were met by a fine but persistent drizzle. The doorman offered them umbrellas.

"Shall we walk?" he suggested.

"All right," said Jane, laughing. "It's an adventure. I'm in New York and I refuse to curb my enthusiasm!"

At first they walked in silence, and then she said, "So, Arky, why do you live here, not in LA where the movies are made?"

"Well, there are a lot of movies made here. And it's a good town for music, New York, and a better lifestyle."

"So are you between jobs?"

"No," Levin said. "I'm working on an animation."

"For children?"

"No, adults."

"Is that unusual, an animation for adults?"

"It's a Japanese film. There's more of a tradition . . ."

"But it's not going so well?"

"What makes you say that?"

"Oh, because you've been watching Marina Abramović. Every day for a week, did you say?"

Levin grimaced.

"Is this how you do it? Distraction as a form of gestation?" she asked.

"Well, it's a difficult project. I've never done an animation before."

She nodded. "Still, you've made a lot of music with great success. Does that help? Knowing that?"

"Not really."

They paused at another set of lights. As they waited for the traffic, Jane said, "You know, in the twenties there was an artist called Tamara de Lempicka. She was Polish, but she'd studied in Paris and developed a remarkable style. She became one of the most famous painters in Europe. In a way she was a precursor to the whole fame thing that Warhol exploited. Her technique was very bold, almost photographic. Despite all her early success, by the time she was thirty-five she never produced anything of significance again."

"Is that meant to make me feel better?" Levin said.

"No, and yes. I mean, I think every artist . . . well, I'm only a teacher, so I don't know. But what I've observed," Jane said, biting her lip and looking sideways at him, "is that all art seems to belong to a time. And some of those time frames are quite short. Either because the world moves on, or the artist does—either metaphorically or literally. So when we do see longevity in an artist's output—when they go on for decades producing brilliant art—I think it's more the exception than the rule. What you've achieved already, well, it's incredible. Incredible. And I am sure that whatever this gestation is, while you sit and watch Abramović or whatever, you just have to trust it. Everything is important, that's what I've observed. You have to be alert, and you'll get going again."

Levin felt an incredible urge to tell her about Lydia. Several times of late he had been overwhelmed with the urge to blurt the story out to a complete stranger. Someone on the subway or a waitress serving him coffee. Some days it felt as if it was a weight swinging inside him like a pendulum, and if he didn't tell someone, anyone, it would knock him right over.

This last week he had discovered that if he went out and spent the day at MoMA watching Abramović, he could return to the apartment as if he was some other man, a man returning from a day at the office, a composer who must work a day job and then squeeze his imagination into the silence of the evening. An artist quite alone, quite unobserved. A widower perhaps. Or single. Never married.

He'd been tinkering with new ideas. He'd made an album after he and Tom had made their last film together. His first in almost twenty-five years. That album had garnered mixed responses. One reviewer called it "overly complex." He had worn it as a badge of honor. The next album was referred to as "an acquired taste." Worse had been the review that said, "It can be disturbing watching an artist change vehicles. Tom Washington's onetime composer is now foraging in modern music for truffles of genius. What he's lacking, in this wandering ode to everyone from Joe Hisaishi to Philip Glass, is direction." Levin had been furious, had even thrown something at the wall. His phone. He remembered how Lydia had got the hole replastered.

Still, it had sold, if modestly. Just enough for Levin to think the next album would be the breakthrough. He had started to yearn for a different kind of acknowledgment; not simply for his work, but as revenge. He wanted the Carnegie Hall night. He wanted what Peter Jackson had given Howard Shore when he'd offered him the *Lord of the Rings* films. He wanted to prove to Tom that he'd been a fool to end their partnership. Levin knew he could have done that last film of Tom's. Could have done it better than the young hopeful Tom had employed. Levin was ready for something big. What was the point of turning fifty if you weren't ready to peak?

This is where I watch artists stumble, as they oscillate between force and submission. You would be amazed how rare it is for artists to feel moments of true satisfaction. When they're inside their craft, inside color or movement or sound, words or clay or pictures or dance, when they submit to the art, that is when they know two things—the void that is life and the pull that is death. The grand and the hollow. The best reflects that. To be such harbingers of truth is not without its cost. It's no easy task to balance a sense of irrelevance with the longing for glory, the abyss with the applause. Artists run their fingers over the fabric of eternity.

11

I HAVE STOOD BESIDE ARTISTS a very long time. I was there at the rape trial of Artemisia Gentileschi. I was there as she drove the painted blade through the neck of Holofernes. I stood beside her as she wrote, "I shall show you what woman is capable of. You will find Caesar's courage in the soul of a woman." Imagine that, five hundred years ago!

I was there for two decades as Dorothea Therbusch gave her life to her children until at last, when her vile mother-in-law died, she resumed the career she was born to. It was I who visited Camille Claudel in the insane asylum, her brilliant hands idle. I watched her die slowly for thirty years, while I could persuade not a single man, not her lover Rodin, nor her brother, to offer her freedom or clay. I stood beside Meret Oppenheim when she covered the spoon and cup with fur and Max Ernst proclaimed that she, at the age of twenty-three, had outstripped them—Duchamp, Breton, and all the Surrealists.

I have seen young women gifted beyond measure—Sofonisba Anguissola at just twenty years of age, Catharina van Hemessen too, Clara Peeters at just thirteen. All of them born before the year 1600. Seek out their paintings if you do not know them. Each had a father who understood their promise and celebrated their value. Each had a mother with talent too, but a life of housekeeping, wifery, and child rearing expected of her. So many women were neither offered nor able to acquire paint or palette, canvas, ink, tuition, paper, time. And so we have the great imbalance.

Marina Abramović has been learning to reject expectations her whole life. It is day thirty-one on the road she has titled *The Artist Is Present*. She has been hallucinating since day one—sometimes for moments and sometimes for an hour or more. It doesn't look painful, this business of sitting, but believe me it is.

It's sure to get worse before it gets better, the hallucinating, the pain. The body is never forgiving in such circumstances. It does not like to be ignored. There are systems at work that rue the dictatorship of the brain. Endocrine, nervous, circulatory. Lymphatic. Exocrine. Digestive. Urinary. Respiratory. Muscular.

We see Marina's stillness, her gaze, her focus, and inside a war has begun. All those systems trying to function while she remains motionless. And her mind? Well, for all the illusion of calm, it is no less busy than everything else. She is full and she is empty because that is the paradox too. She is swimming in sensations, thoughts, memories, and awareness like everyone else, but while this happens she looks into the eyes and hearts of strangers and finds a point of calm. It is her metier to dance on the edge of madness, to vault over pain into the solace of disintegration.

12

AT THE RESTAURANT JANE AND Levin commented on the rustic decor, the luck of getting a table, the menu. They both ordered foie gras to start. Behind them a table of twelve women continuously erupted in laughter, making the opportunities for conversation strained.

"What is it about Abramović's work that fascinates you?" Jane asked.

"I don't know," Levin said. "She's still a new discovery."

"Upstairs in the retrospective," Jane said, "there's a table laid with all sorts of things—like a rose, a bottle of olive oil, a chain, a whip, a bottle of wine, a knife, a hacksaw. A gun and a single bullet. It was a show she did back in 1974. In Italy. She invited the audience to do anything they wanted to her using anything on the table."

"And what happened?"

"Well, they undressed her, they cut her, they decorated her, wrote words on her body. They carried her about, chained her to the table. Finally, someone loaded the gun with the bullet and held it against her head and tried to get Marina to pull the trigger."

"What did she do?"

"She remained entirely passive. She could have died. Some people in the audience stopped the others from harming her."

"That's horrible."

"When you see the photos, she's weeping. But she didn't run away. She stayed passive for the whole six hours. I can't help but think it must be how she survived her childhood."

"Was it bad?"

"During the Second World War, her mother and father saved each other's lives. You'd think with such a romantic beginning it might have worked out. But it didn't. They hated each other. Her mother ran the home like a military camp."

The meal went on, washing on the shallows of history, lapping against memory, dipping into the puddles of parenting and career, but avoiding the darker waters of marriage and grief. They stood often on the knoll of Marina Abramović and surveyed the view. The percussion of female laughter from the back table continued, jarring Levin's thoughts and clattering in his eardrums. He and Jane were two observers, gazing across the divide of the table, making eye contact and then slipping away. The wine was good and the food was good, and yet it all fell short. It was an elevator music night, Levin thought as he helped Jane into her coat and they stepped out onto the cobblestones. It had ultimately been unimportant. An attempt, he thought, at normality.

The rain had stopped and he walked her back to the Greenwich Hotel. The evening had the balmy texture of early summer. They stood on the pavement for a moment before she reached out and shook hands with him. He thought to kiss her cheek but the moment passed. She smiled and thanked him again, and the doorman opened the door.

Levin walked the few blocks across to Washington Square. Night had softened the streets and darkened the doorways. Above him the sky was umber-glazed and all about him were streetlights, headlights, taillights, lit windows, neon and illuminated signs. The stars were defeated. A ruckus of electricity and engineering had beaten them back. By the fountain people lingered, laughing and talking. Children ran about despite the lateness of the hour. Two men played guitars and sang "Hey Jude." Several bystanders joined in. The pavement smelled of steam, rubber, and oil. Levin continued on across the street.

He wondered if Jane would have had sex with him, if he had suggested it. It had been a long time since he had suggested it to anyone but Lydia. The idea of getting naked with a stranger was somewhat alarming. But he'd been giving it some thought of late. He thought of Healayas and how he had always wanted to have sex with her. He imagined every man who met her thought the same thing. He would never ask her, but that didn't stop him thinking of it. Tom had been dead wrong not to follow her to New York.

He wasn't sure Jane would be good in bed. She had very plain hands. He wondered what Jane would have said if he had told her his wife was Lydia Fiorentino, the architect. Perhaps Jane had stood in one of Lydia's buildings. Perhaps she had read about Lydia in a magazine.

My wife is in a nursing home, he imagined saying. *She's been in a coma but now she's not. She'll never walk again. Or talk again. She was the most energetic person when she was well. We knew it was coming. It's genetic. No, I don't see her regularly. I don't see her at all. She wants it that way. She took out a court order. We were happily married. I think so. Our daughter, Alice, is twenty-two. I never got to know her when it was the right time. When was the right time? When she was little? When she was a teenager? It always seemed difficult to know what to talk about with her. She talked to Lydia and then Lydia talked to me. That's how it worked. I didn't like the music she liked. She went through a whole heavy metal phase I didn't understand. I was busy. I worked. Wasn't that the right thing to do? Didn't that count for something as a father? No, I don't think about challenging the court order. Do I want to see Lydia? Yes and no. Do I miss Alice? I think of her.*

He knew if he was a potential client calling Lydia's practice, the receptionist would tell him Ms. Fiorentino was on extended leave. She would not tell him that Ms. Fiorentino was currently residing at an address in the Hamptons. She would tell him that Lydia's business partner, Selma Hernandez, was taking care of everything. Was he able to make an appointment for when Ms. Fiorentino returned? No, the receptionist would reply, not at this time. Because—although she would not say this—Ms. Fiorentino's absence would be permanent.

13

ALICE HAD CALLED TWO DAYS before Christmas. "Dad, I think you'd better come to the hospital. Mom's not so good."

He'd been watching snow falling over Washington Square and feeling as if life was suddenly new and full of possibility with the new year almost upon them, a new album taking shape in his head, a new apartment. He needed Lydia to reassure him this was really theirs, all three thousand square feet of it. The movers had finally left. He'd been trying to get the television sorted so he could watch the game at 8:30. It was a critical match if the Giants were to get into the playoffs.

Lydia had called from the airport when her London flight arrived. She had told him she was going to the hospital. These sudden plunges into ill health were becoming more frequent.

He checked his watch. He weighed up how long it would take him to finish programming the channels and whether he could steal another fifteen minutes to get the game to record. The Christmas traffic would be worse with the snow. He gave it up and went to wash his hands, and find his scarf and hat. He'd just have to be back by 8:10 to finish the setup. It wasn't enough time.

At the hospital Lydia was wired to monitors and drips. Alice pulled back the sheet to show him a bruise on Lydia's hip that went all the way to her ankle. Levin hated the bruises.

"When did that happen?"

Lydia shrugged wanly. "Yesterday, I think."

He tried to remember the last time they had made love. Perhaps the morning before her trip. He wanted to remember. He wanted to make love to her in their new home. To have her back with him, not here where she didn't belong.

"So you're in overnight?"

"Yes," Lydia said. "For a few days probably. They think the creatinine percentage is too low. Elisabetta will be back soon with the results."

She had always had a medical power of attorney in place. For years, he'd been the one she named in case anything happened. But when Alice turned twenty-one, Lydia had changed the paperwork. He'd been hurt by that. They'd had a fight. In the end he'd let it go. It was what Lydia wanted.

"The apartment looks great," he said. "You'll be home for Christmas, won't you?"

"I'm planning on it. Did the unpackers get it all done today?"

He nodded. "I'm wrecked. You were lucky to miss it."

"I'm sorry. I know it was bad timing. But it went well in London." She took his hand and squeezed it. "I hate not being there for our first night together."

He traced the veins that ran across the top of her hand with his thumb. "I bought a bottle of Veuve. But we can have it another night."

"Don't you have a big game?" she asked.

"Eight thirty," he said.

"You go. It's going to be awful getting back downtown in this. And I know it's depressing being in here with me."

"Mom . . ." said Alice.

"Are you sure?" Levin said.

"Of course."

"Did you bring Mom pajamas or anything?" Alice asked.

"Do you need them?" Levin said, irked by Alice's tone. "Don't you have your suitcase?"

"Yes, yes, I have it."

"Fresh pajamas would have been nice," Alice said, pulling a face and not meeting his gaze.

"Give me a break, Alice," he said. "I spent the day moving house. I'm not perfect." Looking at the hospital clock, he saw the numbers click over to 7:31.

"Well," said Lydia.

He had bent to kiss her, then kissed Alice on the top of the head. "Goodbye, my girls. I love you both." And to Lydia, from the doorway, he said, "Get well."

She'd needed plasma exchange and then dialysis. Christmas Day came and he spent lunchtime at the hospital. She was still in the critical care unit so the dozen red roses were put in a vase on the reception desk. She looked gray and feverish beneath the covers and wasn't up to the movie he'd downloaded for them to watch.

She said, "There's so much I love about you."

"Meaning there's a lot you don't?"

"Please, that wasn't—"

'No, really. What did I do wrong this time?"

"It's Christmas Day and I'm eating hospital food. I'm imagining those turkey pies from the deli."

"I didn't think you'd be hungry."

"It's more the idea of it. I know bringing me food means another thing for you to do. Stop at the deli. Make decisions. But it's Christmas Day."

"I bought you roses."

"I know. Thank you. But I'm not allowed flowers in here. You know that. I know you can't understand how sad it makes me feel when you're so . . . I keep thinking that if this is the last time, it doesn't matter that you don't understand. We've been happy. We've done our best. Both of us. But if I get well again . . . there's so much I still want to do . . ."

He held her hand and she looked sadder than he'd ever seen her look.

"With me? Do you still want to do them with me?"

She said, "Arky, sweetheart, it isn't going well. I can feel it. I've come back from this thing so many times. I'm not sure I'm going to pull it off this time."

"You're tired. It's depressing when it's Christmas and you're in here. You'll be fine." He kissed her forehead and smelled the flat odor of drugs leaching from her skin.

"You need to listen to me, Arky. Please. There's a center, a facility."

"What do you mean?"

"I need to get well. I need some time out to do that. Somewhere that means absolute rest."

"Why can't we just get nurses again? I thought this was what you wanted, the apartment . . ."

"I do."

"What am I meant to do there without you?"

"I want to be there. I do. I know this is terrible timing. I know it's been a huge move and you've done it all without me and I'm sorry."

"Where is this . . . place you want to go?"

"East Hampton."

"East Hampton? But it's going to take me hours to come and see you . . ."

"I don't want you to visit. Not at first."

He was stung. "Why not?"

"If I'm lucky, I'll be home in a few weeks. If things get worse, they have everything I'll need."

"But why can't I visit? And what if you do get worse?"

"Alice knows what to do. You won't need to do anything."

"But I want to."

"No you don't. You hate every minute of me being sick."

"Darling, that's not true."

"Isn't it?"

"You could give me a chance. I mean, East Hampton?"

"Arky, sweetheart . . . I love you. But I can't look after you while I'm trying to look after me. Not anymore. It's taken me a while to understand that. This way will be easier for both of us."

"Wow. Do you ever get how tough you are?"

"I don't feel very tough."

"So I'm meant to wait around in an apartment that you wanted to buy, that you've never even spent a night in, and one day I'll get a call to come pick you up in East Hampton?"

"Arky, I'm frightened. Please don't make me fight with you over this. Please understand. This is what will work for me. And I know it will work for you. Can you trust me?"

He had loved to watch her walk. It was as if there were extra muscles in her feet and legs that lifted her. When he heard her voice, he felt it was an instrument he would never tire of. When she smiled it was as if he had finally found the one safe place in the world.

If he had been a scientist, the things on his petri dish would have been Lydia and Alice. On the periphery were Hal, his agent. Healayas. The traitor Tom Washington. When he looked at it like that, all the acquaintances, the film producers, the musicians, and editors, ultimately none of them meant anything. Not when it all came down to it.

When he visited her on New Year's Eve, Lydia said to him, "Sometimes I just want to die so I don't have to go through getting better again and again. I'm always trying to pick up where I left off. But every episode it's harder. I can't get back to where I was, Arky. I'm being washed downstream . . ."

"Why have you loved me all this time?" he asked.

"You're funny. You're very sweet. You're a musical genius. You love me. No one will ever love me the way you do."

"But not the right way."

"Is there a right way? You might have been better without me. Without your noisy, busy, bossy, crazy wife."

"I never want to live without you."

"You can."

"I don't want to."

"But you must. For a little while."

"But why are you doing this? Why do you have to go away?"

"I never want to be in a wheelchair . . . we need to talk about that."

He'd offered her his handkerchief and she blew her nose.

"It's okay," he said. "We don't have to talk about anything now. Nothing like that's going to happen."

"On your birthday," Lydia said as the hospital staff were preparing her for the trip to East Hampton, "you want to open the door when they ring at eight o'clock. I know it's early, but it will be worth it. Short of a blizzard, they'll be there."

"Okay," he said. "But I'll see you before that, won't I? I'll catch the train. Let me know when I can come and see you."

"We'll talk about it. Just let me get well. Write. Make music. Please be happy. I love you."

He had stood on the pavement and stared after her as the ambulance drove her away. He'd been so busy trying to succeed that he hadn't noticed that he'd failed, probably long ago. He just hadn't noticed.

Three days after she arrived at Oakhaven, Lydia had a stroke and slipped into a coma. When she came out of it, nothing was the same.

As soon as he heard about the stroke, Levin made plans to take Alice and drive to East Hampton, but then he'd had a call from Paul asking him to bring Alice and come in for a meeting. Paul Wharton had been Lydia's father's lawyer. The firm had a division for medical law and another for divorce. Paul introduced a younger lawyer who, with thirty-something clarity, talked Levin and Alice through the legal landscape that ensured Lydia's wishes were met.

"I'm so sorry, Levin," Paul said as they left the room. "If there's anything I can do . . ."

Levin had been too numb to reply.

Out on the street, he said to Alice, "I have to see her."

"Dad, you can't. She doesn't want that. Weren't you listening?"

"How can you be sure?"

"I'm not going to get in the middle of you two. I told you that in there. But you have to listen to what she wants."

"What about what I want? You all seem to have decided everything without any concern for me or how I might feel. She's my wife. We've been married almost twenty-four years."

"Dad, what's her condition called?"

"TTP."

"What does it stand for?"

"Thrombo-something. It's unpronounceable."

"Thrombotic thrombocytopenic purpura, Dad. It's not so hard." She said it kindly.

"I guess that's why you're going to be the doctor in the family."

Levin didn't want to think about how Lydia looked. Was her head lolling? Did she make those terrible sounds he'd seen stroke victims make as they tried to talk? Did she dribble?

If Lydia came home, *Kawa* might be his last score. New York was no place for walking sticks or wheelchairs. They'd have to go somewhere suburban. To some place called Sunshine Gardens or The Evergreens. They'd never travel. They'd need to live somewhere with tepid summers and flaccid winters. To live that way would be like being dead, Levin thought. She had saved him from nursing staff coming and going. From a house with railings in the hallways, handholds by the toilet and rubber mats in the bath. She had saved him from a plastic chair in the shower. She had saved him ramps and mushy food and the smell that sickness and decay brought with it.

He had found it difficult enough when she got ill to catch the smell of her. He didn't like what their bedroom became or how the malaise of her illness seemed to sap him of creative energy. Suddenly he was meant to tiptoe in his own house. Had to share the kitchen with medical staff he didn't know and would never remember. He couldn't stay up late playing the piano because she needed to sleep. He had to work on his keyboard under headphones.

There was no Lydia to go out with. Meals became some arrangement on trays like old people. And he would order exactly what she'd wanted, only to have her eat barely a mouthful. Or be too tired to eat at all by the time he got back from buying takeout. And if he went out with friends while Lydia was sick, it put a pall on the whole evening. He quite liked it when she went to the hospital for transfusions because at least that way he could imagine she was traveling. He could watch the season reruns and stay up as late as he liked, turn the music up, sleep in their bed instead of in the guest room, which was always depressing to wake up in.

He hated how the whole world seemed to be set up for two things: illness and death. Lydia's mother had died of the same condition when Lydia was a child. Her father had ensured Lydia had the best of everything—schools, specialists. New York was good for that. And then Lydia became an architect and her work was extraordinary, despite everything. She might have had her mother's physiology, but in other ways she was her father's daughter.

Once Alice was in her teens, she did the runs to the hospital with things Lydia needed. But Lydia's absences, knowing she was in the hospital, watching the increasing frequency of attacks, the complication of medications, had always been terrible for Levin. It wasn't how he'd imagined life would go. He had thought of them as they got older taking walks, seeing movies. Spending summers in Europe. He wanted to go back to Vienna with her, to London, to Spain. He wanted to have her beside him when they heard the Berlin Philharmonic again.

Was he really meant to give up his own life to care for her every hour of the day? Had he really signed up for that? She didn't want him to. That was why she'd done what she'd done. She'd given him his freedom. Something better for both of them. Wasn't he doing just what she had prescribed? That's what she'd said. *Go and write. Make wonderful music. Know that I love you. Have no regrets.*

She might live another five years in her current state. Or another two. He had no idea. But she wanted to do it without him. She hadn't asked for a divorce; she'd simply ensured he could not come and visit. Alice could visit. But Levin was freed from the obligation to spoon wet goo into her mouth or help her to the toilet. Maybe now she wore diapers. This was a hideous thought and he put it away again immediately. For better or worse? It was old-fashioned, he decided. Worse could be dealt with in a modern way. Care could be bought. Services could be acquired. Science, technology, it had all created options. If there was money, then why should anyone lose dignity? He did not have to see Lydia when nothing about her now was the woman he loved. And he could continue his life. It was tragic to lose her, but it would have been more tragic for them both to be prisoners to the one fate. Surely.

Unbridled selfishness. The words came back again to haunt him. Was living his life selfish? Was his one quiet life really doing harm to anyone else? Lydia was looked after. She had the best care money could buy. Science might yet save her. Alice visited. Alice was her medical power of attorney. Alice would know if there was anything that wasn't being done properly.

"She'll really never walk again?" he had asked Alice during one of the rare meals they'd shared after Lydia's stroke.

"They say not. I mean, they have to help her sit up. They strap her into her wheelchair because she likes to . . . Are you okay? You must have imagined that one day it would come to this."

"You know, I never did. I really never did. But I'm fine. Really, I'm fine."

"Really? I'm not."

"Are you angry with me, Alice?"

"No. Maybe. Disappointed, I think."

"What do you mean?"

"Well, I'm not sure what to make of anything really. I think that other husbands . . . look, forget it. I think she wants you to be happy."

"So that's a crime? You think I don't feel guilty?"

"I don't think you do, Dad. I'm not even sure you should. And part of me even admires that you can be so selfish. That she can be so . . . generous."

"Generous! I'm complying with her wishes, and all I get is criticism."

"I guess you've got no excuses."

"No excuses?"

"For not getting all the music done that you ever wanted to."

But somehow it was still about Lydia. If his next album was a success, it would be because Lydia had bought him the Steinway for his birthday. Lydia had given him space and time and all the money he'd ever need.

PART THREE

Only put off until tomorrow what you are willing to die having left undone.

PABLO PICASSO

14

HEALAYAS BREEN WATCHED THE PATTERN of the Marina Abramović performance. The way the artist dropped her head as soon as a guest left and closed her eyes. Then she lifted her shoulders a little, stretched in minute ways, breathed, settled, and when she was ready, she lifted her head and met the gaze of the next person.

Healayas wondered what Abramović ate for breakfast to sustain a day's sitting. Quinoa? Almonds? Spirulina smoothies? Fish? She'd read that Abramović had been a vegetarian since scrubbing all those cow bones in Venice. The performance that had won her the Gold Lion.

Healayas waited, her legs crossed, her scarf pulled over her hair. The old habit of the hijab. And so effective at stopping all conversation with the people in the line. MoMA had made Abramović mass market. MoMA had given her a new following and the following was growing. What it would grow to, Healayas didn't know, but she suspected Abramović would become a household name, even if they didn't pronounce it correctly. She had heard all sorts of variations. This show was too brave, too simple, too hard not to be noticed far and wide.

The pain Abramović was in wasn't obvious. And there was no nudity. No suggestion of sexuality. Up until now, Abramović's work had been an acquired taste. Not everyone could relate to the rigor or the endurance. Cutting herself with razors. The flogging. Eating onions. The strange crystal phase Abramović had gone through after the walk on the Great Wall of China. But suddenly all sorts of people were magnetized by her.

Abstinence, Healayas knew, was the last thing most Americans wanted to experience. Discomfort too. Much better if someone else was feeling it for you. Even better if you could laugh at it. Reality TV. The *Jackass* phenomenon. Johnny Knoxville and Spike Jonze had tapped into the powerful urge to use pain as a device. Mass market it may be, buffoonery for boys, but it was hard core and she understood that.

The first time Healayas had ever come across Marina Abramović was a photograph of a performance called *Rhythm 10*. Abramović was kneeling on the floor with a large kitchen knife in one hand. Her other hand was splayed out on a piece of white paper.

The black-and-white film had been grainy, the sound indistinct. Abramović had fanned twenty knives in front of her. She primed one tape deck then, taking the first knife, she tapped the point fast between each of her splayed fingers like a Slavic drinking game. Every time she cut herself, she chose a new knife. When she had used all twenty knives, she stopped the tape recording. She then listened back to the rhythm of the blades as they beat the floor. Priming the second tape recorder, she let the original tape roll and mimicked the exact pattern, cutting herself in exactly the same place at the same time, changing knives with each cut. Then she played the two tape recorders together listening to the original pattern and the new pattern. The mistakes of the past and the mistakes of the present were synchronized. It had taken place in Edinburgh in 1973, the same year Healayas was born.

Healayas had questions but Abramović wasn't talking to the media for the seventy-five days of *The Artist Is Present*. Healayas wondered if she was talking to anyone at all or if she remained silent in the mornings and the evenings away from here. How hard was that silence? Hardship was in her blood. But hardship had been learned as well. Healayas wondered if the years away from Serbia, the years crossing Europe, living in Amsterdam, teaching in Germany, the life she had here in New York, had filed down the ravages of Abramović's childhood. Had a life of intense experiences smoothed her like a pebble on the ocean floor, polished her into the radiant woman sitting at the heart of the atrium, this statue of herself, immovable, unknowable?

Abramović had once said that in theater the blood wasn't real. The swords weren't real. But in performance art, everything was real. The knives cut, the whip ripped skin, the ice blocks froze flesh, and the candles burned. For one piece, called *Lips of Thomas*, a naked Abramović had lain on her back on huge blocks of ice forming a cross. Then she stood up and used a razor blade to slowly cut a large five-pointed star into her stomach. After each cut she ate from a kilo jar of honey and drank from a bottle of red wine. She whipped her back over and over with a cat-o'-nine-tails until her skin burned in a mass of red welts. Donning a soldier's cap, she stood and listened to a Serbian hymn of war while holding a white flag stained from her bleeding stomach. For seven hours she repeated these actions in a cycle of freeze, cut, honey, wine, whip, song. When she'd first performed *Lips of Thomas* in Germany, she had been thirty-two. At the Guggenheim in 2005 she had been fifty-seven.

Did Abramović leave MoMA each afternoon for a five-star hotel where she was cosseted by room service, masseurs, and shiatsu therapists? Or did she go home to her Greenwich loft with her own pillow? What were her dreams? Healayas wondered if, when Abramović closed her eyes at night, she saw the faces of all these strangers looking into her, wanting to catch her soul amid the shadows, wanting to draw a little piece of courage from her, wanting to scratch a length of skin from her cheek and eat it like a wafer from the altar of truth.

Healayas heard one of the people in the line enthusing about the David Altmejd giant at the New Museum. She had loved it too. He was one of the sexiest men she had ever seen, all fiberglass and steel, a bird on his shoulder. Someone behind her was saying how inconvenient it was that the National Library reading room was closed while a performance took place each afternoon. And two people to her right were discussing the pleasures of reading *The Elegance of the Hedgehog*. As the morning stretched on into afternoon, the line continued to deliver people to Abramović's table. She is teaching them about time, Healayas thought. I have sat here for three hours, the morning has slipped away, and I have done nothing but think. She couldn't remember the last time she had done such a thing.

At last her turn came. She discarded her scarf, slipped off her shoes, crossed into the square, and took her place. Abramović lifted her head and their eyes met. It was the same tangible effect as the previous time, earlier in the week, as if she'd been plugged into an old resonance.

She settled into the gaze between them, aware of chatter and movement in the atrium. But it was peripheral. She focused on the world of Abramović's dark, moist eyes and pale mouth. She noticed her own eyes blinking, but Abramović hardly blinked at all. Healayas stilled her breathing and reached into the darkness beyond Abramović's eyes.

She saw white linen on the table, silverware, and red wine. She began spreading a sliver of toast on her plate with parfait. She bit into it and the toast crunched between her teeth. The texture hit the roof of her mouth, the flavor languid and creamy. She detected salmon, black caviar, sour cream, dill, black pepper.

Instead of Abramović, Tom sat opposite her in a white shirt, the way only Tom could wear a white shirt. He was smiling at her. Instantly her eyes filled with tears. He looked as he had looked that last winter, the shirt ironed, the salt-and-pepper hair just curling above his ears and swept back, the careful close two-day beard, the scent of something citrus on his skin.

"Alone?" he asked.

"So it seems," she replied.

"Well, you know why."

"Yes, I guess I do." She gazed into his eyes.

"Not celibate?" he asked. "Like being on a diet for you."

"My senses become dull without sex. So of course I am not celibate."

"You are still terrifying."

He put the glass of wine to his lips and drank. The same lips that had done such wonderful things to her body.

"A man can never really love a woman who is an artist," she said, leaning in across the table, drawn to smell him.

"Is that what I said?"

"Yes," she replied. She wanted to bite his skin until she could feel the texture of it in her mouth. She wanted to suck the smell of him inside her. He had gazed into her eyes as he orgasmed, and told her that he loved her as he exhaled.

She smelled steak and looked down to see chateaubriand, green beans, a truffled pommes puree, sauce Bernaise, and a red wine jus. It was a meal they had shared in Australia. Two weeks in the heat and tropical rain making love and every night eating the most exquisite food at a little restaurant with canvas awnings, a giant fig tree, and the raucous noise of fruit bats.

"So, are you singing?" he asked.

"Not much. We've got the Lime Club starting in June, but I haven't heard from Arky. Lydia . . ." She trailed off.

"Are you still angry with me?"

"Yes." She sipped the burgundy and felt the oak run under her tongue. "I have never given my heart to anyone like I gave it to you."

"Ditto," he said.

"Why wasn't it enough?"

"Sometimes it was."

"How will I ever trust a man again?"

"That's not a question for me."

"How do you know?"

"You were asking it before I came along."

"That's not true."

"Yes. It is. It was claustrophobic."

She became aware of the buzz of people. The face before her with its pale skin and shining eyes. She felt tears on her face. She saw tears in Abramović's eyes. How had that happened? How had she slipped into some other place with Tom in a restaurant?

She continued to gaze at Abramović but the vision did not reappear. It was over. There was nothing more. She inhaled, dropped her head, closed her eyes, stood up, and crossed the room back to her shoes and bag. She had no words. She went down the stairs, across the lobby, out into the bright street, past trestle tables selling celebrity coffee cups and film scripts. Then, only then, did she laugh. It rippled out of her like a huge wave of relief.

"My god," she said. "My god." She checked her watch. She had sat for over an hour. She must hurry. She was due at work by five.

15

BRITTIKA VAN DER SAR, A PhD candidate from Amsterdam, sat next to Jane Miller. Brittika had a laptop perched on her knees and was grabbing screenshots off the webcam. Sitting opposite Marina Abramović was the writer Colm Tóibín. Brittika hadn't recognized the author or known his books, but Jane did.

"I love his face," Jane said. "It's as if he has absorbed all the stories of the Irish and it has made him sad and a little perplexed."

Tóibín was looking at Marina as a child might. Curious and slightly confused.

"I'm going to do a blog on it. Tell me again the titles of his novels?"

Jane did and Brittika tapped away furiously as the writer and the performance artist sat without words, without sweet tea and biscuits, without vodka and olives, and gazed into each other's eyes.

Jane turned to Brittika and said, "What is it like to be out there, with her?"

Brittika replied, "I felt acutely exposed with the crowd watching but that made me think that the whole thing is about exposure. I didn't really understand that until I was there, on that uncomfortable chair. I know that's kind of obvious, but I never really got the impact of that before about performance art. It's about total exposure. The audience is this enormous force watching you. The first time I only lasted eight minutes. The second time twelve minutes. I think I could do it better."

"You must feel like you know her, though, after so much research," Jane said.

"In a way, but I still wasn't prepared . . ."

"What do you think she's trying to say with this piece?" Jane asked her.

Brittika had neon-pink hair, red lips, purple contacts, and false eyelashes all decorating a delicate Asian face. She was wearing a T-shirt with a cartoon character Jane only vaguely recognized, a short skirt, patterned leggings, and platform boots.

"She did a version of this with Ulay, her partner," Brittika said. "It was in the seventies, in Australia. They sat at either end of a really long table and stared into each other's eyes. It was called *Nightsea Crossing*. They were going to perform it one hundred times. But Ulay got sores on his butt from sitting all day. He lost too much weight. A doctor told him his spleen was going to burst from the pressure of his ribs, if he kept sitting. One day, when the pain was too great, Ulay just got up and left the room. He didn't like it that Marina kept sitting without him. I think it made him hate her a little bit. Knowing she could be stronger."

"Still, what is she trying to say?" Jane asked again.

"What she's been saying since the start, I think. That everything is about connection. Until you understand what connects you, you have no freedom."

"Are you an artist too?" Jane asked.

Brittika shrugged. "Not really."

At age nine, Brittika van der Sar had glimpsed that knowledge was everything. Her only currency was to have more of it than other people. She'd had one or two teachers who had been pivotal in driving her on. And now her PhD subject was becoming more famous by the day. Brittika knew she was in the right place at the right time. If there was no time for the sketches she had done as a child, if the paints and brushes were stacked in a cupboard in her parents' house, if there was barely time to do a quick observation of a face on a train, then that was where she was at in life. When you came from the Amsterdam of immigrants and unemployment, there wasn't time to linger on what might be. There was what had to be. She worked the normal social media channels, ensuring her supervisors were kept abreast of how her research was progressing. She regularly wandered the line, making sure she met the right people—scanning faces, asking questions, introducing herself. The place was a magnet for art curators, critics, and academics. Her looks took her a long way with people. People found it hard to ignore her.

Colm Tóibín departed the table and the next person crossed the floor to sit. Marina appeared to look carefully into the woman with the weathered face haloed by white hair.

Jane was struck by the kindness the older woman exuded. She said to Brittika, "Don't you think that woman has a question, but she can't ask it, not even with her mind? Did you have questions you wanted to ask? When you sat?"

"I wanted to understand how she manages her energy. I think what I got from sitting was that it's all in her breath. I mean, that's not new, it's what yoga teaches, but seeing her sitting there, the only thing that's really happening is her breath."

Brittika imagined for a moment Marina getting up from her seat and doing a little dance for the audience, rubbing her breasts and singing a song of fertility, like in her film *Balkan Baroque*. But Marina stayed completely still. There was none of the wild green Serbian hills, the embroidered peasant finery, the humping naked carnality, or the fecund earth about this performance. There was just this enforced solitude of the gaze, the visitor who remains silent, the unspoken connection between two faces, two minds.

Jane watched the question leave the old woman's face. Soon she rose from the chair and was gone. And so it continued with the next person, and the next person, while Brittika wrote beside her.

"Do you think," whispered Jane, "that to Marina, all the people become one person?"

"Maybe she thinks about the people who won't come. Paolo, you know, her husband. They separated a few months ago."

"How long were they married?"

"Eight years."

"Mourning," said Jane. "Maybe she's in mourning. How awful."

"I can't imagine many men could live with Marina," said Brittika. "I mean, she'd be tough."

"Yes," said Jane. "She's tough. But I don't think it's toughness that keeps her there. I don't think that's what makes all these people come and want to sit. All the great art makes us feel something quite indescribable. Perhaps it's not the best word—but there doesn't seem to be a better one to capture how art can be . . . transformative. A kind of access to a universal wisdom."

"I'm going to use that," said Brittika, tapping away. "I mean, she's using the audience to create this effect, but the audience has also created this experience by how seriously everyone has taken it."

"So what makes it art?" Jane asked.

Brittika smiled.

"Why does most everyone who ever sees your Van Gogh's *Sunflowers* kind of sigh with happiness?" Jane asked.

Brittika had never thought of him as *her* Van Gogh. There was an old Netherlands where everyone was blond-haired and blue-eyed, she knew. Then there was now. Everywhere you looked there were Africans and people from the Middle East and Asians like her. The blond-haired, blue-eyed Dutch were a lingering oddity. Like the bowler-hatted man in London.

After a while, Jane said, "I wonder what would have happened if they had stayed together—Marina and Ulay."

Brittika shrugged. "I think she's been a better artist beyond him. When you look at what's upstairs . . . the retrospective, this performance. Her father, her mother, Ulay. They were steps along the way. Now she's alone."

"So it's a funeral?"

"Yes, she's always liked the idea of her funeral," said Brittika.

"And she invited us!" Jane laughed. She grasped the younger woman's hand briefly. "I will go home and never forget this," she said.

I feel as if I know her, Brittika thought. I'm sitting here on a concrete floor. I've made two trips from Amsterdam to see this and I'll probably make another one yet. I've spent three years of my life writing about her. I know what she has said and done, but being here, I look at her and realize that even though I thought I knew who she was, maybe I don't. It's hard to tell what's fact and what she's told over and over again so it seems like truth, but maybe it isn't. I want her to remember me. But she doesn't know me. She doesn't know what it's taken these last few years. I may never meet her, though I've stared into her eyes longer than I've done with anybody. Perhaps I am just another art student. Maybe she is only nice to people who have something she needs. She knows Amsterdam. It was her home for years. She and I have almost certainly walked some of the same streets, visited the same galleries, eaten in the same restaurants, braced ourselves against the wind off the North Sea, seen the same canals frozen over, seen the daffodils in spring, maybe ridden bikes on the same paths. All that time she was in Amsterdam, she was the same Marina Abramović who would one day be here. I have no idea where I'll be at her age. Or who I'll be. Will I have slept in a field or stood naked before a table of implements in Naples? No, unlikely. I couldn't do what she does. I have no appetite for pain. Or deprivation. Perhaps I got all that out of my system young, before, back in China, before being adopted. What did I love then? I'll never know. Maybe I loved nothing. Maybe I learned to love, but coming late it's harder. I wonder if I ever waited a very long time for someone to come back. I think I probably did.

Later, the man with the angel eyes sat again. He wept and Marina wept with him. Then the announcement came over the loudspeaker before Brittika was ready for the day to end. *The gallery is closing in fifteen minutes.*

She thought of Marina in the greenroom slipping off the red dress. Perhaps Davide, her assistant, would tell her it was raining outside. She would put on pants and a sweater. He would hold out her coat.

"Come. Time to go home."

Brittika knew that on some level she was quite terrified of Marina Abramović. That was part of what kept her working on her PhD. She wondered what terrified Marina. At 1 a.m., did Marina wake panicked and straighten the sheets, fold under the corners until there was no trace of her body as her mother had made her do, midnight after midnight? Did her heart still pound when she woke? Did she have to tell herself that she wasn't seven anymore? Nor ten. Nor twenty. Her mother was dead and could never wake her again. Could never hit her again.

Yet when her mother had lain dying, it had been Marina who had massaged her feet with lavender oil. Tended her bedsores. Loved her.

Brittika and Jane found a nearby diner and ate chicken burgers and key lime pie. Then Brittika returned to the tiny 43rd Street hotel room with its noisy air-con and dry white sheets. She typed, her back up against the stained flock-papered wall. At 11 p.m. she put away her laptop and did some relaxation poses. She could put together the pieces of Abramović's life this way and that, but what was at the heart of that unconquerable gift for endurance?

At 2 a.m. she woke and browsed again the faces on the Flickr website showing everyone who had sat with Marina since March 9. The boy with the mop of black hair, the girl with the vivid green eyes, the woman with the splatter of freckles. The expressions were so bare. Each of them spoke of days lived, life unfolded and refolded, opened and shut, and all of the days weathering a face. She saw her own face, the curious light in her eyes, the mouth that was tight. The worry that seemed to sit on her brow. She didn't want to look worried. She wanted, next time, to smile.

At 3:33 a.m. she closed the laptop and switched off the bedside light. The day was running toward her, coming at her from Europe, traveling relentlessly on, and she must sleep while she could. She wished she had melatonin. Something about the performance was turning her into an insomniac. She wondered where Marina slept in Manhattan. Did she have sleeping tablets? Marina who could not take a nap through the long afternoons, couldn't pee or stretch or yawn or sneeze or roll her shoulders or tap her feet or scratch her nose. What were her nights like?

Brittika set her alarm to wake her at 8 a.m., giving her time to grab a blueberry muffin before she lined up outside the gallery for day thirty-five. If she was lucky, she'd get to sit again today.

16

HERE IS MARINA, AGED FOUR, in Belgrade. This is a true story. This was, I like to think, her first public performance. Playing to an audience of one. Me.

Marina was seated at the kitchen table. Her grandmother said she would be back. But already it had been a long time. Her grandmother had gone to the shop. The shop was not far. The shop was down the stairs, past the little garden and the barking dog. Her grandmother would talk to the other women. Talk about bread. Talk about sausage. Talk about the neighbors. Finish shopping and talking. Then, holding the bag of groceries, walk past the little garden and the barking dog back up the stairs. Put the key in the door.

Marina heard people coming up and down the stairs but none of them turned the key in the lock. None of them was the sound of her grandmother arriving home. She thought about going outside and asking if anyone had seen her grandmother but she was not tall enough to turn the handle on the door. She could get on a chair to do it. But she did not. She sat.

Her grandmother had said to sit and wait. So she sat and waited. She could hear the sound of a fly caught between the glass and the curtain. She could hear her own breathing. The tap in the bathroom dripped. The pipes creaked and gurgled. Someone upstairs was playing music. Soon it would be time to light the candles.

Marina observed the glass of water on the table. She was very thirsty now but she did not touch it. She thought that if she drank the glass of water, her grandmother would not come back.

She wanted to pee. She needed to pee. But she would not pee. If her grandmother didn't come back, who would live with her? Her mother and father might take her to live with them and the new baby, when it arrived. She did not want to live with a baby. She wanted to live here. She wanted her grandmother to come home.

Her grandmother had gone. The door had closed. The door would open again. Her grandmother would come back. If she sat very still.

The clock ticked on the wall. It was the sound of no time passing. In the glass of water she saw tiny specks of color. The table through the glass was moving as if it wasn't really a table at all.

"What are you doing?" her grandmother asked. Suddenly she was there and Marina had not heard the footsteps, nor the key in the door. Her grandmother smelled like outside.

"I said to sit and wait, but I didn't mean you couldn't leave the chair. They didn't have what I needed. I had to take the trolleybus. But then on the way home it broke down."

Marina gazed at the face of her grandmother, full of dust and light.

"There, there. You must be hungry. Tsssk. To think you sat there the whole time. What were you thinking?"

Marina observed the glass of water, reached for it, and took a sip. There were no words. Her grandmother had come back and the hours crafted from silence were over.

I looked at that small dark-haired, dark-eyed girl and I thought, "Bravo."

17

HEALAYAS KNEW HER VOICE HAD always been one of her best resources. It was the voice that had convinced teachers she was not lying. It was the voice that soothed her mother when she had been suspicious. With singing, in media and with her lovers, it was her weapon. She kept it supple with daily exercises. Coaching had helped to free it from the confines of her French accent, making her completely accessible to any American ear. Now her vocal lessons were focused on maintaining her longevity: ensuring she didn't strain her voice or develop habits that would limit her life span as a singer or as a media personality.

The microphone was her metier. In the softness of the recording studio, on a TV set under lights, on the stage, the tension between her mind and her body was palpable. She often came away with sweat drying on the skin between her shoulder blades. With Arnold Keeble she had gained more nerve.

Being black, raised Muslim in Paris, she had learned early the peril of defying men. She was too tall, too rebellious. It had not done her any favors. But as an international student at NYU, then as an intern, and through her early jobs at various radio and television stations, she had discovered she could make men pliable. Keeble had been brusque, arrogant, rude even when they had first met. He was handsome and famously opinionated, irritating but also often wise. She had found herself drawn to him almost unwittingly, not recognizing the early signs of attraction—the multiple wardrobe changes before going in to do a show with him, the part of her that lost concentration as she was prepping. It was lingering by the red peppers in Whole Foods and imagining him at her table that did it. It was because he was powerful, she told herself. The most powerful person she had worked with to date.

In the audition, when she'd surprised him by making him laugh, he'd finally been charming. He didn't think they'd make him have a co-star. Why would he need one? But for all his power, he was another pawn in the ratings game. When she started, he spun her questions back at her. But she had measured up. Especially during the making of the TV show. The art world was a savage and self-serving oligarchy with a few key players pulling all the strings. Keeble was one of them in New York. What mattered here was anyone who could make you famous. Gagosian, Zwirner, they all wanted Arnold Keeble to review their shows. They were inviting her too now. The TV series would be out in June and she knew it was good. There would be more invitations. Keeble might look old in comparison to her. She smiled at the thought, but not unkindly. She had always liked older men. Her father complex, no doubt.

But they were on air and Keeble was completing his introduction. She had to be present. If he caught her inattention, he would be like a viper snapping at her vulnerable ankle.

"Abramović's objective," he was saying, his voice redolent of an English university with gargoyles, "is to achieve, she says, a luminous state of being—an energy dialogue with her audience. Whatever that means. She does have her clothes on for this performance, even if this feels rather like an Emperor's New

Clothes kind of moment. I mean what is an "energy dialogue"? And is she really going to make it through to the end of May?"

Healayas said, "At this halfway point, I think it is already an extraordinary success. *The Artist Is Present* will be the longest-duration solo work of Abramović's career—a marathon of seventy-five days. She has said she does not allow herself to contemplate failure."

Keeble was wearing the shirt she knew his wife had given him for his birthday and his black-and-silver hair was slightly mussed with some kind of wax. The time was 7:37 p.m. Her tea was finished and her lips were dry. She sipped water from a white plastic cup as he spoke. The red On Air light was refracted in the studio glass.

Keeble said, "This is Abramović's attempt to confess something publicly. I mean, is this really any different to Tracey Emin's bed? If she wants to meditate, that's all very well and good. If she wants to sit about for days at a time and contemplate her mortality, the problems of the world, or whatever she's doing, fine. But why should anyone go to see this as art? Perhaps on one level she's giving us an impression of how it is to look at a painting. Fair enough. But why spoil it all with this operatic construct of the ball gown? The Swedish furniture? She's gone from works that were tough, terrifying, and extreme to a surfeit of emotion in a diva's gown."

Healayas observed in near profile Keeble's dark eyes and fierce eyebrows. Such good eyebrows. A large, lovely nose.

"This work," she countered, "gives us both the sum of all those parts we see upstairs in the retrospective and also the evolution of that into something else. It belongs to this time, to this city, to this artist at this time in her career, and I think we won't see its like again."

Keeble countered her argument, expanding on his pet theory of the inadequacy of postmodern art to move beyond theory into genuine substance.

Keeble's wife, Isobel, was beautiful. Healayas had met her at work functions and gallery openings. Isobel understood that women desired Arnold and she gave Healayas no time at all. Isobel was regal, cold. But that coldness, Healayas thought, was probably in part due to the effect of living with Keeble. He was not a person to live with. He would eat a woman's confidence. They had no children.

Keeble liked to put his face between Healayas's legs and he had liked it for some months now. She didn't know whether it was she who had succumbed, or he. She simply knew that one night she took him home with her and he had been eating her pussy ever since. And that was just the place for him, she decided. Where she could see him.

"This show is an evolution of the *Nightsea Crossing* works begun in Australia in the seventies, which she and Ulay performed over four years," offered Healayas. "And 2002's *The House with the Ocean View*, which was such a potent evocation of stillness and rhythm."

Keeble said, "There was the dreadful standing version at the Guggenheim when she wore that gigantic blue dress. Does she really need to inflict herself on us again in this way? I have never been entirely convinced by Abramović. I think the early works—*Rhythm 0, Rhythm 10, 5,* and *2* all had clarity and focus. The work she did with Ulay had context. It was explorative. But afterward there were some very silly things. Crystal shoes, snakes, and scorpions."

Again Keeble extrapolated, and Healayas gave him further opportunities to show off his knowledge of the life and times of

Marina Abramović, in case the audience had forgotten his glittering intellect, his savage opinions and salted caramel voice.

Healayas knew his shoulders beneath the fabric of his shirt. His skin had the veined translucence of marble. The hair under his arms, around his nipples and his balls, was as dark as ink with traces of gray, just as it was at his temples. He was a Jewish atheist and she . . . well, she had decided to believe in very little. He spoke three languages. She spoke five.

"So what you are saying is that because there is no blood or knives or nudity, *The Artist Is Present* is less worthy?" she asked.

He swung back to her, glancing at the clock as if he had things he must do. She had analyzed his style, watching and listening to years of interviews before she'd auditioned. He liked to distract his guests, catch them unawares. In those early weeks of working together, once he realized she was here to stay, at least for now, she had persuaded him she could make him look good. She rarely agreed with him and even more rarely in public.

"Of course not," he said in that elegant, reasonable tone he had perfected. He wasn't nearly so right about things when he was naked. He was curious, childish, and carnal. "I don't think you can divide art into meditative or non-meditative categories. But you must agree that performance art falls into self-indulgence with ease. You cannot avoid the undertone of what she's doing here. Is she mimicking some sort of Indian guru? A Zen master? Is this something she's picked up on her travels in Vietnam, China, or Japan? We have seen Chris Burden being shot, Stelarc's suspensions, Bob Flanagan's sado-masochism, Tehching Hsieh's *Cage Piece*. Is *The Artist Is Present* truly an evolution of performance art? Or should this show be in an Orthodox church?"

Healayas smiled. She wanted to keep looking into his eyes, but she looked away, her mouth always maintaining its correct distance from the microphone. "Abramović has been exploring the physical and mental limits of her being. She has withstood pain, exhaustion, and danger in a quest for emotional and spiritual transformation for forty years. She has taken psychiatric drugs to show us their effects, she has whipped herself, sliced a star into her belly innumerable times. Maybe for an artist, in an evolutionary context, what follows after forty years is stillness and silence."

"And the need to simply sit down?" Keeble suggested. He clearly wanted her to laugh, but Healayas did not.

"As a woman, and as part of her artistic expression, she also embodies the heroine. The warrior. The sufferer. There is this tension between intensity and passivity."

"And now we are the supplicants?" Keeble pursued.

"I think people cry during *The Artist Is Present* because they are genuinely moved."

He was most comfortable when he could be superior, condescending, certain. His face became contorted when he orgasmed.

"For several centuries now art has sat beside religion," he said. "When we get overlap we get outrage. Take *The Black Madonna. Piss Christ*. Wim Delvoye tattooing the Madonna onto a pig's back. I'm uncomfortable with how religious it feels to walk into MoMA right now and see all those people literally kneeling or sitting about and staring at Abramović as if she was a saint."

"She simply invites us to participate," Healayas said. "It may be therapeutic and spiritual, but it is also social and political. It is multi-layered. It reminds us why we love art, why we study art, why we invest ourselves in art."

She knew she had him. He had been distracted. Had it been when she had imagined him supine, erect, bleeding from his lip where she had bitten him, hungry still, as she mounted him?

"So will you sit with her before the show is over?" Healayas smiled.

He laughed silently but his voice was calm. "I could."

"Will you?"

"All right. Two weeks from now, we have a show featuring interviews with the clothed—and unclothed—re-performers. We will find out what it feels like to be fondled in public."

"And I will take a walk though the retrospective and report back on that."

"That's the show for tonight. You're listening to *Art Review from New York* on NPR. From me, Arnold Keeble . . ."

"And me, Healayas Breen . . ."

"Goodnight."

"I've sat with her," Healayas said as they finished up, waving to their producer and pushing through the soundproof doors into the corridor. "Twice."

"Why didn't you say so?"

"It was personal."

"If I buy you dinner, will you tell me about it?" he asked.

"Perhaps another time."

She walked away, tingling, knowing he was watching her go. Somehow they had gotten in deeper than they'd planned. Sex did that. The drug of skin and lust. But she kept walking.

18

SNOW HAD BEEN FALLING AT record levels. It was February and Lydia had been in the Hamptons for a month. Levin had received only the barest reports from Alice after Lydia's stroke. There was no good news. The city was slick with ice and everything felt hunkered down. The days barely became light and the nights were whipped and chastened by Atlantic storms. That day everyone had been braced for a blizzard born in Canada. The weather stations were calling it a Category 1 hurricane. But New York, despite snowdrifts up and down the city, was dauntless. The lights were still on and he'd received an email from Hal.

Where are you? Can't reach you. Call me. Work.

"Arky, hi," said Hal. No one ever sounded like Hal on the phone. Hal had constructed a New York drawl from a Kansas twang (his father) and a New Zealand clip (his mother). His vowels were organic. "Where have you been? Did your phone get stolen by reindeer? I've been calling you for weeks."

"I've been busy."

"Okay," said Hal. "So how are you? How was your weekend?"

His weekend? Levin's one trip out had consisted of a brief foray to eat breakfast at the Grey Dog. The city was dirty with trampled snow and bitterly cold. Tourists were in for the winter sales, filling up the Village, flocking into Bloomingdale's, congesting Spring and Canal and everything in between, trawling the little boutiques selling Swiss Army knives and designer satchels, tea towels and shirts, moving from one warm retail cell to the next. Every cafe and restaurant within a half mile radius of NYU was filled with students back after the holidays. But this was what Lydia had wanted. She had wanted to live on the square a stone's throw from the campus.

Without Lydia, Levin had lost the rhythm of the week— the certainty of Monday to Friday, the habit of Saturday, the reprieve of Sunday. It was all gone. The day could be any day. If he wanted, he could take three Sundays in a row and wander through the city, take in a gallery, walk for hours along Riverside. Without Lydia coming and going from her office, the structures of the working week were abandoned like stone walls where the grass had won out and the whole edifice had fallen into disrepair.

But wasn't creativity the grass that did just that? Worked away at structures. What sort of brainwashing, he had wondered, had created a world in which people worked fifty or sixty hours a week, every week, no matter how beautiful the day outside, no matter what thoughts they were having? Where would the paintings come from? The novels and sculptures? The music?

Levin had been thinking of ideas for his next album. He'd retrieved something he'd begun a few years before, a suite for orchestra—almost a little symphony—of four movements. He had an idea for an opera too, one drawn from an early film score he'd done for Tom.

"I have an offer for you. It's not cars and guns." Hal's voice was too loud in his ear. "As your agent, I need to remind you that people move on fast in this game. Two years is a long time between drinks. Time to jump, Arky."

"I'm listening," said Levin. If it had been a director he'd worked with before, they wouldn't have come to Hal first. And if it had been a big money deal, Hal wouldn't have called, he'd have come to see him. So he waited, half-irritated he'd bothered to respond to the email.

"Here's the thing," said Hal. "You know how Disney teamed up with the Japanese company—Studio Ghibli?"

"A disaster in my mind. Why would Ghibli allow that? Watch how clichéd everything will get."

"Well . . ." Hal paused as if he was about to argue, but instead he continued. "Now Warner is quietly undertaking a few explorative projects with a company called Izumi. The one they want to talk to you about is an adult fairy story."

"Ah."

"Turns out Seiji Isoda, the director, is a fan of your work. He thinks you're the man for the job. He's been working for years to get the project up and then, voila, Warner comes along."

"It's an animation?"

"Yep. But Warner, Levin! And it's for adults, not kids."

"So is it more like *Ghost in the Shell*?"

"Not really. It's a myth. It's pretty unusual. I'm sending you the script over now. It could be good. They're certainly keen to have you. Call me when you've read it."

"Okay."

"Arky, that means call me tomorrow. And turn your phone on. This isn't the Dark Ages."

When he switched off his phone again, it occurred to him that Hal hadn't mentioned Lydia. That must have taken something. Hal was very fond of Lydia and Alice. The day Lydia had her stroke, he'd called Hal and cried on the phone. Hal had come over, brought wine and cheese, and listened to the whole saga. Levin didn't remember the details of the night, but he did remember Hal hugging him at the door. The next day the legalities were made clear, and Levin cut himself off. Yet today they had spoken as if everything was normal. There was something reassuring in this pretence. The Hollywood adage of *fake it until you make it*. He and Hal had faked it, and it had been okay.

They met in Hal's office. There were blizzard warnings from Washington to Long Island. Schools were closed, airports too. Hal had sent a town car to pick him up. It was 11 a.m. and already the day was concrete, the sky ash above the Chrysler Building beyond the boardroom windows.

Two twenty-something women and a thirty-something man in a blue pinstripe accompanied the young director. Levin felt unbearably old. This was partly to do with having watched The Who do the half-time entertainment at the Super Bowl the day before and thinking that being an ageing muso looked like hard work.

Isoda himself looked all of seventeen, with straight shoulder-length hair and sculptural Japanese features. Levin immediately felt like they'd met before. Tom had been like that. An instant connection.

Isoda spoke careful English with a captivating catch in the vowels. Hal hadn't been exaggerating. He did, it appeared, know all Levin's work. Had every album—even *Light Water*, which must have taken quite some doing. And he'd seen every film.

The young director smiled and said without apparent guile, "I think the work you did with Mr. Washington was intriguing. Very interesting scores. It must have been a great loss. I admire the partnership you created. And I admire your composition very much. If you give me this opportunity, perhaps we might take a first step in collaboration together."

The woman in a blouse patterned with cartoon apples looked at Levin and said, "Joe Hisaishi wasn't available, so Mr. Isoda thought of you."

Levin blanched. Joe Hisaishi? It was like not being able to get Howard Shore and thinking on who would do next. Nobody came after Howard Shore and nobody came after Joe Hisaishi. Like Clint Eastwood or Ennio Morricone. John Williams. Randy Newman. As composers, they lived in their own stratospheres. Levin had always wanted to be in that league. Believed he was good enough to be and was surprised that it hadn't happened by now. Maybe he was that good and nobody realized it. Like Van Gogh or Prokofiev. Or maybe he wasn't. That troubled him so much he refused to think about it. Now someone wanted him to score a fairy tale?

"As you know from the script, it's a myth, a fable. We want you to evoke an ancient forest removed from time, and yet bordered by a world that threatens it."

"I've read the script."

"Yes. Did you ever see a fish become a woman?" Isoda asked gently. "When you were a child?"

"No," said Levin.

"I think I did, once. It's what made me love this story. I felt like it was my story. I have spent a lot of time in forests and it feels as if time does really begin there. Maybe stories too. *Willows whiten, aspens quiver, little breezes dusk and shiver, through the wave that runs for ever . . .*"

What sort of Japanese child read Tennyson? Levin wondered. The world had gotten very mixed up.

Levin sifted through the sketches they had placed in front of him. A slender raven-haired woman standing by a river. The woman leaping into the river transforming into a fish. A white bear holding a child tenderly.

"These illustrations, they're amazing," said Levin.

"Thank you," said Isoda.

"They're yours?" Levin asked.

Isoda nodded.

"You know I haven't done an animation before."

Isoda's eyes, dark as wet stone rested on Levin. "And I have not made a feature film before. *Spirited Away* is also an animation. Not really for children. You know this movie?"

"I have a daughter," said Levin. "She was a Studio Ghibli fan."

"So what's our time frame?" Hal interjected, glancing at Levin and motioning with his head encouragingly.

"As you can see, Mr. Isoda is at work on the animations now," said Apple Shirt. Her small perfect mouth was painted with mauve lipstick. "Mr. Isoda will do all the key drawings for the animation team to develop. He has also written the adaptation from the book."

The second woman, in a yellow silk shirt, nodded and spoke. "Studio Izumi has placed great trust in Mr. Isoda."

"I am a great fan of Hayao Miyazaki," Isoda said. "Who of course writes, draws, and directs all his own films. This time I am taking something from literature, but if it is successful perhaps I will be lucky enough to direct one of my own scripts."

"So, the time frame," said Apple Shirt in response to Hal's question.

"I think the expression is that you either have time or money. It's a small budget. So we would like to give you time, Mr. Levin," said Isoda seriously. "I imagine that is usually quite rare."

Levin nodded.

Yellow Silk said, "The studio is developing several projects consecutively, and quite truthfully, *Kawa* is the one Warner is least interested in. But Mr. Isoda intends to prove them wrong."

Apple Shirt slid a DVD across to Levin. "This is some of Mr. Isoda's previous work. Music clips. Some shorts. His work on several games. These are for you."

"That being said," began the man in the pinstripe suit. Until then he had been silent but now he spoke in an unexpected Bronx accent. "It's February ninth. We're scheduled to have animations completed by the thirtieth of April and we would like the initial score by the twentieth of May. When Mr. Isoda is happy, we'll discuss with you how the thing is going to be orchestrated."

Isoda nodded and smiled at Levin. "I would like us to build the music and pictures together."

"And if it gets a release date?" Hal asked.

"That depends on Warner," said Isoda. "I'm hoping next February, when people are ready for something a little more . . . thoughtful after the Christmas blockbusters."

"And you would prefer to record in New York?"

"If that is your preference. Or you could come to Tokyo." Isoda smiled. "I would very much like to record in Tokyo, but of course that will create some difficulties for you, Mr. Levin. Maybe I can take you to our forests. Let's discuss this as we proceed."

Levin considered the album he'd begun toying with. But maybe, just maybe, he could still do it around the edges. It would be good to work. It might bring some sort of structure.

Isoda said, "Mr. Levin, if you will agree to do the soundtrack, I'll do everything I can to make you proud."

Levin stared at the young man with his eager face.

"Just a moment," he said, and left the room. He found the bathroom, closed the door of the cubicle, and leaned his head against the tiled wall. He couldn't say why he began weeping, only that he thought this was possibly the saddest moment of his life.

There was something so ridiculously innocent about Isoda and his hopefulness. Levin thought of the first film score he'd ever worked on, and how he too had done it with so much hope. Did he still have hope? How could he do this without Lydia? He wanted her home. But if he had her home, he'd never be able to say yes to this film or the next. That was the decision she had made for him. Now he had to make something of that. Otherwise the price was too great.

The wall was cold and white against his cheek. He gripped it as if he was floating on a plank in a wild sea, and wailed silently.

After a short while, he gathered himself, opened the cubicle, washed his face at the sink, dried his face and hands, pushed back his hair. He looked bad, he realized. But suddenly it didn't matter. If they thought he was a little unhinged, they were right. He walked down the empty corridor and went back into the meeting room.

"I'll do it," he said.

19

"MY LAST DAY," **JANE SAID,** pulling a face.

"What time is your flight?" Levin inquired.

"Five p.m. I'll stay as long as I can."

Levin thought to tell Jane that he could hear, just beyond the strain of human ears, music playing inside the square. The sort of music that happens when children run through water, or a flock of birds takes off above a lake into an evening sky, or when sunshine strikes the petals of flowers. Sometimes he thought he heard a sitar or the clear melody of the oud, with its half-pear back and its broken neck. He had once been a boy in Seattle trying to catch the music of the wind. Now he was a man stretching his fingers toward his potential before it slipped from his grasp.

"I would have liked to see Frida Kahlo paint her," Jane said. "I wonder what implements of pain she might assign Marina as she sits in the chair? Do you remember when the Pool of Reflection froze solid last winter and people walked on water, there on Capitol Hill? Did you see the pictures? It struck me as biblical, I guess. And here . . . here, they come and sit with her and it's a little bit biblical too."

Levin nodded, still listening to the music in his head.

"You know Brittika, the PhD student I introduced you to waiting in the line? The Chinese girl from Amsterdam with the pink hair? We were talking about how people give the Pollock on the fourth floor a minute or two and move on. But they stop and stare at Marina for hours. Lots of us come back again and again. And look!" She indicated the crowd about the square and the long line of people waiting to take their place at the table. "They're from everywhere. London, Ireland, France, Portugal, Egypt, Israel, Vienna, Australia. They're spending their precious days in New York coming back here again and again. I've never seen anyone spend this much time staring at an artwork."

Levin nodded.

"She looks tired, doesn't she?" said Jane. "I imagine that hundreds of pairs of eyes staring into yours might do that."

Marina was looking particularly pale, her eyes red rimmed as if she was on the edge of an infection. Her skin was the color of candle wax. A lunch crowd was filling the atrium. Another person sat. He had a shaved head and a broad, keen face.

Jane said, "*What am I here for?* I think this is still the question we want answered. Maybe that's why we come here. Maybe we think she knows."

Levin looked at her. He was about to reply when a young woman on the other side of him, voluptuous in a stretch paisley shirt, asked, as if requiring him to solve a minor argument for her, "What do you see in it?"

He shrugged. "Lots of things."

The girl said, "I think she's like a tree that has rooted herself to this place. A silver princess gum."

"That is such a girl thing to say," the young man beside her said, grinning at Levin.

"Well, what tree do you think she is?" she asked her companion.

"I don't know. A baobab. Something exotic."

"And you two?" the girl persisted.

"Oh, maybe a monkey-puzzle tree," said Jane, laughing. "Arky?"

"I don't really know trees," he said.

The young people went back to their own conversation. Jane fell silent as she continued watching the two people in the center of the room regarding one other. *Regard* was too distant a term for it. It was as if they were drinking each other in.

Levin smothered a yawn. He had slept badly. He'd woken at 1:05 a.m. and hadn't been able to fall asleep again. He'd gotten up and watched an episode of *The Sopranos*. He'd tried listlessly to masturbate as he sat on the couch, then gave it up. It seemed too much of an effort and he didn't want to conjure Lydia for such purposes. Eventually he'd put on his headphones and worked away in his studio. He played over old compositions, thinking of a show he might give one day that featured all his best work. He considered the club he'd hire and the guest list.

The city had buzzed on regardless of the hour. The tribe of New York burning through life. He felt the curve of the world and, standing at the window, he rather hoped someone would drop a line and haul him up.

He had been to the doctor the week before and been given cream for the rash on his hand. It hadn't been their regular doctor, but a locum while Dr. Kapelus was on leave. The doctor had suggested some routine blood and urine tests, just to see if there was anything amiss. When they came back, it turned out Levin's cholesterol was up, but nothing serious for his age. No medication required. Kidney function good. Blood pressure one thirty over eighty and heart rate seventy-four. Everything was fine. "Exercise would be good," said the doctor, "for the insomnia. The sweats may be caffeine-related. But life has a whole bundle of things lurking about for men over fifty. Stress is the most insidious. Exercise is your best friend. And it keeps the weight down. That and not too much Ben & Jerry's. Do you swim, play tennis, cycle?"

"Yes, tennis," he had said, remembering Hal's invitation to resume their summer games.

The doctor had advised him to slow down on the coffee. Even stop altogether for six weeks and see if it helped his sleep cycle. What was he eating that might be stimulating his metabolism? the doctor had asked. "Too much red meat? Not enough water during the day?"

Levin had gone four days without coffee but nothing had changed. Not even a headache. And still he'd woken in the night.

He said to Jane, "Last night on the TV there was a news chyron I kept seeing. It said: *A man who went for a late-night swim was found by tourists.* It was only later that I realized I had missed the first few words. In fact, the chyron read: *The body of a man who went for a late-night swim was found by tourists.* Three words made such a difference."

"Especially for the man," Jane said.

Especially for the man. Levin had wondered all his life what would take him off. Would it also be a random act of fate? Or would it be protracted and painful? He worried that he was starting to forget things. He'd walk into the bedroom to get something and have no recollection what it was. He'd go to the market certain of what he needed and find himself staring blankly at the shelves. His recall of movie titles and actors, even film composers, took longer. Sometimes things didn't occur to him until the next day or even days later. By which time he'd forgotten why his brain had been so urgently searching for that particular fact in the first place.

"I think there would be more forgiveness," Jane said, "If we did more of it. Imagine in Arabic countries, in Africa, even here in America, if men did this with their wife, their wives, every day. Looked into each other's eyes. Or soldiers with soldiers. Children with teachers. Heads of governments. Perhaps it would be good to have someone to practice on before you tried it on someone very important to you . . ." She laughed. "But really, imagine!"

Levin thought of his film score for *Kawa*. He had called the first track "Awakening." The Winter King met a young woman living in the forest. A woman bound by a spell. She had lived in the forest a hundred years or more. (It was a fairy tale, after all.) They fell in love and had a child. But when the child arrived, it was to bring the woman the greatest loneliness of all. Levin didn't know how to write that bit. Everything he tried felt like a cliché.

In the wakeful hours between midnight and dawn, it was as if he himself was looking for a path across the river, a perfect beat of stones that would carry him to the far bank without washing him downstream. The river was not kind or helpful. And sometimes there was ice all around him and he was cold. The forest was death overgrown with life. In those desperate hours when he knew himself more alone than he had ever been in his life, he was sure he would lose sight of the track he had made and never be able to find his way back through the trees. At 1:05 or 3:17 or 4:24 a.m. he was never sure of his footing. And he saw Lydia in all the shadows.

"If you do sit, please write and tell me about it," Jane said. "Here, I'll give you my email." She scribbled her details on a piece of notepaper. "This will all seem so far away and unreal once I get back home."

"You'll be able to watch on the live feed," Levin suggested, indicating the camera on the atrium's wall.

"I'll write my mobile number too. If you are about to sit, will you text me? I would love to watch."

"Sure," he said.

"I don't expect many composers have sat with her," Jane said.

"Maybe not." He was ready for Jane to go. He hated drawn-out goodbyes. He would never email her.

She hesitated and then she said, "Arky, my parents were married for sixty years. My mother never came to New York. She always thought she'd get lost. My father came several times for the races."

He nodded, uncertain of why she was telling him this, now she was about to leave.

"Is your wife home again?" she asked.

"No."

"Is it irreparable?"

He looked at her and was surprised to see kindness there.

"Yes."

"But you still love her . . ."

Levin nodded. "I do."

"So, have you tried?"

"She's made it very clear."

"You know, Arky, we don't know each other very well, but probably as well as we ever will. So I just want to say this before I go. Karl and I, we were together for twenty-eight years. Now I've lost him and there's no chance to say all the things I never said. I think, if I dare be so bold as to give advice—which I know men always hate—you should try with everything you have. I just hate seeing love go to waste."

Loneliness was silent, almost soundproof, he thought. "I need to get home," he said.

"All right," she said, startled, as he jumped to his feet.

"Something just fell into place with the film score."

"That's marvelous," she said, standing up beside him. "Go! Go! Quick!"

He kissed her cheek. "Well. It was . . ."

She smiled. "Thank you. It's been a great pleasure meeting you, Arky. Do let me know if you sit with Marina."

"I will," he said, patting the pocket where he had placed her note, wanting to be the sort of man who would.

At home he sat down in his studio and did what he had done almost all of his life. He wandered through arpeggios, through chord modulations in minor and major keys, letting the mood take him, feeling the augmented colors of both. Seeing the profile of Abramović, the pale silent face. He saw a woman alone in the midst of a forest of faces. Then he heard it. There was a heart song, a step between loneliness and connection. The music of forest and water. There, in the notes, was the music of time and solitude and yearning for love.

His hands ran up and down the keyboard, the crisp notes of the Steinway cool and white and black under his fingers. A rush of energy ran down his arms. He heard the theme that would run in and out of the film, threading the scenes together. Raindrops falling on leaves, a moon in the sky and this melody. He under-stood how the melody could progress into other passages. He glimpsed what might come before and after. He played it over and over, seeing the woman who was human by day and a fish by night slipping into the water at sunset, waking and stepping from the river at dawn, the forest gleaming in tiny fragments as light returned to tree and fern, rock and bird, lichen and fungi. The woman standing in the endless wave of water and holding the stories of the world together.

He thought of Dvořák's Symphony No. 9 in E minor, opus 95, the haunting call of horns, the quiet moments of pause. But this was the piano calling, beckoning to the sun. This was a story about how the world was born and how it would change, and nothing would be the same.

20

NOW THAT LEVIN HAD FINALLY got himself out of the way and allowed the music to come in, I went to see Jane depart New York. There are artists and there are facilitators. I bless the facilitators. They are the lubricants of the artistic process. The engine oil of creativity. Beware the artist who believes they have failed, their genius gone unrecognized or unrewarded in the precise way they demanded, and so turns to teaching. So too the parent or friend who offers the wisdom of experience by telling young artists they will never succeed, that the world is too big and they too small, that their dream is invalid for the usual practical reasons. Or the person who from the lofty perch of no art believes he could have been great if he had written or painted or made the film. How hard can it be, after all?

I have observed that the opportunities to chew on failure are as myriad as fork designs. In each there is a little death, and the first response to such a death is usually anger. But Jane is not angry. Jane is considering the chauffeur.

She smelled a fragrance on him. Sandalwood, perhaps, and a hint of cinnamon. She observed his even hairline and slightly heavy neck above the collar of his white shirt. She would have liked to ask him all manner of things. How had he come to be in

New York? Was he happy? What did he make of God or Allah? What did he think of Obama? What did he most like to eat? What would he have done with his life if he could be seventeen again? But instead she sat and watched the skyline drop into suburbs and the broad expanse of freeway escape the city under a damp colorless sky. She thought it would be wonderful to be home and have the grandchildren ask questions, and put her own to rest for a while.

She had spent sixteen days watching Marina Abramović sit at a table. She had seen people return day after day. Some of them had waited for hours to sit. Many of them had missed out. Hundreds of thousands had come to witness or participate in *The Artist Is Present* and it was only halfway through. It would go on without her. She would not be here to see it end, but she had been a tiny fragment of it. A shoe on the edge of the live cam, a blurred face in the crowd.

She reflected on the visit she had taken to the site of the World Trade Center. The scale of it had shocked her. It wasn't just two buildings. It was an entire city block reduced to a massive pit of gravel dotted with yellow machinery. Best to lay a field of grass, she thought. Best to landscape a high conical hill with a view and the sky for consideration with a water garden that traced a meandering course down every side. She thought of a design she had seen in a magazine. A museum in Cairo with a rain room so that children, who might live their whole childhood without the skies ever opening, could experience more than forty different types of precipitation.

The world was filled with information, Jane thought. It was impossible to do more than scratch the surface in a lifetime. It was too much of a coincidence that roads were like arteries, that buildings were like penises, that clouds were like paintings, that war was a hunt and water like thought. She wondered what it would be like to let nature have a hill of green where the Twin Towers had once stood. To have the sea breeze blow upon the faces of those who came to grieve and pray and reflect. What a small miracle it would be for a hill to be restored to the landscape of Manhattan when only four hundred years ago the whole island had been nothing but hills and forests. But flatness suited roads and the foundations of buildings. Flatness suited grids and underground systems. Flatness suited transport and even walking. The mountains and hills had been pushed outward into the sea, the rivers sent underground, the forests turned into lumber, the birds and deer evicted. To put one big hill back, that would be something. What would old DeWitt Clinton think of that? she wondered.

Marina Abramović had brought something new into the city. She had made of herself a rock in the center of a town where everything moved and had been moving en masse for hundreds of years. She had brought her European history, her family history, her personal history and, like a true New York pioneer, she had bent the city to her will. And she had done it through art.

At the airport Jane bought a *Cosmos* magazine and waited. When she was settled on the plane, the flight was delayed for two hours. She read and she watched night venture in from the Atlantic. In the seat beside her, a young man tapped furiously on his iPad, texted on his phone, busy in his world. At last the flight was cleared. Her champagne glass was removed along with an empty water bottle and snack wrappers. The plane began taxiing, building up momentum.

In that wild rush against gravity, she always felt certain that it could never work, metal and wings and hundreds of people inside a great elongated box being lifted into the sky. But of course the miracle happened. They were above Manhattan, above the soaring grid of buildings, the great harbor with the Statue of Liberty somewhere below. Lights indicating life and activity stretching as far as the eye could see. They curved north, west, south, and she was going home. She closed her eyes and for a moment she was back in the atrium and she wondered, if she had sat with Abramović, what might she have seen or felt? Had it been enough to sit on the sidelines? Had she somehow missed an opportunity for something life-changing, some act of courage?

Her hand reflexively reached for Karl's to squeeze. She had a vivid urge to, for a moment, lay her head on the shoulder of the young man beside her. To pretend for a moment that there was someone who loved her close by.

Maybe I could go back, near the end, she thought. I could come back. I could see her on her last day, when she stands up. How marvelous it would be to see Marina Abramović stand up at the end of her seventy-five days.

PART FOUR

The days you work are the best days.

GEORGIA O'KEEFFE

21

LEVIN HAD BEEN SITTING FOR sixteen minutes at his kitchen table. He was aware of his neck. It felt a little jammed. He'd woken at 4:30 a.m. and by 5:15, having nothing better to do, dug out the black track pants and the white T-shirt he always wore. He arrived for the 6 a.m. Pilates class at the studio on Lafayette by 5:45. His teacher from last year, he learned, had moved to Arizona, but the new teacher, Maddie, had been helpful. His hamstrings were tight, she'd told him, and his buttocks were tight. Most every part of him was tight, and what was tight had gotten flabbier. After the class he had felt as if the world was clearer, brighter. His proprioception needed improving, but Maddie had appeared to be pleased with him.

On the way home, he'd eaten scrambled eggs and coffee at a cafe he'd never tried before, and found it good. Back at the apartment, he removed all but two chairs from the dining table and set the remaining chairs exactly opposite each other. On one chair he arranged several pillows from the bed. When that didn't quite work, he used the three red cushions from the couch and a round white pillow from the spare bedroom. Then he got his black cashmere scarf from the cupboard and arranged that too.

"Hello, Marina," he said. It made a basic enough resemblance.

He sat down on the chair opposite and attempted to relax. He felt a little bit silly, but no one could see him. He smiled at the way he'd arranged her hair, and then stopped himself. He breathed and stared at the white pillow face. He noticed almost instantly his desire to scratch his left shoulder blade. He eased his head gently to the left and to the right. He scratched an eyebrow and rolled his shoulders, rubbed one shoulder blade and then the other against the back of the chair, uncrossed his feet and flexed his fingers. Then he attempted again to sit entirely still.

He tried to imagine Marina's eyes staring back at him from the pillow face. He glanced at the wide rooftop balcony beyond the glass doors. He could be washing the breakfast dishes, getting on with his day in the studio. He could be taking a walk, going uptown. But he had to see about this sitting business.

He began to think about what he'd just read in the *Times* over his eggs. How April 19 was a day on which all sorts of big events had occurred. The Oklahoma bombing. The Waco, Texas, killings. And further back it had been the start of the American Revolution.

There was a lot of store in dates. Memorial Day, the Fourth of July, Labor Day and Halloween, Thanksgiving. They'd rented the same house up in Maine after Memorial Day for years when Alice was small. He usually went only the first few days, but Lydia and Alice had stayed for weeks. He liked New York in summer. The hot heavy nights, the sticky evenings with the windows open. The bliss of air-conditioning and cold showers and a breeze coming in off the Hudson. The quiet of the apartment. The welcome relief of solitude day after day. But then he missed Lydia and Alice. When he thought about that time he thought of John Coltrane, Thelonious Monk, and craft beer.

Again he tried to focus on Marina looking back at him from across the table. After a while he realized he was looking at the wall of glass cupboards. It looked as if a whole family lived here. He could have managed quite well now with a cup, a bowl, and a plate. Yolanda, their housekeeper, put meals in the fridge each week with little notes attached. Twice a week she cleaned out the fridge and everything was new again. Sometimes she left him chocolate brownies or cookies. And she kept the pantry stocked with all the different cat foods Rigby loved.

Lydia had liked to make Sunday lunches for their friends. New friends, old friends, it was all the same to Lydia. Gatherings restored her as if they were exercise. He didn't have the need for people that she did. Found it almost unfathomable that she'd fly in from Buenos Aires or Seoul and have eighteen people for lunch the next day. But that was Lydia. Always living as if there wasn't time to slow down. And perhaps she'd been right.

Pillow-Marina, looking back at him, was entirely still. He squinted at her, and she admonished him for his restlessness. Beneath the table, he unlaced his fingers and put them on his legs. Almost immediately, his hand began to itch. And soon his backside. His lower back was tight, and his hips began to ache. It was the Pilates. He had found all those little muscles that never did any work and everything was going to be sore by tomorrow.

The only movement he had noticed the real Marina make was a little lean forward or back. Or a little roll of the shoulders and head. They were done very slowly. What happened if she got too hot or cold? he wondered. Bad luck, he guessed. She could hardly say, *Hey, bring me a blanket.* The same with urinating. Or, worse, a bowel movement. Surely there came the midmorning need to take a crap? He had no idea how she managed any of it. Maybe Serbians were just made tougher than other people. He shrugged and stretched his neck. Another broken rule.

By now his arms were feeling heavy at his sides. He turned and looked back at the clock. Seventeen minutes. He sighed, shifted, and straightened. But the pain in his buttocks and hips was becoming excruciating.

It would have been better if Lydia had thrown something, he thought. If she had yelled. He wished she had hurt him physically, scarred him somewhere, so he could look at it and say: *That was the day. There it is. The day she told me she couldn't live with me anymore.*

After Alice had called him about the stroke, he had carefully unpacked the last of the moving boxes marked *Lydia Only*. He had placed every precious item carefully, debating with himself the correct arrangement of teapots, sculptures, little bowls, and boxes. For weeks he bought fresh flowers for her desk, trying to fool himself that in doing so he was luring her home.

He didn't miss hearing her discuss the education crisis in schools, or what Obama should be doing in his first term while he had the balance of power in the Senate, or how furious she was at Obama winning the Nobel Peace Prize and that it was the worst decision since Kissinger won it. And how this winter was going to be the coldest ever recorded, which would cause all sorts of havoc for the agricultural sector, and that sea ice was melting at an unprecedented rate. He didn't want to know that everything was going haywire. Hadn't he earned the right to enjoy air-conditioning? He liked well-lit rooms and air travel. He felt helpless to solve any of the things that were going wrong in the world. He was just one person, a musician, a composer. He entertained people. It wasn't really his problem. He sorted the trash.

He was surprised to find he was missing Alice. He missed her more now than during the year she'd spent in France. Her absence then, he seemed to remember, had been something of a relief. He had liked having Lydia to himself again. They had discovered a rhythm of work and movies, meals and walks, bike rides and cafes, as if this was the real reward of staying together for twenty years.

When Alice had returned from France, she'd moved in with friends. Her bed, her desk, posters, books, clothes, jewelery, all the paraphernalia that had saturated her room through her school years had gone.

She'd never visited the new apartment. He'd never asked her to. She'd never suggested it. When they met, it was in cafes or restaurants. Her university fees and monthly allowance were paid from an account Lydia had set up. He didn't really serve a purpose. He saw this more acutely now that Lydia wasn't here to make family dinners or organize for the three of them to go to the theater or concerts together.

Lydia's clothes still hung in the wardrobe. Her jars and bottles were in the bathroom. And there was the piano that had been delivered on the morning of his birthday on January 21. It had come in via the balcony by crane. Lydia had arranged permits, a road closure, all back in November, without breathing a word of it to him.

It drew a crowd on the icy street as the wooden box was hoisted five floors and swung in. He loved the piano. After the Steinway people had left, he'd sat down that first day and played for hours. But as the day had stretched out there was no other acknowledgment. No one had dropped by because there was no Lydia to organize friends. There was no Alice because he was still angry over the legal situation and didn't want to turn on his phone. So he never knew if she'd remembered his birthday or not, or had wanted to catch up. If she'd really wanted to, she had his address. But there was no card. No message at the front desk.

They should never have moved to this new apartment. He was surprised he hadn't thought of it before. It was April and he was still living here alone and Lydia was not coming home. He suddenly knew that with a terrible cold certainty. He would call their real estate agent and tell her he wanted to sell it. He'd find somewhere else. Maybe back on the Upper West Side. Somewhere that would fit the piano but not remind him every moment of the day that Lydia wasn't here.

He got up from the table and went to the storage cupboard and pulled out the last of the moving boxes flat-packed against the wall. He began assembling them, walking to the kitchen for scissors, rummaging through several drawers in the hope of finding packing tape. But he couldn't find it. It was only then that he realized he had left the table. He had left the chair and Marina with her pillow face and dark cashmere hair. He looked at the clock. He had lasted almost twenty-six minutes.

She overrides herself, he thought. Marina must have urges all day to get up, to walk about, to go do something else. But she doesn't.

Unbidden, a conversation with Alice came back to him. She was twelve or thirteen, putting on her boots in the ski room of their old house in Aspen.

"Dad," she said, "I have been thinking that humans need fear."

"Why is that?" he had asked her.

"Well," she said, with the kind of matter-of-factness she employed to inform him of her choice of breakfast cereal, "fear leads to doubt. Doubt leads to reason. Reason leads to choice. Choice leads to life. Without fear you don't have doubt. Without doubt you don't have reason. Without reason you don't have choice. Without choice you don't have life."

But did choice always lead to life? Small deaths happened every day. He had seen that. There was the death of turning twenty-one and never again being able to claim youth as an excuse. The death of idealism when the first girl you loved left you and so did the second and the third. The death of having the audience respond only kindly, not warmly, not ecstatically to his work. The death of losing awards, or not even being nominated. The death of jobs going to other composers with less experience or talent. The death of energy as forty-five came around and he realized he just didn't want to work the hours he once had. His face, which he'd always quite liked, had done double time in the last few years. The once ginger-blond hair was now silver and receding. The skin had grown loose at the base of his neck. In a human life, time was relentless.

He must call Alice. He went to the bedroom, retrieved his mobile, and switched it on. She answered after two rings.

"Dad," she said. "Nice to hear from you."

He suspected sarcasm, which was unlike Alice. He decided to overlook it. "Can I take you to dinner?"

"Um, is everything okay?"

"Sure. Yes. Fine."

"I'm kind of busy."

"Gramercy Tavern? There's something I need to discuss with you."

"Dad, there's nothing to—"

"Please, Alice. I really need to see you."

She sighed. "Oh, so you call after all this time, after all my messages, and you need to see me?"

"Just a father wanting to have dinner with his daughter."

There was another sigh.

"Maybe Sunday."

"Seven o'clock?"

"I guess so."

"See you then," said Levin, and then, though she was gone, he said, "thank you."

He pushed the boxes flat again and put them back in the closet. At any moment Yolanda would arrive. It suddenly occurred to Levin that he didn't know how Yolanda was paid. How was she reimbursed for the food she bought each week? Ever since Lydia had left, she'd kept everything as he liked it. Organic Valley low-fat milk, Porto Rico's French Brazilian Santos coffee. Amy's sourdough. Ben & Jerry's. And meals. Macaroni and cheese, fajitas, roast pork with scalloped potatoes, seafood pie, lasagne. The cupboards were kept stocked with pasta and sauces. There were several cheeses in the fridge, cold cuts, relish. He prickled at the idea of her doing all this while he had neglected her wages. Not reimbursed her. It could well be a small fortune by now.

He penned a note. *Hi Yolanda, do I owe you anything for these past few months? Please advise.* He propped it against a cup on the kitchen bench. Then he added, *I'm so sorry if I've neglected this.* Another thing he had to take care of in Lydia's absence. And the tax. There had been an email from their accountant. But Lydia did all that stuff. Couldn't the accountants just do it for him?

He went out, walked down the street to Francois, and ate a rocket salad, a piece of seared salmon, fries. He listened through lunch to Zoë Keating's album under headphones. It sounded as if she was playing her cello beside a lacquered screen of mother-of-pearl birds and snowcapped mountains. He could feel the wind off a long narrow lake. As she played a whole landscape came to life.

He arrived at MoMA just after 1:30. He thought that maybe if dinner went well, he and Alice might go together to see the retrospective on the sixth floor. He thought she might enjoy it. They could rebuild a little. It had been a very tough few months.

It must be tough for her, seeing her mother like that. Did she go often to see Lydia? He guessed she did. He felt a stab of jealousy.

He looked about for Jane, then remembered that she had gone back to Georgia. Suddenly, he missed her.

22

PEOPLE FLOCK TO RETROSPECTIVES—VAN GOGH at the National
Gallery in London, Kandinsky at the Guggenheim. They flock
to see the *Mona Lisa*, the statue of *David*. They flock to Art
Basel and the Venice Biennale. But when did a city last cast
its collective attention on a single work of one artist? In 1969
Christo and Jeanne-Claude wrapped the Sydney coastline. In
2005 they made seven thousand five hundred and three gates of
saffron fabric in Central Park and more people walked among
them than entered all of New York's galleries in that single year.

Now, every day the crowds are increasing. The line to sit
with Marina Abramović begins to form at 7 a.m. on the pavement outside MoMA. Since the show began on March 9, more
than three hundred and fifty thousand people have come to see
this one work of art.

The artist is at her table. The man with the angel eyes is
opposite her again. They have been sitting together, unmoving,
eyes connecting, for almost half an hour. Marina can see a room
with a floor of confetti made from notes and letters, receipts,
journals, manuscripts, books—every shred of documentation
she has amassed (and believe me there is an amassment—she

throws nothing away, not even a receipt from the dentist). It is the room she imagines her dead body being laid in.

Seated at the side of the performance is Arky Levin in dark jeans and a blue patterned shirt. Farther along is Brittika from Amsterdam, with her silken pink hair and trademark makeup. There are other students with hoodies and laptops, who will trade on this show for months if they manage to write something useful about it. There are the very famous, who are increasing in numbers at *The Artist Is Present*. They are given preference at the head of the line. Of course.

There are visitors from Brooklyn, Bombay, Berlin, and Baghdad. Well, perhaps not Baghdad, because that is a war zone of broken buildings, dust, and heat, and not a bird to be heard. I have seen death scoop up tens of thousands of civilians in that war. The same civilians who once admired Van Gogh's sunflowers, or Monet's lilies. Perhaps they read the poems of Nazik Al-Malaika, Dorothy Wordsworth, Mary Oliver, Christina Rossetti. Perhaps they liked the music of Leonard Cohen and Kadim Al-Sahir. Or the writing of Mahmoud Saeed, Ernest Hemingway, Betool Khedairi, Toni Morrison. War seeks to eliminate commonality.

This is not a war zone. This is commonality. Marina's friends come too. What do they make of this? And what of those who don't come? Who can't quite bear to see her in such pain? For they know her well enough to know the pain she is in. Can see it in the tremor of her eyelid, the tension in her fingers, the pallor of her skin, the glaze across her lucent brown irises.

Francesca Lang is the wife of Marina's longtime agent, Dieter Lang. For the one artist who makes an agent rich, there are many who never will. Agents are like cats. Rarely do they get lucky and catch a bird, but it does not stop them from being fascinated by flight. Marina has not made Dieter rich. He never thought she would. But he thought what she did was important.

"I've said it before," said Francesca to her husband. "Marina was Cleopatra in a past life. Or Hippolyta. Or Élisabeth Vigée-Lebrun. A painter would make sense."

Dieter Lang sighed.

"You must stop going," she said to him. "It doesn't help her and it certainly doesn't help you."

"But I need to see that she's okay. I mean, we know she's not. We know it's hell."

"She will be fine. If there's one thing I am sure of, it's that." She knew Marina's legs were swelling. Her ribs were sinking into her organs. But Marina would be fine. If Francesca wasn't so entirely certain of Marina's ability to succeed, she might, over the years, have been more uncertain of her marriage. But there had never been any cause to be, as Francesca had surmised from the start. Marina was never going to fail. Dieter had made the right decision.

Francesca understood that Marina's success required Dieter to be adviser, business liaison, friend, agent, counsel, and accomplice in all things that promoted the artistic ambitions of Marina. This was not a malicious observation. It was simply true. Despite it being 2010, Francesca was surprised how often she had to defend the desire for success in a woman. If anything, it ought to be encouraged, Francesca thought. How tired she was, after all they had fought for, to find the ambitious woman still painted as the femme fatale, lacking in empathy, selfish, threatening—no matter how much she gave of herself to the world. It was ridiculous but it was still there.

Francesca had known Marina for several years before she had introduced her to Dieter. It had been Francesca who arranged the lunch where at last Dieter and Marina agreed on a working relationship. Of course it had to be. Why ever not? Dieter was the perfect agent for Marina. They both had the same ambitions, the same hunger for New York.

People asked Francesca how she felt about Marina. Wasn't Marina tough? Ruthless? *Yes*, Francesca would say, *and no. Marina's the warmest person I have ever met.* Women's groups tried to claim Marina as a feminist but Marina denied it. She said she had made no overtly feminist pieces, though Francesca would dispute that. Surely *Art Must Be Beautiful, Artist Must Be Beautiful* said a great deal about women and art.

The thing people seemed to overlook was that Marina had watched Yugoslavia turn into a religious bloodbath under Milošević. Orthodox Christians, their crosses around their necks, killing Muslims and Catholics and atheists. Dead Bosnians and Croatians and Albanians on TV every night. Tortured women and girls. Rapes. Sex slaves. Mass graves. Marina knew what it did to people. She had lived with parents who each kept a loaded pistol beside the bed.

Marina had requested but been refused (once they understood what show she intended to stage) the Yugoslavian pavilion at the Venice Biennale. Dieter had found her an airless basement ripe with summer heat and there she scrubbed cow bones fresh from the abattoir. Mounted on the walls of the cellar were photographs of her parents—Vojo and Danica—their images reflected in large copper water bowls. On one wall was a film of Marina dressed in a white lab coat, explaining about the wolf rat who eats all the other rats.

As visitors descended the stairs to the cellar, they were met by the sweet putrid smell of rotting meat. There was the artist in a bloodied white shift atop the pile of rotting bones, scrubbing away the blood and gore. This was a citizen's response and a daughter's response. An artist's response. It was her own form of outrage and lament and possibly farewell to a country she had loved.

"I am only interested in art that can change the ideology of society," Marina said at the ceremony to award her the Golden Lion.

Francesca understood some of that. She was German. It was enough simply to say that. She was German, and nothing could take away the things that statement had come to mean since Hitler. Francesca recalled the writer she'd seen interviewed on *Oprah*. Oprah had asked him what race he was. The young man had responded: "The human race."

Marina did not actively befriend politicians, nor did she seek out the allegiance of billionaires. If such people came into her life, they interested her only if she felt a connection. She did not force anything to be something it was not. If she had ever been Hippolyta of the Amazons, or Freyja the Norse goddess, then in this life Marina had subdued her warring instincts. But not her wanting ones. She wanted fame. And she had sought it through long hard labor, by endurance and pain and heartbreak and love, over decades in which the only thing that kept her going was her commitment to herself not to let this life go unrecorded.

"Didn't you have an Anne Boleyn theory?" Dieter asked her as he poured Grey Goose for them both, adding fresh lime and a splash of tonic. He was off the phone at last. An evening when they could eat dinner on the couch together and watch a DVD.

"Oh, yes," said Francesca, remembering that she had once suspected Marina was the reincarnated second wife of Henry the Eighth. "I'd forgotten that one. But it does make sense."

"If I had been Anne Boleyn in a past life, then I'm not sure I'd be worried about death; I think I'd be worried about love," said Dieter, chewing on a piece of celery. "I think I'd worry about

the cost . . . *wild for to hold, though I seem tame*, to condense
Thomas Wyatt."

Francesca took the glass he offered her. "To our Marina."
And they both drank.

For twenty years Francesca had watched people subsumed
by Marina's greater force. They bathed in her radiance, her easy
humor, her hospitality and magnetism.

"It will be the making of her. You know that," Dieter said.

"I see it happening right in front of us," Francesca agreed.
"And you were pivotal. It was refining it, pushing her to make
it simpler—it worked. It's so utterly simple. The staircase, the
theater of those early ideas, it wouldn't have been nearly so
powerful. This is perfect. All that's left is energy. It's not really
remarkable to think that people are being drawn to it. Or that
those who sit are being profoundly affected."

"I have asked Colm to write something about his sitting."

"Good," said Francesca.

Francesca liked writers. She liked to feed them. She liked to
feed anyone creative. She should have given the wall inside their
door over to signatures and by now it would have been filled
with people who had eaten at their table.

"Antony Gormley is getting the usual attention," Dieter said.

"Ah, yes," said Francesca. "I listened to the podcast."

"And?"

"Oh, Arnold was saying the standard things about Gormley's
use of space and referencing the Mersey and London, and then
Healayas Breen said this interesting thing. She said historically
the artist's role had been to stimulate us and arrest our visual
senses with color, texture, content—but that now YouTube gave
us all that. So Gormley's statues looking down on the city and
Abramović at MoMA were two new considerations for what art

might be into the future. Perhaps art was evolving into something to remind us of the power of reflection, even stillness."

When Marina had done *The House with the Ocean View* in 2002, Dieter hadn't been sure he could bear it. They had constructed three open rooms on the wall. The rooms were interlinked and a ladder rested against each room, but the steps were made of razor-sharp knife blades, making it impossible to ascend or descend. For twelve days Marina had lived up there in those three open rooms. One held a bed, one a shower and toilet, and the third a table and chair. For twelve days Marina had no food, nothing but water to drink and a metronome to keep her company.

Dieter had left the gallery each night and locked the doors, knowing Marina was still in there. If there was a fire, he had locked her in and she had no way out other than down those ladders of knives. In the morning, when he and the staff arrived, she would be there going through her rituals. She wouldn't have it any other way.

Each day she took three showers. Every day she changed the tunic and pants she wore for another of identical shape but a new color. Sometimes she began a Serbian song and, as much as possible, she maintained eye contact with the people in the gallery. *Establishing an energy dialogue*, Marina had called it.

Some people came every day and sat for hours on the floor. Someone offered her an apple, placing it up on the platform. It stayed there until one of the staff removed it. When Francesca had visited *The House with the Ocean View*, the gallery had felt like a church. And now the atrium at MoMA did too.

"Is she reading any of the reviews?" she asked Dieter.

Dieter shook his head. "I tell myself that if I sit with her for a few minutes, that's a few minutes in which nothing is wanted of her," he said.

Francesca held his hand. "On the last day she'll stand up and it will be over. She'll bathe in all the acknowledgment that will come to her and forget what it has cost her. The cost to her organs, her kidneys. Her mind. The hunger. When it's a complete success—and it will be—she will forget it all. You know her. She will be in diva mode, glorious, radiant, and it will all be in the past. And then she'll crash."

When Francesca had met Dieter, he had been getting over a traumatic breakup.

"You rescued me," he liked to tell her in those early years. Abducted his heart and never returned it. She knew he loved Marina. They both loved Marina. He must love Marina. But his heart was hers.

"You have to remember that," Francesca continued. "To make sure her house is ready for her. It has to be stocked. Ready for her to have complete rest. In the end, this may take something from her that she can't replace, but if it wasn't so fraught with danger, and so hard, she would never choose it."

Dieter's eyes filled with tears. They sat there, side by side on the couch. Thirty-four years they had been married. Thirty-four years, four children, five grandchildren, Berlin to New York, and how did they stay this way, where she knew him so intimately that nothing was new, and yet he was still a mystery to himself?

And the reverse was true, Francesca thought. Perhaps that was the way of long marriage. As they got older, they could never lose track of themselves. They had the other to remind them.

23

WHEN LEVIN ARRIVED TO MEET Alice for their Sunday night meal, she was listening to something and reading what appeared to be a large illustrated medical textbook. He leaned over and kissed her on the cheek. He placed the earbud she handed him in his left ear.

"Evanescence," said Alice. "*Fallen.* 2003. Hi."

Levin nodded, listening to a wash of surging guitars and soaring vocals.

"They're making another album right now," she added, closing the book slowly as if it was hard to take her eyes from the page.

"What else are you listening to?"

"Hmmm . . . *Horehound.*" She met his eyes with her own green ones. "So what's up?"

"It's a very strange time."

"And that's what you wanted to discuss?"

"No. I wanted to see you. I wanted to see you if you're all right."

"If I'm all right? Are you serious?"

"Yes, I am."

Alice wanted to hurt him then. It had taken him all this time to think that maybe she wasn't okay. But it was hard to be unkind to him. It was like kicking a puppy and she hated that too, that her father was like that. There were shadows under his eyes. He looked thinner. She would not feel sorry for him.

She said, "I cut up a cadaver last week. Well, not all of it. Some of it. The thigh, the gluteus maximus, the little sinews around the hip joint."

He looked at her fine white fingers and imagined them unfurling nerves and arteries, her clinical eye observing the simple complexity of that weight-bearing joint.

"I think it's normal," she went on, "to feel a little unhinged when you have to deal with a cadaver for the first time. They told us that, and I'm sure they are watching for it too. I think if you enjoy it, they'd be worried."

"I guess they don't want sociopaths qualifying with degrees in medicine," said Levin, thinking of *Dexter*, and how sociopaths, even serial killers, had become the subject of Oscar-winning movies and prime-time viewing on television.

"I'm sure a few have," Alice said. It was hard to say which of her fellow students would become the sociopath, or the murderer. Certainly several would become drug addicts. Some probably already were. It was the law of averages, after all. All of medicine was based on it on some level. How many people you had to immunize before the population was safe. How many would die of cancer and how many from heart disease. How many would have a child with a birth defect. How many would contract late-onset diabetes.

Alice was wearing a red floral dress and a white cardigan embroidered with blue and green butterflies. She had a thing for old-fashioned dresses and mismatching patterns. Levin could never see her without thinking of Björk. But where Björk had a bone wildness in her face, Alice had the sheen of Ingrid Bergman, with those big eyes and big smile in a cream and pink complexion. He'd worried through her teenage years that one day she'd realize that she wasn't a stick-thin girl in the latest tiny jeans. He worried that she'd get anorexic or bulimic or depressed. But Alice never did. She discovered retro clothes, put them together in a peculiarly individual style, and found friends wherever she went. She had been in and out of love half a dozen times with boys who had made his palms sweat, but nothing and nobody had yet dimmed her kindness, or the light in her eyes—except perhaps him. And this troubled him.

He hadn't considered Alice when he'd complied with Lydia's wishes. He hadn't thought he needed to. She had her own life. Her own apartment. He had thought, perhaps wrongly, that his job as a father was done. He knew he had tried to be a good father.

After Alice was born, they had decided it was too great a risk to Lydia to have another baby. So Alice was it. Levin had been relieved. It had been a shock how much noise babies made. It had upended his life. Alice the baby, named after Lydia's mother, consumed Lydia's attention. Alice the five-year-old had a calendar scheduled around her. Alice the teenager became a vegetarian and suddenly he was eating tofu. Alice determined Lydia's life. The lateness of the hour she got to bed, the washing that needed doing, the movies they watched, the places they vacationed. Alice toyed with the idea of architecture and worked for a couple of years in Lydia's firm after senior year, before going to France. Then she applied to medical school at NYU and was accepted. And here she was, and Levin didn't know how he had gotten so much older that his daughter was this woman.

Alice ordered the duck ravioli (vegetarianism having gone the way of the Goth phase that happened about the same time) and Levin the grilled pork chop. After the wine arrived, and the food soon after, she said, as if complying with a social expectation, "So, what have you been doing?"

He told her about the performance at MoMA.

"Oh, Marina Abramović," Alice said. "I really want to see it. Is it good? What's she like?"

"Very still."

"Did you see the naked people upstairs?"

"No, I haven't seen that yet."

"It's been all over the news!" She laughed. "How long does she have to sit there for?"

"Until the end of May," he said.

"Wow. Really? Did you sit with her?"

"Oh no. No."

"Why not?"

"Well, there's a line, for one thing. There are usually at least twenty people waiting to sit by first thing in the morning and the line just grows after that. Some people sit for hours and the rest of them all wait for nothing . . ."

"And she never gets up? She just sits there?"

He nodded.

"But what do people do?"

"We watch her. It's very strange." He shrugged.

There was a silence and then he thought to say, "So, how goes the world of medicine?"

"It's big. My brain has to keep taking in all this information and trying to organize it. But the prac work is great. It's amazing to actually work with a real body and see all this incredible construction of muscles and ligaments, bones and blood vessels."

"Do the cadavers you work on have names still? Are they John or Nancy?"

"No, they have codes."

"Is it yours then, for the duration—the body?" he asked.

"Yes, but we share them. There are two of us working on ours. And the third-year students have already removed the face and explored the head. At first we had one that didn't have much muscle so we got another one. Most of them die quite old so there's not much muscle left."

"Of natural circumstances?" he asked with a smile.

"I think they have to die a certain way for them to be suitable," she said, frowning slightly. Clearly this wasn't an area where jokes were made.

"Is it possible to go all day without urinating?" he asked.

"If you don't drink," she said, "but I think it would be hard. You mean Marina Abramović, right? We've been talking about it at school. I mean, she's got to be getting dehydrated. Unless she drinks all night, but she couldn't stay awake all day if she did that. We're all betting she has a catheter. Has she done something like this before?"

"I don't really know very much about her,' he said. "Do you want to go together one day?"

"And see the nudes upstairs?" She smiled.

"If I must."

"I'll think about it. I'm so busy."

"Okay," he said.

"I saw Healayas the other day," Alice told him, scraping the last of the chocolate cake and ice cream off the plate. "Have you seen her? Are you guys doing the club again through summer?"

"No. I haven't seen any of them since . . ." Levin trailed off. "It's probably too late."

"You should. It's such a good gig."

"Would you come play with us some time?"

"Hmmm . . ." She looked away.

"This is what Mom wanted, Alice," he said. "As the person with power of attorney, you know that better than anyone."

"Yes," she said, turning to him again. "But how would any of us know that's what she wants?"

"Well, she put it in writing—she made it legal."

"That was when she was well. That was before she stopped being able to change her mind."

"Do you think she wants to change her mind?"

"I don't know," Alice said, and tears filled her eyes.

"What would you have me do?" he asked, finishing his espresso.

Alice said, "I just feel like she's so alone out there and I can't visit every weekend."

Across the room a baby had started crying. The noise penetrated Levin's ear with a particular ferocity.

"Shall we go?" he asked.

On the sidewalk she kissed his cheek and said, "You know, Dad, I'm not really okay about any of this. I just have to keep trusting it will all work out."

"Okay," he said.

"So, thanks for dinner."

She walked away and he wanted to cry then. It wasn't okay with him either and he didn't trust it would work out. He wanted it to be like it was. He wanted Lydia to come home and see the way he'd arranged everything. He wanted her there in the morning drying her hair on a towel. He wanted her voice on the other end of the phone talking about what they would have for dinner. Maybe if the *Kawa* score earned him nominations . . . maybe if his new album took off . . . He needed some sort of sign. But without stars, or God, there was nothing to wish upon and nowhere to ask for help.

24

THE NEXT MORNING, HE TOOK an early Skype call from the film director, Seiji Isoda, in Tokyo. Then he carefully arranged the three cushions on the chair again, red, red, and red, then the round white pillow and the long black cashmere scarf for Abramović's hair.

"Good morning," he said. I'm frightened of a pillow, he thought. But why was he frightened? Was he always frightened? Yes, he thought with startling clarity. I am always frightened. He wanted to forget that thought right away.

He wasn't a bigger man. He knew that. He was an average man, and something was wrong with him. Where was the feeling that everything was all right? Surely by fifty you were meant to have that locked in?

Who was he, when all was said and done? Who did people see when they saw him? People said he had nice eyes. Would Marina think he had nice eyes? He wasn't impressively tall. He wasn't impressively handsome. Lydia used to remind him to smile. "You know, you even frown in your sleep," she said. "And I whisper to you that I love you, and sometimes your frown goes away."

She had been certainty. When everything fell apart, she would be there. It was partly why he always felt so angry when she got sick. He didn't like that the whole world wobbled when that happened, and he felt small. Small and alone. And now everyone knew. They knew that somehow he had failed Lydia. When she might have needed him the way couples seemed to do when life got tough, she had shunted him to the side.

He continued to gaze at the pillow face and imagined the dark eyes of Marina Abramović looking back at him. Today he felt more comfortable on the chair. There was a blade of sunshine coming in across the floor and illuminating the edge of the Danish dining table. He liked nice things. He liked the things they had bought that would always have style.

Mostly Lydia was right. He didn't like people. Hardly at all. He certainly didn't like thinking about people. He didn't want to know about starving people who lived on one corncob a day if they were lucky. He didn't care about people who would be swallowed up by climate change. He didn't care about the plastic take-out containers of his life stretching out behind him in a great wake that probably reached from here to the moon by now. He didn't even like living on this planet particularly. It was complex and often violent.

He hadn't liked growing up either. He'd loved his mother but he hadn't liked her. She had meditated. She had silent days. Days when he was not allowed to speak to her and she did not speak to him. They ate in silence, washed up in silence, went to bed in silence. The piano was the only thing allowed to disturb the house because Levin, his mother assured him, was destined for greatness. She was sure there was some sort of plan at work in the universe, a plan that would see the stars align, and her nights nursing to get him through school, and her weekend shifts at the aged-care facility, would no longer be necessary because Levin was going to be famous.

He hardly remembered his father. He remembered the night his mother had come into his room. He had been four. He remembered the light from the hallway and the weight of her pressing the sheets down on him and her voice in the dark whispering, "Your father is dead, Arky. He's dead"

Perhaps she said more. He didn't remember. He only remembered that afterward she had left the room and he had lain there in the darkness. He wasn't sure he was going to be able to keep breathing. Or if he was even allowed to breathe when his father was dead.

Levin had a dim memory of his father holding his hand as they walked down a flight of stairs. But perhaps he had made it up. When his mother died, it had simply consolidated his thinking. Bad things happened at any moment. It was an almost unbearable effort being human. Did it matter that he'd loved Lydia? Did it matter that he'd tried to be a good husband and father?

He had made some nice film scores. He had made some people happy with his music. Other than that, did it really matter how he lived his life? It was hard enough knowing which lightbulb to buy. How to navigate new software. How to buy the right phone plan. How to document work and travel expenses. The list was endless. If the little things made no sense, what hope was there for big things like marriages?

He'd done his best. Clearly it hadn't been enough. He felt immensely sad. He felt as if he'd missed something very important. Lydia had tried to get him to go to therapy. "Can you imagine what it would be like to have some freedom around all your worry?" she'd said. "And look what happened to you. It could really help."

But he didn't need help from a stranger. He didn't want to be some clichéd New Yorker with therapy every Friday morning before the weekend came and everything went pear-shaped.

Pillow-Marina looked back at him. She said nothing. But she was there. That seemed to matter. Even in her pillow form, it felt good to know she was there. He took a deep breath, closed his eyes, dropped his head as he'd seen them do at the museum.

He got up from the table, noting that he'd sat for almost half an hour, which surprised him because it had felt shorter. He made coffee. He thought about dinner with Alice and decided it seemed to require a follow-up. He didn't know how to help. He'd never known how to help. It was his great flaw. His father had died and he didn't know how to help. His mother died and maybe she wouldn't have if she hadn't needed to get out of the house that night. He suspected she had driven away because she had needed to be alone. She'd often taken drives at night. He must have been hard to live with. There was no help for that. It was long ago. He didn't know how to solve anything but music.

He sat in his studio, coffee cup in hand, and listened again to the melodies he was discovering for *Kawa*, and the one melody that might repeat throughout the film. The soundtrack had to evoke love and loss in a world cloaked in snow and he thought, I'm writing the music of this winter. The winter when everything went away.

Isoda had liked both theme track options he'd sent. The completion of the new scenes would determine which melody they finally chose. Or it might take longer to be sure. They had discussed the possibility of him going to Tokyo next month to Isoda's studio. With the new scenes he'd have more than forty minutes of footage, but they weren't consecutive scenes. It was hard to gauge precisely the emotional arc of the story. If he could see the work in progress—see the sketches taking form, see what Isoda was seeing—then he could be sure that the melody would draw the pictures together. If it did, there was the score to write, an orchestra waiting for its parts, and a studio to book. He'd need vocals and session musos.

He began considering which orchestra, the pros and cons of recording in New York or possibly Chicago. Maybe even Tokyo. This was what he loved, when the process began to escalate and the outcome began to appear.

Lydia had been the same about architecture. He had stood in her buildings and been in awe of her. Floors played music, ceilings rained, and rooms were divided by live fish, butterflies, crickets. Holographic symbols were pinned to the night sky, a pedestrian bridge rolled up like a caterpillar, filaments of light made an ever-changing ceiling of rainbows, corridors rippled with laughter. In her buildings there was no separation between the interior and the exterior worlds. The private homes she designed had Japanese maples inside the front door, waterfalls on rooftops, fragrant vertical interior gardens, and streams running through bathrooms.

By her mid-thirties she was so in demand that she could choose one or two commercial projects and a house or two to do each year. She liked to be there when Alice came home from school. She had a waiting list two years ahead. Invitations to travel and speak piled up on her desk. Awards and citations cluttered her shelves. Some days Levin wondered how to reach out and touch her. She seemed to belong to other people. Was he even visible when she had flown in from Shanghai or Madrid? She kissed him, hugged him, was gone into the bathroom, dressing, asking him how he was, how Alice was, and all the time she was watching the clock, considering how long his answer was taking in relation to the traffic that would catch them at 51st on their way uptown to see the Philharmonic and the things she had yet to prepare for the next day.

When they made love it felt like the only time he could really hold her. When she woke in the night, she would reach out and curl herself around him, and he felt as if he was the luckiest man in the world. When he woke she was often gone to her desk. In her pale blue hooded dressing gown she had the look of a nun at prayer.

Washington Square had been her dream. He didn't know why she wanted to live on Washington Square. She just liked it. Of course it had to be the right building, have the right bones. So they had thrown themselves into the New York real estate Olympics. For every co-op they had to provide his work history, her work history, their financials for the last five years, everything that captured them on paper: references, qualifications, memberships. Their personal details laid bare for strangers to assess, compare, and pass judgement.

"There are new apartments on the river over in the Meatpacking District," Anastasia, the Russian real estate agent, advised them. "They're very sizable. Views over the Hudson. Near the High Line. They're also in your price range."

"Lydia wants Washington Square," Levin said.

"Okay," Anastasia said, picking up the red leather folder. "Some very nice places on offer just now, plenty of movement and good prices."

Several times they missed out. And then this apartment had come up.

A gracious (approx. 3382 sq. ft.) home. Rarely does a home come on the market with such a large interior space and vast, luxurious outdoor space . . . parallel and herringbone-laid hardwood flooring . . . huge master suite bathed in sunlight with eastern and southern exposures . . . marble, granite . . . large private study also opening to balcony, two additional bedrooms . . . storage . . . magical view over Washington Square Park.

Lydia saw the possibilities the balcony and the southern light afforded them. They had talked of ideas to reconfigure it at some point in the future. She had gone back and forth across town. Produced endless paperwork for him to sign and complete. And then they got the call. It was theirs.

Lydia had been looking drawn as fall faded and winter wrapped the city. She'd been back and forth to London all year, working on an interactive installation for children commissioned after the launch of her Rain Room in Cairo. Because no English child needed an education in varieties of rain, it was to be a horizontal and vertical flower and fruit garden within a vast bee house. She called it the Pollen Project. It was meant to be ready for the London Olympics in 2012.

He was used to her translucence by the end of a project, as if she had poured the substance of herself into it. She had flown to London for final meetings ten days before Christmas. Two days before they were due to move into the new apartment, she had rung from London to say she had to stay another day. She was so sorry. There was a new hurdle with the Department of Agriculture.

"We'll have to cancel the move," he'd said.

"No, no," she'd protested. "We can't. The settlement is done. Everything is booked. It will take weeks to reschedule. Everything is ready to go. They'll pack and unpack. I've fully briefed them. I've told them it has to be done by the end of the day. You just need to let them in uptown and welcome them downtown, okay? You shouldn't even have to wrap or unwrap a cup. But if you want to do your studio, you just need to let them know."

He wanted to do his studio. And he told her so.

"If they put stuff in the wrong places, we'll sort it out in the new year," she said. "We can do that together. What matters is getting it all moved. I'm so looking forward to two whole weeks off to just enjoy our new home. I'm not even going to check my email."

For two days the packers had been in their old apartment and he had made himself scarce packing albums and equipment in his studio. When he was done, and the reality of leaving their home of twenty years, the chaos and the effort of strangers in every room, was all too much, he had taken a room at the Algonquin and drunk a bottle of good French wine while watching *Inglourious Basterds*.

He'd thought it an unnecessary expense, hiring unpackers, but when he saw the scale of the boxes that were arriving at Washington Square, he'd been relieved. He had all the boxes marked *Arky's Studio* sorted first. Then he'd taken a Stanley knife and, slitting open the packing tape, he'd begun untangling the leads and considering how he was going to set it all up. From time to time he'd listened for a plate lowered too heavily on a stack, or wineglasses being irreverently handled. He'd wondered if he'd find a favorite jacket was missing. Or a box of CDs. But no such thing seemed to have occurred.

When he went to inspect the work, the wardrobes looked like a Benetton shop. Everything was color coordinated and folded. There was the familiar linen on their bed and the liquid soap Lydia liked in the bathroom. He did not know the smell of this place, the noise the water made refilling the toilet, the snap of the light switches, the sound of his shoes on the parquetry or the door to the bedroom closing behind him. But it now housed their furniture, their art.

He spent the day determining the exact position of the iMacs and the speakers, reconnecting cables and plugs. By mid-afternoon he had settled on the best location for the Kurzweil keyboard in relation to his main Mac keyboard and the angle of his chair to the door. He had even placed a few photographs.

His music collection remained in boxes but he thought he could unpack that over the coming weeks. The packers had asked his advice on arranging books and he had explained Lydia's system. Every book in the house was marked on the spine—*A* for architecture, *H* for history, *M* for music, *N* for novel, *P* for poetry. Then they were arranged alphabetically within subject or type. Lydia would do that bit. If they could just put them in groupings according to letter . . .

By the time the unpackers left at 5:45 p.m. there were only three boxes left in the living area. They were all marked *Treasures—Fragile—Lydia Only—DO NOT UNPACK*—written in Lydia's sharp square letters. He had always liked her handwriting. It had buildings within it.

Out on the deck, snow had begun falling in the darkness. The city disappeared. The neighboring apartments were gone along with the trees fringing the square. The swell and push of traffic was muted and distant. He had Veuve in the fridge, glasses waiting on the counter with a bowl of fresh strawberries. He had been ridiculously happy it was snowing, as if it indicated some kind of good omen for their future. He'd been trying to get the television programmed when she had called.

"Hi, sweetheart," she said. "I've had a tough twenty-four hours. I'm going to go straight to the hospital. See if they can sort me out."

She had never seen it, everything he had done to make this their home.

25

THE PHONE RANG AT 9:15 the following Sunday morning. He'd turned it back on the day before and decided to see what happened. Hal happened.

"Just checking you're still alive, Arky," he said. "Have you remembered?"

Levin thought quickly. Was there a meeting he'd missed? Had Isoda or his people wanted something he'd forgotten?

"Tennis?" prompted Hal with his normal irony.

Tennis! Levin laughed, relieved. "Oh, yes. Of course. I'll be ready in twenty minutes."

"So you did forget," said Hal. "Okay. See you on the corner."

They took the Williamsburg Bridge accompanied by Ella Fitzgerald singing the Gershwin songbook. The roof was off the convertible and the day was fine.

"So, what gives?" Hal said.

"I'm making progress," Levin said. "It's coming along."

"I've got another job you might like to look at. It's a new TV series. Some kind of medieval sci-fi thing, like Henry the Eighth meets *Twilight*."

"When would it have to be done?"

"I could push for end of June."

"Hal . . ."

"I know. You want to focus on *Kawa*. Sometimes a little multi-tasking helps. I keep telling you, it saves those expensive gaps between jobs. If I only had you as my client, I'd have been back in Kansas long ago. Hey, by the way, several people have asked about you of late. Did you get on Facebook or something?"

"No," Levin said.

"Well, stranger things have happened. Did you see Obama gave us the right to make medical decisions for our loved ones? We can now be by the bedside of our partners when they're dying."

"Oh, good."

"Good!" Hal said. "It's appalling. We vote him in and that's the best he can do? He's got the Senate. I'm still waiting for something meaningful. Get out of Iraq."

Hal had a square face and a body that was steadily getting squarer. He wore large yellow-framed glasses and his face was very lined now, much more since 2001. He had been right in the thick of it, covered in ash, one block away, on his way to a meeting on the forty-third floor. He had once said to Levin: "Only missed being a jumper, or dying in the collapse, by five minutes. That ash on me, later I thought about it. That was people. Probably people I knew."

Hal continued on, talking about a new judge for the Supreme Court, fiscal reform. From time to time his hands did star-jumps off the steering wheel to emphasize a point. Lydia always said how good Hal would have been in office, a good politician, and how frustrated she was that being gay was a hindrance. Hal was never going to pretend. He was never going to hide Craig or find a rent-a-blonde wife to see him into office. Hal and Craig had been together for twenty-seven years, longer than almost any couple Levin knew. But America wasn't ready for gay politicians, let alone a gay president. Or an atheist. Hal and Lydia loved talking politics. Levin just poured the wine and turned on the football.

Breakfast on hope, dine on fear. It had been a line on a poster for one of Tom's early movies. And since the crash that sentiment had gotten a whole lot worse.

"So, you want to tell me how it's really going?" Hal said.

"Well, Seiji says the production time's getting blown out of the water. They're using his illustrators on other projects that have priority. I think he's just hoping if he sits tight, it will get done without anyone really noticing, and he'll get a release. Some days I get three scenes and then a week goes by and I get nothing. And then I get revisions."

"Anything I can listen to? You using some of those Japanese wooden flutes?" Hal said.

"Shakuhachi," said Levin.

"Yes! Good!"

"No. No shakuhachi." Levin laughed. "So far it's mostly piano. Violins and a little percussion. I thought I really had it but then I look at the latest scenes and it's awkward, clichéd. Like everyone has heard it before."

"This is not the time to lose confidence, Arky."

"Annie Lennox singing 'Into the West'—you know, from *Lord of the Rings*? Perfect. In fact, almost anything from *Lord of the Rings* would do right now. Howard Shore just got it right. Ludovico Einaudi's *Nightbook*? That too. How about Marianelli's soundtrack to *Atonement*?"

"Am I meant to be getting worried?" Hal asked. "You know, Arky, you're not going to like me saying it, but think about the music you'd write for Lydia right now, the way things are."

"Wow." Levin felt as if he had been winded.

"Just think about it."

"Hal . . ."

"We love you both. I don't want you to wake up and realize you let the best thing in your life go, Arky."

The car had become ridiculously small and Levin felt as if he was suffocating. But Hal went on. "I know you. You love each other. I know she's the most independent person in the world, and she pretends she doesn't need anything, but she needs you, Arky. I walk into the hospital and you're asleep with your head on her lap. She's just sitting there looking like death warmed up stroking *your* head. It's not meant to be that way."

"But hospitals always make me tired."

"But you're *not* the one who needs looking after. No, that's not true, you're old enough to be the one *doing* some looking after."

Levin had nothing to say.

"It just breaks my heart to see you guys apart . . . And look at you—you're looking terrible. I don't mind saying it. You look like a wreck."

"I'm okay. Really. I'm . . . and she needs to be there."

"Yes, but not alone. Not without you ever visiting. And don't talk about the legals. God, if there was ever a case for challenging a legal document . . . I know you're going to say that she wanted you to do this; she wanted you to make music. But is that enough?"

Music. It sounded feeble suddenly in the face of the yawning gap between life before Christmas and life these past four months.

He'd always known music as an electrical circuit running through every pathway in his body. When music came to him, the world grew calm and clear and silent. It was why he loved New York. The pavement, the streetlights, the subway, it was all a kind of circuitry fueled with energy. It wasn't that anyone could be great here, but everyone could try, and so he had kept trying, and felt that the city, sometimes the city alone, believed in him. It would all have been worth it. How else was the Brooklyn Bridge built? The Empire State? The certainty of a vision.

Marina was doing it every day and hundreds and thousands of people were sweeping their lives in her direction to feel the dream she held inside her. He must look into her eyes. He felt a cold flush of electricity up his arms. It had to be done.

Hal paused. "So, what else have you been doing, apart from convincing yourself you're a terrible composer?"

"I've been going to MoMA. To the Abramović thing."

"Oh, yes," Hal said. "Have you sat?"

"No."

"Craig and I went. It's fascinating. The queue was huge so we went upstairs and wandered around for ages. I came home exhausted. What a life! I literally collapsed on the couch and didn't move until Craig brought me a Bellini. I was so in awe. I mean, she is the canvas, isn't she? And she's a kind of muse or oracle. I want to take Abramović vitamins. I just love that intensity in everything she does.

"By the way," he continued, "we had a night at the Standard bar. You know—the one with the hot tub. They sell bathing suits from a vending machine! Of course, after midnight no one cares. I don't think there was a single real New Yorker there. The place was full of twenty-year-olds speaking crazy German, girls in micro-skirts and boys with unbelievable form. It was great fun. I think we've become the new Silicon Valley. A geographically contained focus group for every new app developer. It's really the end of the shabby. At breakfast this morning they asked me if I wanted my grapefruit brûléed. I mean, really?"

At the Tennis Center they played three sets on an outdoor court. Levin lost 4–6, 5–7, 3–6. He hated to lose. And he was disturbed by how out of shape he was.

"I think we should get back on the squash court," he said to Hal as they made their way back to Manhattan for lunch.

"You know more men our age die on the squash court from heart attacks than any other sport?" asked Hal.

"Maybe not, then . . . I have started back at Pilates."

"I don't mind winning," said Hal. "Don't get me wrong."

He surveyed the skyline ahead. "I never get over that Lego-block sky, as Craig's nephew calls it. He has this passion for the water towers and tells me they're tin men all asleep and at night they get up and walk about. They'd make fabulous little studios if we drained them and did them up. We'd have to change the fire regulations, of course, but . . . perhaps that's where the artists of New York could start again. In fact, keep the water towers and start dropping trailer homes on the rooftops. Make them rent-subsidized, just for creatives. Kind of like a grant. Where will New York be in twenty years if creative people, who have always been the lifeblood of this town, can't afford to live here anymore? It will all be about money and the Chinese. Who wants that?"

"You want to live somewhere else?"

"Are you kidding?"

Over *penne all'arrabbiata* Hal said, "You really going to stay in the new apartment? It must be pretty lonely."

Levin grimaced.

"Maybe you should go to Tokyo and meet up with Isoda's team there," Hal suggested. "It might speed things up a little."

"Maybe next month."

"Well, okay. I'm counting on you to pull this thing off."

As Hal dropped him off at the square, he asked Levin, "Do you ever wonder what your life might have been if you hadn't loved music?"

"No, I don't," Levin said. "I've never wondered that."

"You know, that's the gift. You've never had to wonder. Me, I keep being an agent and the birth date on my driver's license gets further and further away. It's like the end of *Annie Hall* when the guy who plays Woody Allen's brother thinks he's a chicken. The psychiatrist asks Woody Allen why he doesn't get his brother locked up. And Woody says, 'I need the eggs.' That's me. I do what I do because I need the eggs."

"Are you quitting, Hal?" Levin asked, his hand on the door handle.

"No, Arky. I think what I'm trying to say to you is, you don't need the eggs. You've got real choices. Maybe it's time to choose."

26

HEALAYAS BREEN WALKED SLOWLY THROUGH the Abramović retrospective—through rooms of video installations, huge photographs, glass boxes arranged with memorabilia. It was 9 a.m. and she was entirely alone. She had a Sennheiser microphone plugged into her iPhone. It was a prerecord for the show. Her headphones conveyed what the microphone was picking up. She walked quietly, having removed her shoes and tucked them into her orange tote, which she abandoned against a wall.

She took a small sip of water, relaxed her shoulders, and then began her introduction, recalling for her listeners how some of the artists currently re-enacting the works of Marina Abramović had reported being groped by visitors. One of the artists stated that several men had fondled her breasts as she stood nude in a doorway re-performing the work *Imponderabilia*.

"*Imponderabilia*," Healayas said into the microphone, "was first performed in Germany by Abramović and her partner, Ulay. It was meant to remind people that the artist was the doorway to the gallery. Originally Marina and Ulay, both naked, were so close to each other that people entering the gallery had to squeeze between them. But at MoMA, thirty-three years later, it is so controversial to have nude performers that visitors have been given an alternative entrance. The two nudes stand far enough apart that a visitor can slip between them without making any actual contact with skin. Even so, only about forty percent of visitors choose to walk between the nudes. The remainder choose the traditional entrance at the other end of the room. So the original point about artists and galleries seems to have been lost. And in New York nudity is still considered so shocking that it has made the front pages of the major newspapers.

"Male performers," she continued, "have also received unwanted advances, having their genitals stroked and squeezed by visitors. One male performer was apparently removed because he became visibly aroused."

Everyone had their own forms of submission and rebellion, Healayas considered. All her life people had confided in her. Told her things of an acutely personal nature. Even as a child, it had happened to her. Perhaps they sensed even then that there was nothing they could say that would shock her.

She stopped at a black-and-white film of Abramović lying down, her head toward the camera.

"*Bubbles, scales, fish, monotone, monotonous,*" said Abramović, the pace of the words slow and deliberate. Looking very young and dark-eyed, Abramović was speaking Serbian while the English subtitles translated: *Molotov cocktail, eyes, eyelashes, eye focus, pupil . . .*

The task was to voice all the words Marina's mind could muster without repetition and without stopping. If she repeated a word or couldn't think of any more, the performance ended. Healayas was fascinated by how the words connected to one another. "*Key, wall, corner, preserves, knife, handle, bread, moussaka, apple cake, condiment, whisky, humidity, embroidery . . .*

"*Children, names, milk, youth, whisper, yogurt, legalized abortion, never, travel, puberty, misunderstanding, disagreement,*

politician, position, struggle for power, German, Australian, panic,
picnic, pistol, tank, machine gun . . . lieutenant colonel, soldier,
private, regular, menstruation, masturbation, honey . . ."

Healayas thought that if she had long enough, she could map
Abramović's mind by observing the word associations she made.
It was words that gave people away. Silence, she knew, after years
of interviewing people, was the only safety. Sergio, a former
neighbor in Paris, admitted to her that hate came naturally to
him. He was a famous academic, but found himself surrounded
by hardly anyone intellectually adequate or passingly interesting. Particularly his wife and daughters. Sarah, a friend from
California, liked to find YouTube clips about birth defects and
torture. Senegal had more than thirty devices for pleasure. Yvette
cooked vegetables her husband didn't like, but was reproachful if
he didn't eat them. He was dying of bowel cancer and confined
to bed. Two weeks before he was diagnosed, she had found the
little red book of names and numbers and the dates he'd visited
that he kept in his glove compartment, but she did not tell him.

Meredith's husband, Barney, spent the insurance money after
her death on a holiday in Antigua. Upon returning home he
expanded his interests from the girl he visited on East 116th to
another farther uptown. Margaret shoplifted books. She had
several coats specially adapted. She said it was orgasmic leaving
with a hardback. John whispered to his father, in the palliative-
care center, "No one has ever loved you," and his father had
nodded and said, "I know."

Healayas knew that all guilt ultimately corrodes.

She remembered Abramović's re-performance of *Seedbed*—the
Vito Acconci piece—at the Guggenheim in 2005. Healayas had sat
on the raised stage while underneath the floorboards Abramović
had masturbated unseen, but not unheard. A microphone under
the stage captured the narrative. On the platform, the people

sitting avoided making eye contact. Couples and friends giggled. One man lay facedown on the floor and started to hump against it while underneath Abramović moaned, her words colored by her Serbian accent. *Do you like to see another man making love to me while you're masturbating? . . . Pull my pussy lips out of the way so my clitoris is exposed—spreading legs wider, pinching nipples. Who are you? . . . Can I come? . . . I need to know you're there. Are you with me? . . . Are you my fantasy?"*

Healayas had often thought about playing that recording on *Art Review* and seeing what people made of it. Was it art and not pornography because it was in the Guggenheim? When Acconci had performed it back in the long summer of love in 1972, it had been winter. He'd given four performances over two weeks, each lasting six hours. His cock must have been rubbed raw.

Healayas continued through the retrospective, recording her observations. Abramović and Ulay in a film running naked at each other in an underground car park. They slapped their bodies together, then retreated back to their separate concrete columns almost as if they were on a long length of elastic. Then running toward each other they collided again. A crowd observed as the whack and slap of flesh against flesh went on and on.

There was a film where they breathed into each other's mouths, locked together until one of them began to pass out from oxygen deprivation. In another film they were kneeling face-to-face and Ulay slapped Marina's cheek. Marina slapped Ulay. Hand to cheek, hand to cheek, slap, slap, slap. The slaps became harder, the sound of the sting greater. Each of them was reeling a little. Until at last Ulay gave a slap so strong that Marina's head swung with the impact. She responded with her own slap to his face, just as hard. They both bowed their heads, unable to go on.

In another film they screamed at each other, guttural screams directly into the other's face until they went hoarse.

Artists were more honest than most people, Healayas thought. The performance artist Stelarc had grown an ear out of his left arm with the help of a team of doctors and scientists. A microphone was inserted and Stelarc's conversations could be heard, making the ear a remote listening device for anyone who cared to listen in on Stelarc's life.

Most people, Healayas knew, didn't want to look inside themselves, let alone magnify that inner life for the world to see or hear or criticize. Perhaps that was the invitation at the heart of *The Artist Is Present*. "Come and be yourself." And the people who sat found out how hard, how confronting, and how strange that was.

At the back of the retrospective, Healayas sat down on the floor and watched the video showing Abramović and Ulay walking the Great Wall of China. *The Lovers*. Two figures in red and blue walking toward each other over thousands of miles to say goodbye.

For eight years Abramović and Ulay had planned that walk. They were to begin at either end of the wall. After three thousand miles they would meet and marry. Instead, after thirteen years together, they had used it to formally end their relationship and their artistic collaboration. Abramović had said: "We spend so much time focused on the beginning of relationships, why do we not give equal consideration to ending them?"

Ulay walked on a cliff above a distant snake of silver river, he tramped across a sienna desert. His gangly frame was cloaked and his face shadowed. His stride was steady and light. He traversed broken fragments of wall and fissures caused by earthquakes. He walked across grasslands where the wall had disappeared, and places where it had long fallen into disrepair.

Marina, starting at the eastern end of the Great Wall, had the familiar rammed-earth wall, the stone balustrades and staircases. Step-by-step, staff in hand, she climbed. She appeared diminished by the scale of the ancient fortress and the steepness of the steps. Up and up, down and down, up and up, on and on she walked, her red clothing moving in the wind. The light beyond was golden. Her head was set, her gaze impassive, her step resolute.

Three thousand miles to say goodbye. Healayas watched as the film continued through to the final moment when Ulay and Marina met.

Healayas thought of her sister pleading with her to come home for their father's funeral.

"Why do you have to be so difficult?" Airah had asked her. It had always been her mother's complaint. That she, Healayas, was difficult. "I'd like you here to help me sort everything. I don't know what to do with it all."

"Throw it away."

"He loved you. He loved you more than anyone. He never blamed you," Airah had cried. "Why can't you come home and say goodbye to him?"

"There's nothing to say." Not to her father nor to his grave.

In the afterlight of the call, she thought she could have volunteered some shared memory. "Do you remember how we'd toss those little stick boats he made into the Seine from the bridge? Remember when he came in at night and how he smelled of bitumen after rain?" But if she started that conversation it might never end.

She didn't want to see her father's name on a grave. She didn't want to see the house without him there playing music. She didn't want to see his clarinet. She remembered how, as a child, when he played she saw rainbows. How his eyes had been the saddest eyes she had ever seen. How his hand had closed about hers like a wing about a body. How even when she was almost as tall as him, he'd take her hand to cross a street. How he'd remained sure of her course, sure that she was capable and wise, long after she'd proved to him she wasn't.

I would walk three thousand miles to see you again, Papa, she thought. I will wear red and you will wear blue. I would walk beside the Yangtze, across desert, up and down stairs, fending off bureaucrats and a million tourists, just to see you again. You are not dead. You are simply ahead on the path. When my time comes, I will be ready and you will be there. You with a flag bearing the Maltese cross. Me, I carry no flag. See, I have taken no other country than yours. Your warm, dry fingers will fold around mine and I will be safe.

"Healayas," a voice said. It was Octavia, the MoMA media person they'd assigned to her. "Are you all right?"

"Yes, yes, of course," Healayas, said, standing.

"We're about to open. It's ten twenty-five."

"I'm sorry."

"It's very moving. Don't worry. Lots of people cry."

27

MARINA HAS A MONTH TO go. On the radio they're playing Antony and the Johnsons. It's "Hope There's Someone" and Antony sounds like a sixteenth-century castrato. At least one person listening through headphones in the line is feeling as if she wants to drink petrol and set herself on fire for the sheer beauty of vivid, searing extinguishment. The city has slipped through a misty dawn and is now poised beneath neatly arranged Pixar clouds. Alice Levin is arriving sixty seconds early to a lecture. Healayas Breen is drinking Gatorade after swimming sixty laps at the pool.

Marco Anelli, the official photographer, is carefully repositioning his Canon EOS-1D Mark IV. Every evening, after he has reviewed the photographs from the day and made his recommendations to Marina, who checks them all before he uploads them, Marco has time to sleep. He can live on six hours, although he sleeps until midday on Tuesday, the one day of the week MoMA is closed and they all get a twenty-four-hour reprieve to recover a little normality. Sometimes on Tuesday night he cannot imagine how he will resume the schedule for another week and another.

There is no time for friends. No energy for friends. All day he is surrounded by people. All day he spends observing faces.

His dreams have become strange police lineups. Sometimes he is weeding faces in a giant garden, other times he is scooping them up as if they have fallen like moonbeams onto the river's surface. Last night he dreamed of a party where he went from room to room looking for someone in particular, whom he never found, and everyone was dressed as iridescent bluebirds with dark masked eyes and beaks of sparkling beads.

He passed the clipboard with the permission slip to the next person in the line, and she filled it out, signed it, and asked him, as they all asked him, "Will it be long?"

He smiled, and said to each person who asked, "It is impossible to tell."

He tried not to engage in conversation in the atrium. He was not a spokesperson. He was the photographer. When he and Marina had discussed this show, they had imagined the chair opposite Marina would often be empty. They had never imagined people would be so compelled to sit that they would wait for hours and hours.

He checked his watch, a gift from Marina. How perfect that she should have given him time. It was the thing they shared. While ever she was here he was also here. For seventy-five days he was her constant witness.

They had met in Rome when he had asked to photograph her and she offered him ten minutes the next day. It was all the time she could give him, she said. She had greeted him at the appointed time and he had surprised her because it was not her face he wanted. It was her scars.

The scars told her real stories. The scars that came from knives and ice, fire and scalpel; years of work on the tightrope between art and spirituality. Years of trying to create a philosophical bridge between east and west. He did not pretend to understand her, so he admired her. She was *squisita* the way older women could be *squisita*. They knew their own voice, the way they moved, the way to dress. They knew their curves and their own face and if they had lived, really lived, there was something like a well in them that, as a younger man, he wanted to drink from. It wasn't entirely sexual but it was entirely sensual. That was what he felt. The sensuality of *devozione* for Marina. Her strength, her humor, her solitude, her impromptu meals—*pollo arrosto, melanzane ripiene, risotto ai funghi*. She had a way of making him feel like family. Making them all feel like family. *La famiglia di Marina.*

He looked at her through the lens of his camera and saw in her dark eyes generations of Slavs and Arabs, Greeks and Persians, who had migrated on foot, on donkey, taking with them the possessions that would see them through the next winter. Into that crumpled landscape they had gone, at the crossroads of Europe and the Middle East. Being Italian he understood the sense of country people had. He imagined it wasn't easy for your country to change names, have different masters, be a pawn in the games of monsters. Italy had known all that. Even now, Italian soldiers were dying in Iraq for Bush's war that was now Obama's war. The war Berlusconi, *il buffone*, had signed them up for. Italians understood how people who were once your neighbors could become your enemy. Italy had not united as a nation until after the First World War. But in Yugoslavia the fighting had been long and bitter and of a different order. There was a particular voltage of hatred between Serbians and Bosnians, Croatians, Albanians, Montenegrins, Slovenians. Between Muslims and Christians—*una vecchia guerra*.

People had picked up axes and killed women and children who lived in the same street. That was Yugoslavia. A no-longer country. A fairy story place of madmen and musicians, lovers and killers, on a stretch of peninsula between Austria and Macedonia.

Marina came from the once-Yugoslavia, a place that had been squeezing and twisting and folding itself up longer than places had names. A peninsula of steep-sided valleys, rushing rivers, blue lakes, winding villages, snowcapped mountains. An origami landscape with endless *segreti*.

After the first ten minutes of the photographic shoot, Marina Abramović had given Marco her whole day.

She had said later, when the day was done and they were on the terrazzo drinking limoncello, that if you dipped your fingers in the pockets of Yugoslavia, you could pull out stories of warm bread, onions and mincemeat, vine leaves and plum brandy, corn bread and strudel. You could unravel myths of the sun drawn from a palace by white horses, a young God dropping corn in spring, summer as a woman newly in love but abandoned each autumn. You could cut yourself on ancient mountain ranges and skin your knees on lost valleys, yet there were fields of red poppies and homemade wine and someone singing ballads of virgins wandering in the moonlight and old women who carried the bones of animals to stave off disease.

There were other myths Marina had told him: of large black cats that barked like dogs to protect the cows in the barn through the slow white winter; spirits in the bathhouse, by the front door, by the fireplace; rat-catchers and shepherds, soldiers and priests, the world swathed in black, green, gold, red, magenta.

When she planned this show, he said, "I will photograph everyone who comes to sit with you."

"Seventy-five days," she said. "Are you sure? Can you do it? *È un periodo lungo.*"

"*Sì,*" he had said, not understanding then how long seventy-five days could be. Perhaps Marina hadn't either.

They conversed always in Italian. He spoke English badly. His Serbian was hello, goodbye, thank you, tomorrow, hungry, delicious, one, two, three, love. She spoke German and French too, and Dutch, and in every language she was funny, intense, and her accent rumbled with Balkan vowels and consonants.

"I will stay with you for the entire show," he said. Even then he felt his devotion to her. "Every day, so that nothing, no one is missed. Every face. We will capture every face."

So here he was, and spring was gracing the city outside. The children in the strollers who came into the atrium had bare legs and were no longer swathed and booted. He smelled rain on trench coats and wind in the wraps and scarves.

For seventy-five days he was an archivist. Every day he took the clipboard and moved along the line of people and had them sign the permission form to be photographed, making their images available to Marina for any future works, books, films, performances. Nearly everyone signed. Then he returned to his camera and photographed face after face. Every face. He captured the moment when they first sat and their eyes connected with Marina. Then he waited until their emotions began to surface, and he captured them again and again.

A sitting could last two minutes or two hours. Or an entire day. He hadn't expected people to do that. Nor had any of *la famiglia di Marina*. So many expressions crossed the faces of those who sat. He looked for intensity. He looked for the moment when the person sitting was consumed by the indecipherable. He felt as if he was inside a world of raw truth. Who would have imagined there would be such faces? He had photographed architecture, history, musicians. Now, day after day, he looked into the human face, painted with curiosity, and he saw the abyss of history within a human heart. Every one was its own beaten, salvaged, polished, engraved, carved, luminous form.

He captured this ephemeral thing, a communion between an artist and her audience. The chair opposite her was an invitation. *Come sit if you wish.*

Here in New York, where time was everyone's currency, and to gaze deeply into the face of another was possibly a sign of madness, people were flocking to sit with Marina Abramović. She wasn't so much stealing hearts, he thought, as awakening them. The light that came into their eyes. Their intelligence, their sadness, all of it tumbled out as people sat. Marco, with his long lens and archivist's eye, captured them all. *Il devoto ed i devoti.*

28

WHEN BRITTIKA VAN DER SAR returned to New York for the
third time, she went straight to MoMA, ignoring her desire for
a shower after the overnight flight from Amsterdam. Marco,
the photographer, recognized her and nodded when he saw her.
Carlos, who must have sat fifteen times by now, was sitting
again. Carlos had a social media following. On Twitter there
was an IsatwithMarina hashtag. She saw the silver-haired film
composer on the sidelines too, the one Jane had introduced
her to. He was in his usual position, seated on a red pillow.
He was entirely absorbed in the two people at the table, as
if he was watching a movie. She wondered what was going
on in his life that this was what took up his time. She must
interview him.

Today she was lucky and the line moved fast. By midafter-
noon it was finally her turn. She strode to the table. She wanted
to get it right this time. She gazed into Abramović's brown eyes,
sure there was a flicker of recognition, a warming. Brittika smiled
and hoped Marco had gotten just that moment.

She was aware of the noise of the crowd milling and staring.
She hoped she looked confident but she felt only nervousness.
Why didn't other people seem to be afraid of the crowd when

they sat? It was the hardest thing to pretend confidence when you didn't feel it.

Her heart was beating hard in her chest and her hands were shaking. There was a sort of tremor running down her spine. Did people on TV get nervous? Did Marina get nervous? Was she nervous right now?

When I get my PhD, I'll stop feeling like this, thought Brittika. Six more months. Then I won't feel like a fake anymore.

Marco had told her that Marina's team had taken bets, before the show started, on how many people would sit. Marina's assistant, Davide Balliano, had predicted more than half a million visitors and fifteen hundred sitters. They had all thought he was way too ambitious. But *The Artist Is Present* was over halfway through and Davide had already won the bet on the visitor numbers and more than a thousand people had sat in the chair opposite Marina.

Brittika readjusted herself. She took a breath and let it out slowly. She maintained the gaze with Abramović but her heart wouldn't settle. She thought of stories about Marina to distract her. She wanted to get to twenty minutes. Let the record show she had made it to twenty minutes.

She thought about the time Marina had brought a friend home from school and they had taken one of her father's revolvers from the glass display cabinet. Marina had loaded a single bullet into the chamber of the gun and spun the cylinder. Then she held the muzzle to her head and pulled the trigger. Click. No shot. Then her friend spun the cylinder and held the gun to his head. He pressed the trigger. Click. No shot. They had both fallen about laughing.

When Marina was still living at home at age twenty-eight, she wanted to do a show where she would walk on stage dressed the way her mother would have liked her to. In a nice skirt and blouse, or a dress and gloves, with hair and makeup done. Marina would stand and look at the public and then put one bullet in the chamber of the gun. She would spin the cylinder, put the gun to her temple, and shoot. If she didn't die, then she would dress in the clothes *she* wanted to wear, looking how *she* wanted to look, and leave.

She had also wanted to make a room where, when people entered, they would undress and all their clothes would be washed, dried, and ironed, then returned. The naked visitors would then dress in their clean clothes and exit the room. Laundromat as performance art. The university had refused to permit it.

Brittika thought of the little Citroën van parked at the entrance to the retrospective upstairs. Marina and Ulay had driven all over Europe in it, with their dog, Alba. It no longer held the narrow mattress they had slept on for five years, the cooking equipment, the books that came and went as they traveled, the retsina bottles, Marina's latest knitting project. Alba was long dead. Gone too were the pale headlights pinning the road to their van, the goats that gave them milk in the morning, the walks on cliff tops, through forests, and across town squares listening to conversations. Watching games of backgammon and boules. Making plans for this show and that. Gone was that relationship.

Brittika wondered if she would ever meet someone who made her feel the way Marina and Ulay had once felt about each other. She couldn't imagine living and working with someone. To let them hold a bow and arrow to your heart like Marina had in *Rest Energy*. Or take your breath, like in *Breathing In/Breathing Out*, until you were almost poisoned by the other person's carbon dioxide. Or to bind your hair together. That one made her particularly claustrophobic and she grimaced.

She hoped Marco hadn't caught that. She realized her heart had settled and the quiver down her spine was less insistent. She refocused on Marina's eyes and tried to be open.

I don't want to love like you've loved, she thought as she looked at Marina. Brittika knew she became way too intense with guys. Her last relationship had ended badly. She had basically stalked him. It embarrassed her to think back on it. She hoped Marco hadn't taken her photograph just then either.

She saw that Marina's gaze was lingering in the space just before Brittika's face as if there was another world right in front of her that Brittika couldn't see. What was Marina seeing?

Art did not stop, that's what Marina had said. Art did not get to five o'clock and say, "That's it, the day is done, go think about TV or making dinner." It wasn't like that. It was there all the time: when you were chopping vegetables, talking with a friend, reading a newspaper, listening to music, having a party. It was always there offering suggestions, wanting you to go write or draw, sing or play. Wanting you to imagine big things, to connect with an audience, to use energy, to find energy. It wasn't ready when you were, it didn't come when you wanted it or leave when you were done. It took its time. It was often late, or slow, or not what you had in mind.

Brittika thought about how when she arrived home late her mother had always thought to put food aside for her. How she always left the lamp on in the hallway. Put fresh linen on her bed. As if her mother wanted Brittika to be sure that she was loved. That was the problem of adoption. You weren't. Not first off. Not enough to keep. Her birth mother had been a woman in China who had probably already given birth to one child. Or who had wanted a son, and so had given Brittika up in the hope that next time . . .

But she had been adopted and knew nothing other than her parents who had done so much for her. She was trying to do everything she could to make them know she appreciated them. But it wasn't easy to do that. She had urges to do things that she didn't understand. Without a sense of history, she didn't know why she'd had such an interest in sex from such a young age. It had already got her into trouble.

She wasn't sure she was essentially a good person. She thought when she could afford it, it would be good for her to live alone because the idea of it frightened her. She imagined a cottage by the sand dunes on the little island of Terschelling in the North Sea. Maybe she'd try to go there to finish the last draft of her PhD.

Brittika had a theory that Abramović didn't like being alone. Sitting at this table was part of that fear. Marina had been a solitary child, living with her grandmother for the first six years of her life, and seeing her father and mother only on Sundays. She had returned home to live with her parents when her brother was born. Not long after, she was hospitalized for a year with a blood condition. Her mother never came to visit.

Nobody might have come to *The Artist Is Present*. The show could have opened and, after a few days, once the Abramović fans had come and gone, it might have wilted and died. People might have stood on the sidelines, frowned, scoffed, and dismissed it. That was always the risk. The work might not have connected with anyone. Marina Abramović might have come all this way, from Belgrade to New York via forty years of art, to be alone at this table for three long months.

And then, for a long time, Brittika simply sat, and there was a luminescence that descended as if the skylight six floors above them was sending a cone of sunlight down into the atrium.

Marina's face looked as if it was made of stone as ancient as the face of the Sphinx, but now it was a man's face, and now an opal.

At some point Brittika saw a small square package in the air between Marina and herself. The package floated toward her and she could see it was gently vibrating. Without moving, somehow Brittika was able to reach out and take the package between her fingers. It smelled of wool wash. She thought of her mother in a pool of lamplight practicing her calligraphy. She saw her father hanging out washing. She felt the smallness of herself. She thought of how she would lie awake and talk to Jesus as a child and several times she was sure Jesus had talked back.

She unwrapped the gold leaf around the package and within it she saw her soul. It was dark and eternal like starlight but shaped like a small mochi ball. She slipped it into her mouth and swallowed it.

When she finally stood and left the chair, the room had become a place of strangers. She had forgotten what language she was meant to speak. She went out into the street.

Later, lying on the grass in Central Park and staring at clouds, she felt as if parts of herself had flown away, or come home.

PART FIVE

Every artist was first an amateur.

RALPH WALDO EMERSON

29

"HEALAYAS? IT'S ARKY."

"Arky? Hi! Are you okay?"

Her voice was the same as ever. Suddenly Levin didn't know what he'd been afraid of, or why he hadn't called her months ago.

"I saw you sat with Marina Abramović," he said.

"Yes, I have—twice now."

"Could we talk about it?"

"*Bien sûr.* Will you come over?"

"Umm . . ."

"I could make something."

"Really? Thank you. I'd like that. Okay. What time?"

"Anytime. Tonight? Just come over. I've really missed you."

"I thought you might like to do the vocals. On the new soundtrack I'm working on."

"Let's talk about it."

"I'll bring a few tracks."

"Okay. So does seven work?"

He looked at his watch, calculated the trip and his need to shower and shave. "Sure."

"*À bientôt,*" she said.

Healayas lived on Malcolm X Boulevard, a few blocks north of the park. New apartments were multiplying inside old civic buildings. Cafes were replacing locksmiths. A new movie theater had opened. But Harlem had been making itself over for millions of years. Before white and black, there were Indians, and before Indians there had been mastodons and bison. Before that there had been dinosaurs and glaciers and before that a great inland sea just waiting for the Appalachian Mountains to rise up out of the ocean and make Manhattan Island.

Levin took the A train express to 125th and then walked. He'd finally unpacked his old vinyls and had come across some Morrissey, Nick Drake's *Pink Moon*, and several Leonard Cohen albums that Tom had given him years back. It had felt good to play music loudly with the doors open onto the balcony and let the sound ripple out over the treetops on Washington Square.

Healayas's apartment was at the top of a brownstone fenced with polished steel, interrupted only by a gate with a video keypad and a slot for mail. The owner had gutted the first two floors but Healayas's apartment on the top floor remained unrenovated. Levin pressed the intercom. Healayas buzzed him in and he walked down the laneway and climbed the side stairs.

The door was open to the warm evening. She came toward him, embraced him, kissing him on both cheeks. "It's good to see you, Arky. You don't have to be quite so good at avoiding everyone, you know. We all miss you. I'm making gazpacho. I thought in this heat gazpacho followed by pasta with garlic prawns."

She moved about the kitchen in cutoff blue jeans, a small red T-shirt, colored leather ties on her wrists, her hair pinned back and falling between her shoulder blades in black ringlets. She was chopping garlic, parsley, grating lemon rind, tossing them together in a bowl, slicing bread.

Tom had met Healayas at a party in Aspen at Hunter S. Thompson's place. Healayas was years younger, but that hadn't stopped Tom. She had also had been with someone else at the time, but at the end of the holiday, she and Tom went back to Los Angeles together.

They had been a vivid couple. He knew Tom had asked her to marry him, and Healayas had not given him an answer. Once Tom had said to him that Healayas was Teflon. Everywhere they went, men slid off her. Did he mind? No, he said to Levin. He had to keep reassuring her that *he* wasn't going anywhere. But he did. He used to say Leonard Cohen must have been thinking of her when he wrote:

> I met a lady, she was playing with her soldiers in the dark
> oh one by one she had to tell them
> that her name was Joan of Arc.
> I was in that army, yes, I stayed a little while;
> I want to thank you, Joan of Arc,
> for treating me so well.

Levin had played that song again just this afternoon and heard other lyrics that had stuck on repeat in his mind.

> And the skylight is like skin for a drum I'll never mend
> And all the rain falls down amen
> On the works of last year's man.

On the table was fresh ciabatta, a dish of olive oil and another of dukkah. Healayas opened the bottle of wine he had brought. Plucking two glasses from a shelf, she poured for them and sat, looking at Levin across the wooden countertop.

"So, tell me, what's new, Arky?"

"I've been working on a soundtrack. It's a feature-length anim-ation. A company called Izumi that's partnered with Warner. Japanese director."

"An animation? Is that a first for you?"

"It is," said Levin. "But I like it."

"So how does it work with the Japanese director? You go there? He comes here?"

"We Skype. But I may go there soon. We may even do the final soundtrack in Tokyo."

"You want to play me something?"

"Later. I've got some lyrics I'd love your thoughts on."

He explained the script Seiji Isoda had adapted about a woman who was a fish by night and how she falls in love with a man who is also a bear and the King of Winter.

"What is the problem? What makes the tension?" Healayas asked.

"They have a child, and the child has to choose whether to be a bear like her father, which means leaving, or stay and be a fish like her mother."

"To become your mother or your father, that is the eternal question," said Healayas. She stared out over the low rooftops of South Harlem. The heat hung damp in the air. A thunder-storm was brewing.

"So no happy ending?" she asked.

Levin shook his head.

"A truthful story." Healayas shrugged. "And the music? It has to be evocative, no?"

"Yes, but not biblical like *The Mission*, or fantasy like *The Lord of the Rings*. And not like *The Last of the Mohicans* or *Dances with Wolves*. I want it to be stranger. And wondrous. Like combining Guillermo del Toro with Terrence Malick in music. I haven't got it right yet."

"Have you seen Lydia?" Healayas asked as if this was a casual question.

Levin blinked and shook his head. "I really don't want to talk about it."

Healayas put English spinach into a colander and rinsed it. Then she wrapped the leaves in a clean tea towel and flicked the water from them before arranging the salad in a red bowl. "Then we won't," she said slowly. "Best to get the elephant out of the room, though."

Levin said nothing.

"So, you want to talk about Marina Abramović?" Healayas asked.

"Yes. What was it like to sit with her?"

"Well, completely unexpected," said Healayas, then laughed. "I found myself talking to Tom. It was as if he was right there in front of me as real as you are. We were having a meal together. I'm serious. We were just chatting as if it was completely normal."

"You mean it was a hallucination?"

"Well, I guess so, but it sure tasted good."

"What did he say?"

"Same old Tom. But so vivid. It's stayed with me ever since. I wonder if everyone is having these experiences."

Levin frowned.

"Did you see the Colm Tóibín piece?"

"No," Levin said.

"I'll get it. Wait."

She went into the living room and he heard her rustling about, then she reappeared.

Holding a copy of the *Times*, she read aloud. "*It was like being brought into a room in Enniscorthy when I was a child on the day after a neighbor had died and being allowed to look at the corpse's face. And then this—listen to this," she said. "*This was serious,* *too serious maybe, too intimate, too searching. It was either, I felt, what I should do all the time or what I should never do."*

She looked at Levin. "It's because it feels so on the edge. Like church or a ceremony that you're not sure you're really invited to, but you go anyway. It's remarkable. Haunting. You haven't sat?"

"No."

"You must, Arky. You must."

"Must I?" he asked.

"You will love it. Don't miss out."

"I might."

"Or you might not." Then, changing the subject, she said, "Are you going to do the Lime Club with us? I would really love you to. We all want you to do it."

"I'm thinking about it."

"I know I can get another pianist, but it wouldn't feel right without you."

"Okay," he said.

"And I know Alice is interested in doing some dates. I saw her the other day."

"Okay."

"Okay, *yes*, or okay, *I'll think about it?*"

"Yes, I'll do the season."

"Gee, Arky, we try to get an answer out of you for six months, and now you just say yes?"

He shrugged. "Sorry."

There was a pause. Levin sipped his wine and looked about the kitchen at the saucepans hung from hooks on a rack above him, the melted candles on the benchtop, the knife block, the metal sink, the block of soap on a dish on the windowsill, pomegranates in a bowl and tomatoes in another. He felt like he was in a still life. As if sitting here he had caught up to some other part of himself that had been here waiting for him. Last time he'd been here Lydia had been with him. Healayas had cooked them dinner. It was bizarre when he thought that was only a few months back.

Healayas cut bread. Then she took a container of soup from the refrigerator and put it in a blender. "Sorry about the noise," she said, and he braced as she turned the machine on.

She poured the bright red soup into two dark bowls and tossed small cubes of cucumber and red peppers on top.

"It's really good to see you, Arky," she said, sliding one bowl toward him. "It's been much too long."

From Healayas's speakers came the music he had brought with him. The simple piano, the counterpoint of viola, the introduction of oboes, the answering cellos. A mellow trumpet rising up out of the strings and soaring over treetops.

"It's definitely water and forest," she said.

"Oh good," Levin said.

"So, I'm thinking that now it just needs . . . hmmm . . . love?"

Levin sighed. He looked up at the large print on the wall. It was a photograph of Healayas singing. Her hair was loose and she was in a silver singlet, her skin ebony. She looked magnificent as she leaned toward the microphone with her eyes closed.

"It's there. It just needs unearthing," she said.

Levin sipped the coffee she had made. Turkish, sweet and grainy.

They worked into the night. He on her upright piano, and Healayas feeling her way with the lyrics he had penned. She had an organic, impulsive response to music. She had made him feel at times, over the years they had played together, that classical training had ruined him. When she sang she gave him goose bumps. She had a sound in her voice that sometimes moved him to tears.

After midnight the thunderstorm broke, hammering on the roof too loud for them to continue.

"I'll call you a cab. Or you're welcome to stay. I can make up the sofa bed. We can go out for breakfast?"

He had no idea how he would sleep with her in close proximity. He was unanchored. He wanted desperately to ask her just to hold him, to take him to bed and hold him. But he couldn't ask such a thing.

"It's okay. I'll get a cab," he said.

Was she in a relationship? He never liked to ask. She had sometimes introduced him to men at gigs, but no one had been constant since Tom.

"So I'll come over tomorrow afternoon and we'll put the vocals down?" she asked.

"Yes. Okay. See you then."

"You know, I've never seen it, your new apartment."

"I haven't had anyone over."

When she kissed him goodnight, she said, "You know, Arky, Lydia loves you very much."

"Does she?" he asked.

"Of course," she said. "Have you talked to anyone? I can recommend someone good."

"A lawyer?"

"No." She smiled. "A therapist."

"I'm fine. Really. I hate it, but it's fine."

"No one is okay through something like this. It eats away at everything. You're in pain."

"Really, if it's what Lydia wants . . . you know Lydia. She doesn't change her mind."

"We wouldn't know if she did," said Healayas.

"Oh, God," said Levin. He wished this whole topic had not come up.

"She loves you. I think maybe she wanted to see who you could be . . . who you both could be . . ."

"So, like a test? Or an experiment?"

"No. No. Not like that."

"I want to see her," he said.

Healayas nodded. "There's a tiny chance, I know it's remote, but still, that she could come out of this, enough to talk, enough to listen to music together . . ."

"You mean she'd come home?"

Healayas shrugged. "Here, a little poem: *Even after all this time, the sun never says, 'You owe me.' Look what happens with a love like that. It lights the whole world.* You never know what love can create, Arky."

She hugged him intensely at the door then let him go. "See you tomorrow. Here—the umbrella!"

The cab sped downtown past melting lights and through new puddles, the traffic hissing and muted beyond and, inside the cab, the windshield wipers clicked like a metronome in the storm and the rain fell down. Amen.

30

UPSTAIRS ON THE SIXTH FLOOR, parked at the entrance to the retrospective, was an old van. It was empty inside. Alice liked the idea of living in a van, being on the road with a band or a boyfriend or both. Marina Abramović had been a kind of rock chick in those days, she thought. Going from gig to gig, performing across Europe.

Above was a huge black-and-white picture of Abramović. Screams and moans could be heard coming from inside the exhibition. A warning advised that the show *may be disturbing for some.*

Two women stood nearby looking at the sign and one was saying, "I tell him to wash his face five times, to clean his teeth five times, to get dressed, and still it isn't done."

They nodded together and moved forward. Another couple passed by. The man was saying, "Well, I question what these kind of people are doing in art. The business types wanting to make money. That's a whole other art," and they both laughed.

"Oh, well, here goes," Alice said to her father.

Levin smiled and together they moved into the crowded room. Large screens were showing videos of Abramović. The first had her vigorously brushing her hair. She was saying, *"Art must be beautiful, artist must be beautiful"* as she dragged the brush savagely through her long, dark hair. Alice agreed with the sentiment, but was it okay for a beautiful woman to be saying it?

Ahead there was a bottleneck at the doorway with the first of the nude performers. To get a better view, Alice moved away from Levin to the side of the room. A young woman with golden skin and small, awkward breasts stood opposite a lean, immobile man who was also naked. The nude couple held each other's gaze unflinchingly. The crowd was hesitant. Some people clutched their bags and darted between the two nudes. Others took their time, but rarely did anyone look into the eyes of the performers. Almost every visitor, male and female, turned toward the woman as they stepped through the opening into the next room. Only one person, a man, faced the man, but he did not make eye contact. There was a brusque passing, no consideration of buttons or belt clasps against soft flesh.

Alice chose to face the man too and felt the heat of his naked body. It was over before she had remembered to look into his eyes. She turned to see Levin looking down at the floor, moving through facing the woman. Alice did not want to think about her father as a sexual being.

Ahead there were two people pointing at each other in a small alcove, their fingers almost touching. Farther in, a man and a woman were entwined by their hair, back to back, in a recess of white wall. They also showed no sign of movement other than the blink of their eyes.

In a darkened room a light shone on a huge pile of white plaster cow bones. A large screen showed Abramović in a lab coat and glasses. She appeared to be giving a lecture. Then she took off her coat and began dancing wearing nothing but a black slip, stockings, and high black shoes.

Alice wasn't sure what it was about, but she liked it. It was sort of funny. She moved toward a man lying beneath a skeleton. She became aware, once she was beside him, that he was also quite naked, and she felt a little embarrassed that she was so close to him. As he breathed, the skeleton appeared to breathe with him.

Alice gazed briefly at the glass cabinets that held letters, photographs, and medals. Then she sat on a leather bench and listened under headphones.

Marina was saying in her distinctive accented English: "*I went to monastery in Ladakh because I wanted to see preparation for lama dancing . . . we are just normal human beings, then when I put the mask on my head I become a god and a god can do anything.*

"*How to catch the moment of here and now? It's all about present. A performer can still be distracted—the body performs but the mind is everywhere . . .*"

The fat woman beside Alice took off her headphones. "It's breaking up so badly," she said loudly. "They should fix that. I can't understand what she's saying."

Alice nodded and returned her attention to the voice.

"*Rhythm five. I construct a five-pointed star—construction is made in wood shavings soaked in one hundred liters of petrol . . . communist star, Tito time. On my birth certificate . . . somehow a curse for me. I make a ritual to exorcise the star—cut all my hair and put into the star, cut toenails, cut fingernails . . . big mistake . . . then lie in the center of the star . . . didn't know no oxygen in the middle of the star . . . lost consciousness. A doctor saw something wrong. I was being burned and not reacting . . . took me out of the piece and revived me.*"

What did her father see in Abramović? Alice frowned. He liked solitude. She remembered the nights when her mother was away on business and Yolanda had left, and she'd hoped he'd come and talk to her, but he just played music. He could go for weeks without ever having a conversation with her, other than telling her about a new film he was working on, the next bit of music he was trying to solve.

When she had begun to learn cello, she thought it might be something they could do together, or maybe that had been Lydia's plan. But it wasn't until Alice got back from Paris and he heard her play in her band that he asked her to come play with him in Healayas's band. She realized before then he simply hadn't rated her as a musician.

Abramović's voice in the crackly headphones was saying: *"Failure is so important. You have to experiment. Failure is part of the process."*

New York attracted extreme things, Alice thought. The French guy who tightrope-walked between the Twin Towers when they were still standing. Abramović sitting for seventy-five days in silence. To fall, to fail, the possibility of disaster was so close.

Alice didn't like to fail. She had worked hard not to fail. She thought she may be failing her mother but she didn't know how to solve it. She rose and moved on through the retrospective. In the next room a girl about her own age was naked high on a wall. Alice observed a tiny seat between her legs, a little clear plastic bicycle seat almost invisible in the girl's pubic hair. Her arms were outstretched. People were standing at the back of the room watching. Alice walked forward and the young woman met her eyes. Alice did not look away. The girl's arms moved infinitesimally. Her feet were on tiny supports and as Alice watched she saw that the girl was moving incrementally to keep herself pinned to the wall. Alice worried for her so high up and exposed to the concrete floor, people staring at her nudity.

Alice visited her mother every weekend she could. It took three trains, but she read and studied, and it was a new pattern. To dress your mother was a strange thing. It had about it a sense of continuum. Her mother did not make eye contact. Her expression was entirely passive, as if she was daydreaming. She didn't speak, although sometimes she sighed. Her mother was taken to shower in a wheelchair. The nurses spoke to her, the poem of the health worker recited to reassure the patient of the small and essential tasks of day and night: *there we go, sliding you into the chair, now lifting your feet, one, two, that's it, and now off we go into the bathroom, here we are, that's right, now off with your nightdress, and shower on, oh lovely, not too hot, not too hot, that's right, nice and warm, let's wash your hair, that's right, let's close your eyes . . .*

They returned her mother to her in towels. Alice had dried the skin between her mother's toes. She clipped her mother's toenails and blow-dried her hair. Later, when her mother was again in her chair by the window, wearing a fresh kimono in patterned green silk over white cotton pajamas, Alice took out nail polish and with careful strokes painted her mother's fingernails and toenails a sparkling turquoise blue.

She shifted and the artist on the wall gently released Alice from her gaze.

Alice walked into a larger room. It was a performance called *The Room with the Ocean View*. Her mother had an ocean view now. Her room took in the dunes and the sea and the sea took in Lydia. Lydia liked to sit by the window. She had made noises, appeared in microscopic ways to be agitated if she was moved elsewhere. If Alice sat on the floor and placed her mother's hand on her head, Lydia made tiny motions with her fingers as if she was attempting to stroke Alice's hair. This she could only do with her right hand. She could not grip a cup or hold a pencil.

"Are you sure you wouldn't like to go home?" she had asked her mother, but there was no reply. The apartment on Columbus that had been their home for twenty years was gone. Alice had seen the new apartment only before her parents had purchased it. She had not been there since her father had moved in. He had never invited her.

Her mother was the sort of person who was greeted by the greengrocer. Who remembered the names of everyone in their building, including most of the maids and nannies that came and went from various apartments. When they ate at Cafe con Leche, the staff gathered around them and made a fuss, knowing Lydia would order the black bean soup, Levin the roast pork, and she, Alice, would order the *chicharrón de pollo*, which as a child she had loved to say almost as much as to eat.

Home was a different notion now. Home was her clothes and books, the little window by her desk looking down onto a rooftop garden where no one ever sat. There were rituals of Cointreau late on Saturday nights after their weekly gig and huevos rancheros on Sundays. Home was her cello and her bass guitar. Home was being able to rehearse with her fellow band members in the tiny studio below street level on Seventh. Home was the squealing plumbing when the shower ran, and the creak in the floorboards by the fridge.

In *The House with the Ocean View*, Marina Abramović had created a home comprising three white rooms attached to the walls of the gallery, accessible only by three ladders with knives for steps. From the speakers Abramović's voice narrated every step and action she had taken over the twelve days she lived up there. "*I take a deep breath and my chest rises. Then it falls. I remain sitting still. My feet are flat on the floor and spaced hip width apart. My back is straight against the chair. My head does not move. Only my eyes blink. The rest of my body is motionless.*"

Alice could have made a similar account of her mother's days. She suspected her mother was on a long journey away from the grace of ordinary. She might suffer another stroke. She might die somewhere while her mind was far away. Alice did not know how she would live without her.

Lydia was on the dialysis machine each week. They had completed another round of plasma exchange. To look at her, she appeared as fragile as mist. There was a calm about her that may have been life leaving, or life returning, Alice could not tell.

Yesterday, Alice had laid a brand-new Moleskine notebook beside her mother's chair and a 4B pencil that she knew her mother favored. Her mother had shown no sign of recognition or acknowledgment when Alice arrived. Only her hand on the top of Alice's head moving ever so gently seemed to indicate that, somewhere inside, she remembered.

When she was a child, Alice's scrapbooks had been full of clippings from brochures of taps and door handles, wall and floor claddings, architectural magazines, houses lit for the evening, foodless kitchens, bathrooms without toys, beds without evidence of sleep. Every birthday her mother constructed from cardboard and foam core a new doll's house according to Alice's latest ideas—a tree house, a stable, a house five storeys tall, a lighthouse.

She had spent a great deal of time watching her mother go from one hundred miles an hour to a complete stop. There was fast Lydia and slow Lydia. Slow Lydia slept a great deal of the time. Slow Lydia lay in bed and watched movies and played cards with Alice. Slow Lydia spent days in the hospital. Slow Lydia was there in bed when Alice arrived home from school. When Alice had realized it was only medical knowledge that could save her mother, she had set her sights on becoming a doctor of hematology.

In the quiet room behind the dunes of Long Island, Alice had unlocked the clips on her cello case. She moved through the Suites for Solo Cello 1–6 and her mother remained entirely silent, fixed by the sea.

31

DANICA ABRAMOVIĆ WANDERED THROUGH THE retrospective, seeing photos of her daughter's life that she knew nothing of. Marina had made her life everywhere but Yugoslavia. Even during Milošević, she never came home. She let herself be slapped by that German, let herself be naked with him, traipsed after him across Europe showing her naked body to the whole world. But it hadn't brought her happiness. Love was a wasteland. That's the way it went, Danica knew. "You want to be a strong woman?" she asked the visitors who wandered by, oblivious to her. "Then you will never find a man who treats you as an equal. You have to play the little games. Oh, giggling, cooking, making them think they have such a huge cock every time they put it near you. The truth is that men are the empty ones. And women are meant to fill them up. I could count on a few fingers the men I ever truly admired. Give them long enough and men are always disappointing."

Danica stared at a photograph of her daughter carrying an armful of firewood. "I shake my fist at that film you made of Serbia, bringing this on our good name. The humping men and naked women showing their *pi'čka*. Your mockery of our songs. I denounce you too, for slicing our beloved communist star into your stomach. And that thing in Venice at the Biennale, scrubbing the bones of cows. They gave *you* the Golden Lion! Has the world gone mad?"

Danica remembered the room in the apartment she had given Marina for her studio and how Marina had smeared shoe polish all over it. But I made her live with it, Danica thought, that ugly smell—but not as ugly as that great pile of rotting cow bones, there in Venice.

People had said to her, "Ah, your daughter is so famous. You must be very proud."

"I am proud," Danica would reply. But she did not say of what she was proud and it wasn't Marina. What mother could be proud of that? Showing her breasts, burning the communist star. Whipping herself naked. And that time in Milan with the gun and the bullet and all those other things they could have hurt her with. It's a wonder she wasn't raped.

She had read Marina's interviews. "My mother bought me only flannel pajamas three sizes too big each birthday. My mother punished me. My mother hit me. My mother tried to kill me. My mother never kissed me. My mother hid my real birth date from me. My mother this, my mother that."

Danica, in her new lightweight form, had been there when Marina had gone to clear out her apartment the day after the funeral.

Marina had found the trunk with the scrapbooks.

"Don't open them. None of that is for you. It's not for anyone," she tried to tell Marina. But death was impotence.

Inside were the newspaper clippings, the magazine articles, everything dated, cataloged, and recorded. Right back to 1967. Every mention of the artist Marina Abramović. Even some little leather clouds, yellowed and curled, stuck into the pages. The first art Marina had made. Danica hadn't meant to leave the box for anyone to find. She had been too sick to remember it.

Marina had taken every little thing from the trunk. Turned over the war medals. Read the citations from President Tito. Read the letters from the survivors. And there she was, a grown woman, nearly sixty, weeping on Danica's bed.

"You see, Marina," Danica had said, too late for Marina to hear her words. "A mother is just a heart. You pain me, every day of my life, with those dark eyes. You reproach me. But discipline is the only thing that protects you when the world goes mad. I thought it would make you safe."

From the sixth floor Danica looks down into the atrium at her daughter far below, alone in the middle of the world.

"You know I would rescue you from a burning truck. I would carry you to safety. Any moment you need it, I would do that for you."

Love was a wasteland. Danica could no more fly down and scoop Marina up than swim the length of the Danube.

32

FRANCESCA LANG COULD HEAR HER husband, Dieter, talking in French on the phone. It was another interview with one of the European media outlets. She peeled apples as the one-sided conversation washed through the open door. Marina wasn't talking to the media for three months, so Dieter must talk for her.

"After the Biennale? Well, she hardly ever eats meat . . ."

"Pre-Ulay I think she was working out how to be an artist. Then twelve years with Ulay. Post-Ulay there was uncertainty of course. And then extraordinary growth."

"She calls herself the grandmother of performance art. And this show, it will immortalize her."

"The thing that may surprise people is that she's a very gentle person. Very funny. Incredibly warm. Superstitious. She's very generous."

"She believes in seven-year cycles. So if something goes wrong . . . seven years."

Right now, Dieter was one of the most powerful men in the art world. More than six hundred thousand people had come to MoMA to see *The Artist Is Present*. Celebrities had come. Sharon Stone. Isabella Rossellini. Andreas Gursky. Antony Gormley.

Lou Reed. Rufus Wainwright. Björk. Antony Hegarty. Matthew Barney. The phones at his gallery did not stop ringing.

"Yes, a huge high to win the Golden Lion . . . Marina was watching the country being destroyed by Milošević. So that was her way of expressing it . . ."

"Yes, *The Room with the Ocean View* was her answer to 9/11. She wanted to create a still point in the aftermath."

"It's all about energy. People talk of her extreme ego. Self-aggrandizement. But she's not tough on people. She's very tough on herself."

"Well, everything matters to Louise Bourgeois."

Francesca took him fresh coffee and a letter and CD from Healayas Breen that had been addressed to her. The note said: *I thought you and Dieter might be interested in some of the coverage we've been giving* The Artist Is Present. *Cordialement, Healayas Breen.*

Dieter ran his hand over her buttocks as she moved away. He put the reporter on speakerphone.

Francesca couldn't stand Arnold Keeble. But of course Keeble was on the guest list. He was on the guest list to any art event in the world. His television series had been a huge hit, but she had smiled when she noticed that the next series featured Healayas too. Arnold had a way of looking at a woman that dismissed, or sexualized. So many men did it without even noticing. On the radio with Healayas he was clever, combative, arrogant, irritating. It made Francesca wonder about his relationship with his co-host outside the studio. Healayas was so very striking. It was hard to know if her looks and her accent had always been an advantage.

"What you need to understand here," Dieter was saying to the journalist, "and I don't mean to claim anything, I don't want to take anything away from her because she does it, but she works best in collaboration. Some artists need it more than others. Some are very self-reliant and that works for them. But Marina . . . it's not a control thing. We're both controlling, but together there's a different sort of exploration. I mean take Michaela Barns and the piece at the Empire State. It could have been terrible but it wasn't. We pared it back over two years and it gained cogency. Marina is like that. It's a journey and we're both on it. I'm sure she'd say she's learned from it. I have learned enormously from her. I mean, you do from the greats."

Dieter beckoned to Francesca to sit with him.

"You each bring a unique perspective?" the journalist's voice asked.

"I see the world through a literary filter, the need for story. Marina sees it in a completely different way. She's a great thinker. She's organic. She responds emotionally. But over twenty-five years, I think we know that together we're greater than our parts. That's how it is."

"How is it that you became interested in art, Monsieur Lang?"

Dieter smiled at Francesca. "Well, it's a cute story. I had a teacher, Miss Stein, in my final year of primary school. She went somewhere on a holiday, and sent us each a postcard of a piece of art she saw. I got Giacometti's *Walking Man*. Some of the kids laughed and thought I'd been unlucky. Some of them had Turners or Vermeers. But I got the Giacometti. I wanted to be in the art world from that moment on."

"Marina has no family," said the journalist. "Her marriage to the artist Paolo Canevari has recently ended. Is *The Artist Is Present* also a form of mourning for her?"

"No comment," said Dieter.

"So art has mattered more to her than love?" the journalist asked.

Francesca frowned. She wanted to say to the journalist that it's never as simple as art or love. Look at the greats in any field. Relationships are hard. She is one of the most famous women in the world and she has millions of dollars in art and property. And there is no one to go home to at night.

When Dieter did not answer, the journalist added, "It seems that her life is a metaphor for performance art. Nothing will remain."

Dieter said, "Oh, I think a lot will remain. There will be books, a film to come. There's a documentary in the making. Things we can't see yet will come from this. But this, what we've seen at MoMA, will never happen again. It's been very special. More than anyone had hoped for, I think. Especially Marina."

She'll be a page, Francesca thought, half a page in the history of art in a hundred years. And Dieter? He would have helped to make it possible.

"No re-enactments?"

"I can't promise that." She saw Dieter allow himself a small smile.

"Has fame always been her driving force?" the journalist asked.

"Yes," said Dieter. "It has. It is for many artists, if you stop to ask them, or they are honest enough to answer truthfully."

After the interview was over, Francesca suggested to Dieter that he offer Healayas Breen an interview with Marina the night the show ended. The world media would be clamoring to get to her.

"Not Arnold? He'll be furious."

"I think Healayas will do it well," Francesca said.

"All right."

She enjoyed swirling these little pools of influence for other women. God knew, the women of the world needed all the help they could get.

She returned to the kitchen and arranged apples in bubbling brown sugar and butter. Slowly she turned them and watched as the white flesh became translucent. The smell rose up and she blew on the spoon and licked it. She thought of Marina sitting in that white room day after day. And then, when she was at home, drinking water every hour to avoid dehydration. And the pain that must be everywhere now. Even for a woman as experienced as Marina, it was a big ask.

My dear friend, she thought. I send you sunshine, and blue sky, and spring becoming summer. Just twenty days to go. Just twenty days and I will make you a feast.

She began listing on a piece of paper everyone that she and Dieter must invite to that meal.

I will never sit for seventy-five days, Francesca thought. I will never slice my stomach with a razor blade or eat a kilo of honey. I will never show my body to the world nor have students who think me wise and brave. But because you do this, Marina, I am stronger. I am more certain of that every day. You live your art and it is inseparable from you. And with it you bring me courage. You are a woman and this is a fact. No matter what people make of anything else, your gender is unequivocal.

33

AS SHE WAITED IN THE line to sit again, Brittika thought about her soul. Was it really a quivering dark shadow wrapped in gold leaf? Had she really eaten it? And where had it come from? Had she left it somewhere? She thought of the Murakami novel in which the soul of a man was in a woodshed dying of cold. This wasn't the time for her to dive into New Age self-analysis. It had been a hallucination. Simple as that. She had to put it behind her and focus. She had to get through these seventy-five days. Ironic that her thesis on endurance should become an act of endurance in itself.

She'd been back to Amsterdam to meet with her supervisors, and she had worked on the latest draft of her thesis. She had done some long shifts at the local co-op, and then booked the cheapest flight to New York for the final days of the show. Her credit card was sagging under the weight of *The Artist Is Present*. The hostel on 46th was no friendlier with familiarity. The air conditioner had become noisier, as had the noise coming up from the street.

Endurance had become the role of everyone in the audience too. Perhaps, after fifty-four days, Marina had moved on from endurance into some other state. In March, Abramović had worn a dark blue dress. In April it became a bright red version of the same dress. Today was the first day of May. The long red dress had been replaced with an identical gown of pure white.

Brittika thought, She has become her own flag. The blue, red, and white of the nation of Abramović.

The nation of Abramović, she observed, had drawn an army of believers. What they believed in was anyone's guess, but they kept coming. The atrium was more crowded every day. Why did they cry? Did they find reassurance, awakening, mystery? Something was happening. It was there in the tears. The endless tears from the people who sat in that chair opposite Abramović.

Already Brittika had waited nine hours in the line and still there were four people ahead of her. She had made new connections, traded emails and shared research, collected quotes, ideas, interviews, and stories. Yesterday she had waited all day, but missed out on sitting with Abramović by five people.

She'd interviewed Carlos, who had sat seventeen times. He thought sitting opposite Marina was like psychic housekeeping. Like cleaning out an old cupboard.

Brittika was sure they'd soon start limiting the time people could sit. There were rumblings now when people sat longer than fifteen minutes. And the stampede up the stairs at 10:30 a.m. had become dangerous. This morning someone had tried to create order from chaos by handing out numbers along the line. She had received number twenty-six at 5 a.m. People had slept on the street outside MoMA. They had been hopping about in sleeping bags trying to warm up, laughing at the madness and the seriousness of their intent.

Brittika inserted her earphones again. She was listening to the Dirty Projectors' "Stillness Is the Move." She smiled at the coincidence. Maybe stillness was the move. A young man in a red-and-white gingham shirt tapped her on the shoulder and she removed an earphone.

"Hi," she said.

"I've seen you sit before," he said, squatting down beside her, "so I wanted to ask you: Are you sacrificial in some way?"

"In what context?" He had lovely eyes. He didn't look like a nut but it was New York.

"Well, this waiting to sit with her, is it a sort of ritual?"

"Wouldn't sacrificial imply some kind of death?" she asked. She could see his biceps beneath his shirtsleeves, the breadth of his chest.

"I'm not implying it," he said, smiling, and it was a wide, white smile. "That's exactly what I'm saying. Even all this waiting. There's a death of expectation. And on the chair, it's a death of personality. People are caught out."

"I'm not sure if we're caught out," Brittika said.

"But I saw your photo online. You looked surprised by what you saw. Even shocked."

"Are you an art student?" she asked, flattered but still wary.

"I'm a butcher," he said. "But I've come a few times. I don't think I'll get to sit but that's okay."

"Are you really a butcher?" she asked. Somehow this disappointed her. And then she considered that he was probably a millionaire butcher in that shirt. Some kind of New York inheritance.

"Yeah, I am. Doesn't it seem enough?" he said.

"No, it's just . . ."

"Where are you from?" he asked.

"Amsterdam," she said. "I'm just here for the show."

"I like your accent. So what have you noticed about New Yorkers?"

"That they're surprisingly patient. Because I really have only seen this show."

He grinned. "Then let me tell you: we're poets. Even the developers, the bureaucrats, and us butchers from Brooklyn. You just have to ask us how we feel about this city and we start getting lyrical. That's the way we are here. New York is a much more romantic city than Paris."

"And you know Paris?"

"I've watched the movies." He laughed. "And I might get there one day."

He gestured to Abramović. "That's why this show works here. I don't think it would work in any other city nearly so well. It would need more. You know, multimedia or whatever. But it suits us. It gives us a little moment to remember we're poets, even if we never write a word." He looked at his watch. "I gotta go."

"Nice to talk to you," she said, wishing he wouldn't walk away. Ridiculously wanting to kiss him goodbye. "I'm Brittika," she said impulsively, holding out her hand.

"Maybe I'll see you again, Brittika."

"What's your name?" she asked in a rush.

He grinned. "Charlie."

"Are you coming back?" she asked.

"Will you be here?"

"I will. I'm in New York now until the end."

"I hope I see you before then."

PART SIX

It takes courage to grow up and become who you really are.

E.E. CUMMINGS

34

IT WAS EARLY AFTERNOON AND Levin arrived to find the atrium crammed with people. Marina was in a long white dress and the table was gone. Now there were just two chairs facing each other. The intimacy of the situation was even more startling.

Levin watched as a slender woman in skinny jeans, a black sweater, and pointy white suede boots rose from the chair. She had a striking wizened face and moved like a dancer. Levin felt he should recognize her. Then a child sat. When she left after ten minutes, she had the look of someone who has just performed an act of bravery and was relieved to have escaped uninjured.

Abramović was looking tired. Other than the almost invisible roll of the neck, and a minute restlessness on the chair, she was inert. Her eyelids rested in a half gaze, steady and distant. The woman on his right had her fingers across her mouth in rapt awe.

"How does she do it?" the rapt woman whispered to Levin. "To be so still all day?"

"She's been at it a long time," Levin said, feeling like he was becoming an expert.

"Since March, yes?" the woman looked at him.

"Since 1963."

Someone behind them said in a loud voice. "So what? She's a real person, right? What will galleries become next? Black walls? Silence?"

"Shh," someone nearby said.

"I'm being shushed," the man's voice continued. "It's not a gallery. It's a library. Worse, it's a damn church. They're all praying."

People squeezed past him. On the other side of the square, two children had sat down, their legs crossed like yogic masters, facing each other in imitation of Marina and her sitter. The woman beside him saw them too, and she smiled and nodded at them. The children sat for a few minutes quite seriously, gazing into each other's eyes. Then the girl fell about giggling and the boy fell on top of her.

Levin observed a man in the crowd with his left arm inked. The one word he could make out below the folded shirtsleeve was the word *kill*. Levin looked at the security guards who were in quiet conversation, although their eyes were ever vigilant. What would they do if the man simply stepped into the square and wounded Marina, drew a gun, a blade, raised a fist, or took her neck between his hands? He continued to observe the man. What would he, Levin, who had no martial arts skills, no military training, who didn't even own a handgun, do if he saw the man draw a weapon? He didn't want to think about what he might become in such a situation.

The *Kawa* soundtrack was almost done. Or as done as it could be until he had the final pictures and an orchestra who knew their parts. Seiji Isoda was planning to arrive in the first week of June with the final edit, which suited Levin perfectly because he didn't want to miss these last weeks with Marina. Isoda had sent him several tests with the draft tracks striped to the pictures and it was better than Levin had imagined, even if it still lacked an essential connectivity. But Isoda seemed so optimistic. In the end, they decided on New York for recording the final score. Anything else felt too hard.

Pillow-Marina was still seated in her chair at the dining table in the apartment. Her cashmere hair now comprised three black scarves twisted into the side braid she favored. The first time Yolanda the housekeeper had come she had dismantled her, folded the scarf, and returned the cushions to the couch. But the next time he had left a note. *Please do not disturb. (Work in progress.)* And since then Marina had sat silently, and each morning, Levin sat opposite her.

At the piano he chased music into the forest, underwater, over rocks, and into fish. He chased it all the way downstream to the sea, and there he had found himself on a long pale beach and quite alone. There was no mythical fish-woman to pluck him up and put him back into the river, so he could swim home. There was only Pillow-Marina and the empty apartment. He had tried to capture that too. The true sound of solitude.

When the music was gone for the night, he looked at the photographs on Flickr of all the people who had sat with Marina. He had never noticed before how the human face could be so varied. And the variation wasn't in the features, or the colors, although that was part of it. It was in the way the person leaned into their face, or didn't, they way they looked out with intensity or resignation, with curiosity or fear, and it seemed to indicate the way they saw the world in general. We live as we see, he thought, and he knew Lydia would have been fascinated by the faces too, and he hated thinking of her in the past tense.

That morning, on the way to MoMA, he'd been following a woman up the stairs from the subway. She was in a long floral halter-neck sundress that all the girls seemed to be wearing now the weather was warm. Her whole back and arms were tattooed with green vines and yellow flowers. When she turned her head, though, he had been startled to discover her face was withered and hard. He thought instantly that she must be a heroin addict and remembered Hal once telling him that the truly poor couldn't afford to live in Manhattan anymore. Manhattan belonged to the rich now. Maybe she was the daughter of old money, or the ex-wife of a famous artist. Still, the contrast of the delicate botanical art and that weary, worn-out face stayed with him. Who had she been when she'd chosen those pictures, compared to who she was now?

His eyes kept returning to the man with *kill* on his arm. Then Lydia's voice said clearly to him, "Arky, you're just seeing the last word. Not the whole sentence. It actually says: *Thou shalt not kill.*"

He blinked rapidly. Of course it wasn't Lydia speaking to him, but it had been so vivid. And perhaps she was right. Would a person bent on killing in public have taken such care to iron his white shirt?

When the gallery closed for the day, Marina was still alive. There had been no scene and the man in the white shirt had disappeared hours before. Levin took the A train but instead of getting off at West 4th Street he went on to Canal and walked to the river. There he sat on a bench and watched the ferries and cargo ships.

After his mother died and he'd gone to live with his grandparents, his grandfather had introduced him to Dave Brubeck, Oscar Petersen, Art Tatum, Bill Evans. And his grandmother had loved musicals. Rodgers and Hammerstein. Gilbert and Sullivan. They both encouraged him to keep composing. Working as an usher at the Arlington in his senior year, he fell in love with soundtracks. He loved Jarre's scores to *Lawrence of Arabia* and *Dr. Zhivago*. John Barry's *Born Free* score and all those Bond movies—*Dr. No*, *The Man with the Golden Gun*, *Thunderball*, and *Goldfinger*. And Bernard Herrmann's soundtracks to *Vertigo*, *North by Northwest*, and *Psycho*. He'd go home and practice them. Take them apart. Put them back together. He learned other instruments. His grandfather taught him drums and saxophone, and he picked up guitar. His grandfather said he made anything sound musical. His grandmother told him friends would come.

Then Levin got a scholarship to Juilliard. He met Tom Washington at a student event. Tom was an actor at the Lee Strasberg school but he wanted to be a director and he was looking for someone to compose the music. Neither of the first two short films they did together amounted to much. Back then Tom wasn't a particularly good writer, and they did all the special effects themselves. But Tom had the same passion for film that Levin had for music. The third film was an eighteen-minute dark comedy featuring a mute girl who tried to get her boyfriend out of prison. It got picked up on the awards circuit. It was In Competition at Cannes and won in Toronto. People praised the soundtrack. An agent in LA wanted to represent him. Tom was offered a feature and he insisted that Levin was signed for the soundtrack. The budget was more than either of them had ever imagined. And that first feature won Sundance. It won Berlin. The soundtrack was nominated for an Oscar and Tom's script was nominated for best original screenplay. The lead was nominated for best actor. They didn't win that year, but Tom was the latest wonder kid and the budgets got bigger fast.

Levin met Lydia one day at a recording studio he and Tom were using. She was looking it over for her father as a possible investment. Levin had been sitting in a back room taking a moment out while Tom was on a call. Lydia said she needed to sit down somewhere quiet because she was feeling dizzy, and was it okay if she just hid away in here a few moments because bathrooms made her feel worse.

She was a second-year architecture student at NYU. He asked if he could call her, make sure she got home all right, and she gave him her number. When he called and said they should have coffee, she agreed. He delivered flowers to her via the concierge in her building, who was Brazilian and liked being part of this little romance. He rang and played piano until she was asleep. She said, "You're too sweet for me. You don't know how complicated this can be."

A marriage was a series of days, Levin thought. He thought of Lydia in the morning. First the underpants then the bra. Rarely the other way around. Standing in the early light, slipping off the long T-shirt she wore to bed. For years she had always done her bra up from the front and then swiveled it about to cup her breasts. Later, he realized she had stopped doing this and was doing it the way women did it in movies: scooping her breasts into the fabric then reaching behind, duck-winged, and snipping closed the clasps. Bras came in so many fabrics—opaque and transparent, embroidered, spotted, striped, delicate, molded, lace, satin, black, cream, red, and orange. Day after day she poured her perfect handfuls of breasts into sculptured fabric. He would have done anything to hold her breasts for a day.

He thought of how rarely he had touched her at such moments, as she dressed and undressed. She had seemed unreachable, distant, something to be observed tacitly, a glimpse of long thigh and buttocks.

The music he heard at such times was Brian Eno's flashes of sound, light touching here and there, the morning's texture having the weight of feathers or the static of nylon. Lydia was not by nature a moody person. Quite the opposite. She had an eternal sort of optimism that he had liked. Needed. It was he who brought the static.

"I have this blood condition," Lydia said the very first day they met, by way of explanation for her dizziness and the red spots he noticed on her arms. Already, there in that little room, Levin knew he wanted to marry her.

When he first proposed, she said, "I don't think I should get married. This thing I have, it's hereditary. My mother died from it. You have to know that it could make things very difficult. I'm not sure I want to put you through that. Losing my mother, it's wrecked my father. And the doctors all say it's too dangerous for me to have children. If I ever need an operation . . . well, it's nasty."

"I'll look after you," he said.

They were married, and one year later Lydia was unexpectedly and worryingly pregnant. It was a huge risk, but she wouldn't consider an abortion.

"It's meant to be, it must be," she said.

So Alice, who was meant to be, was born. The easiest birth in the world.

Levin's grandparents died in the same year, one following the other only days apart, as if they were the head and tail of a kite that had found its way free. In the weeks that followed he had played Beethoven's Piano Concerto No. 5 so often that for years it was the one thing that would always put Alice to sleep.

Being here sounds like this, Levin thought as the sky darkened, turning the Hudson to pewter. The rumbling of traffic, the lift of wind, the passing of joggers, the parents with strollers, the roller skaters, the lovers, the great river moving past, taking itself out to sea. Behind him the city bloomed with night lights. Life was the Leonard Cohen songbook, he decided. Bittersweet love, a little sex, and a moment of God. Then life moved on. You got over the love, sex came and went, and you forgot about God.

Perhaps ignoring things was an underestimated art. A critical survival skill even. Ignoring the bullet wound so you could get to the hospital. Ignoring the phone call so you could avoid the news. Ignoring the memories so you didn't hurt.

He suspected that instead of the Stop sign that seemed to have haunted his life since Christmas, somewhere there was a Go sign, or a Turn Left sign. If only he could glimpse it out of the corner of his eye, he'd follow it. If only a white rabbit would appear, he'd run after it. If only Lydia would come home and be Lydia again, he'd know what to do.

35

BACK IN GEORGIA, JANE MILLER watched the webcam that was her eye into the atrium. The camera was angled to capture the floor of the square. Jane could just see the far edge with feet, crossed legs, bags sprawled amid waiting people. She'd had an email from Matthew, the shabby-shoed lawyer. It had been sweet and funny. And then a text had come through from Brittika, the young Dutch girl doing her PhD. *Next in line. Nervous.*

I'm part of a community, Jane thought. She couldn't see the line, only the young woman currently sitting opposite Marina. She was crossing and then uncrossing her arms and legs. She sat forward and then she sat back. She scratched and then crossed her arms again, but still she sat, as if Marina was her opponent in a silent battle of wills. The girl put her hands in her pockets. She wiggled and crossed her legs again.

"What are you trying to prove?" Jane asked aloud. "Why stay if you're so uncomfortable?"

But despite her restlessness, the young woman did stay, and she appeared to be returning Marina's gaze with a petulant stare. Marina in turn was a rock that loved her regardless of what happened. Jane peered more closely at the young woman. She looked familiar. She opened the monograph of the show she had purchased in the MoMA store. Flicking through the pages she found a girl straddling a bicycle seat, high up on a wall, her arms outstretched, completely naked. She thought it looked decidedly like the girl sitting in the chair. Was the young woman one of Marina's re-performers? One of the cast of thirty or so who had been specially trained by Marina?

The media had all but dismissed the re-enactments, saying the young people lacked the charisma Marina and Ulay had brought to the original performances. Perhaps the young woman was naked and ready for work under her trench coat, Jane considered.

The young woman gave a final irritated wriggle and stood up. She was quickly replaced by Brittika, unmistakable with her trademark pink bob.

The phone rang and Jane answered it. "Hi, Bob, I'm in the middle of something right now," she said. "How about five? Great. See you then."

Brittika settled in the chair opposite Marina. Marina lifted her head and Brittika took off the summer frock she was wearing to reveal her entirely naked body.

Jane's eyes opened wide and an "Oh" escaped her lips.

Within moments the guards were upon Brittika, heaving her from the chair, and Jane lost sight of them as they moved out of the scope of the webcam.

In another moment, an older man replaced Brittika at the table. Marina, who had dropped her head, lifted it again, locked eyes with the man, and the performance continued.

What had Brittika been thinking? Jane wondered. She was certain Brittika was off in some room where she could be charged with . . . what? Public nudity? Indecency? But there were people upstairs naked. Jane hoped they'd let her dress again, let her have that dignity. She wondered if people had clapped. She considered calling Brittika, but to say what? *What were you thinking?* What on earth were you thinking?

At 5 p.m. she met with Bob, their farm manager, and they went through the last month's results. Since Karl's diagnosis she had thought a lot about the chemicals they used every day on the cotton. Known to cause cancers, tumors, mutations in fish, birds, and humans. It had been one of the few things she and Karl had fought about over the years, but they'd stopped fighting once he got the tumor. She thought about their workers and wondered how much longer she could go on just because the world needed cotton. She'd talked organics to Bob, but she might as well have said she wanted him to become a Muslim.

Her eldest daughter had called and invited her to dinner, and Jane was pleased to go. It was so hot and muggy and there were only so many meals for one that she could get excited about.

Coming home later, in the cool of evening, there was a startlingly yellow full moon. The house was no noisier than it had been when she left. The rooms no fuller. The bed no untidier. She tossed two cushions off the couch onto the floor just to give the sense of something having happened. After her daughter's home, with her three little children banging about, the contrast was hard to bear. Jane never thought she'd miss the rattle and roar of a football game on the television. Or spreadsheets on the kitchen table with Karl calling her to come in here and look at these projections because he couldn't make it add up.

She sat again at the computer and went over the latest profit and loss, assessing the costs that had escalated and the subsidies from government that had boosted income. After a while she reopened the MoMA website and looked at the photographs of the latest people who had sat. The expressions were so curiously raw, she thought. Like that moon tonight. Entirely unguarded.

Evidence that life had been going on a long, long time and still no one was any the wiser about how to explain it. The mystery of individuality despite every indication that we were all pretty much the same. It was a fact of human beings, the variation of physical differences and the sameness of motivations.

She wondered if, after all, she was silly not to have sat. She did not think of herself as lacking courage. But she could count on one hand the things she could describe as truly brave acts. Childbirth three times over. And burying Karl. Literally watching him go into the ground. She thought she'd split in two just standing there.

She thought of how Marina and Ulay had walked all that way to say goodbye to each other. And the fact he had come back, on the very first day of *The Artist Is Present*, to sit with her. That had touched her very much. Ulay's face in the photograph. The mischief in his eyes and the look of knowing old love.

She could have flown back to New York to see the last days of *The Artist Is Present*. But it was too late to get it organized now. She had a shareholder meeting next week for a company in which she had invested quite a sum. Still, she felt more restless than she had ever felt in her life.

"Maybe I need to walk like Marina. Maybe a walk would help. What do you think of going walking, Karl? But not toward each other. Let's both go in the same direction," she said, regarding his face in the photograph on the desk.

"How about that walk in Spain that is so popular? You remember—I told you about it last weekend when there was that program on the television. We could do that. I could be a little Catholic again after all these years. Maybe a walk would do us both good."

Would it be crowded at this time of the year? And was she fit enough? Maybe she should wait until September, when the weather cooled. She'd have to go halfway around the world. She'd need a travel agent and a passport. And was a walk in Spain what she really wanted to do? Yes, she decided. I think it is. It would be a year since Karl had died. A sort of anniversary then.

With such concerns occupying her mind, she wished Karl a good night and blew out the candle in its glass jar next to his photograph.

36

MARINA BEGAN AT SHANHAIGUAN, IN the east, where the Chinese said the dragon's head rested in the Yellow Sea. It had been a marriage walk, but now, after thirteen years, it had come undone, this thing that had bound them so intensely.

It had been eight years in the planning. Letters and permits, visas and money, diplomacy, the Netherlands and China, international cultural exchange, itineraries, reissued itineraries, squabbles, bureaucrats, flights and trucks, government hotels and no camping.

They had wanted silence and solitude. Nights under the stars like they'd had in the desert in Australia, a minimal crew that would not interfere with their private, meditative walk. But there was so little time to be truly alone. Only when she walked, when the camera crew was ahead or behind, in the tracts of film they managed to capture when each day they finally arrived at the wall, driven in vans from some obscure location where it had been essential to stay. Then she had time to connect with herself, with this ancient place, with this land. And in those moments the sky and the path and the sense of scale humbled her and sometimes released her.

Ulay began at the tip of the dragon's tail, at Jiayuguan, in the barren Gobi desert. She had no way of knowing if he too was experiencing the chaos of Chinese bureaucracy that corroded the days. She had no contact with Ulay or his crew.

Once she had thought of Ulay as her perfect hermaphroditic union. Her creative and spiritual union. Walking toward each other, they had originally planned to be drawn closer by the magnetic power of each other. Now they walked against the current that had pushed them apart.

Still, they both felt that it was the fitting thing to do. To walk this route of mythology, of dragons and gods and wild men. The Chinese said the dragon connected earth and sky. And the wall was constructed in mirror image to the Milky Way. So they were walking the stars too.

Coming from the east, Marina had to walk the sections of the wall most popular with the tourists. They had little interest in her, being more concerned with snapping each other against the giant stone backdrop. She carved her way through clicking cameras. She climbed the winding wall, the relentless steps, the ancient escarpments. She passed through the towers with their brass bowls for purification. She walked the chakra points of the earthbound and celestial dragon, and the way of human life gone long into the past.

Every day the Chinese bureaucrats and officials who accompanied her, or who joined them in each new province, insisted that paperwork be signed off in triplicate, and that each day begin with meetings and end with meetings. This exhausted her and she retreated to whatever bare concrete cell she had been assigned in yet another bare communist hotel and allowed the discussions and arguments to go on without her.

By day she measured the landscape with her body. Feeling the scale, the beauty, the poverty beyond the wall work upon her, soaking into her eyes. Step by step. Her legs each morning were stiff with yesterday's work. Marina started as early as possible, wanting to catch the sunrise, to have those moments of pure surrender, prayer, and reflection that she yearned for.

Soon the crowds diminished, the tourists evaporated, and she was a lone figure on the wall. She wore red. Ulay was in blue. Red dragon, blue dragon. They had dressed for the film, but also for their characters, for their own personal mythology, for the mythology of duality that they had played out all these years. As the days passed she felt like she lost track of who he was, what went wrong, and even why they were walking. Some days she was more tired than she could remember ever being.

She wanted to see him walking toward her. She wanted him to hold her. She wanted duality but there was only singularity. Each step she took moved her closer to him, and to the end of together, the end of partnership, the end of connection, to the end of love.

She thought sometimes only step, step, step. Every step harder than the last. She tried to climb quickly but on the rough parts of the path, where the wall had crumbled, she groped for hand-holds, slid and slipped.

Marina and Ulay, red dragon, blue dragon, walked on. Now they were twelve hundred miles apart.

Marina was in the middle of nowhere familiar. She felt the fear of that, and the happiness. This was what she loved. To be in the unknown. To be on the other side of fear where everything became possible. She was emptying herself. The irritation of bureaucracy, the hours of boredom as she endured long car rides and nights on hard beds after bad food—it all released her. Her body went on without her feeling attached to it. She might have been the wind or one of its riders, she did not know. Or perhaps the wind rode her.

Why had she loved Ulay? Why had there been such a force between them? How was it that they had the same birthday? That when they met they were both wearing chopsticks in their hair? That he felt half-female while she felt half-male. How was it that he felt like the person she had known through lifetimes? As if she had loved him and hurt him time after time, and that she could love him hard enough to destroy him. What was that? What was her rage and her pain, her grief and hollowness? Because for all they'd been, for all they'd traveled, were traveling these thousands of miles, she had no idea what she was going to do with her life beyond this.

Weeks passed. Months passed. One thousand miles. Five hundred miles. The ugliness of the bad hotels brought paradox and Tito, the excess and scarcity of communism. It brought back the controls and limits and corruption of a world she could not wait to be free of. But still she walked. And tried to shed the numbness every day with the sheer beauty of the landscape and the immensity of the human spirit that had built this wall and fought for centuries to protect an empire.

She might have been another sort of woman. She might have had a child, been a mother, a wife. But she couldn't feel that this time. She didn't want it. They'd chosen not to. She'd chosen not to. She wanted this life, this one life for herself. And if that was selfish, if that was the harder road, then so be it. She would do it alone. She would find the next step and the next step and the next step. She had no future she could see. She would carve it out for herself as they'd carved out the steps for this wall. On one side was the past, the other the future. One side heaven, the other hell, one side black, the other white, one side night, the other day. Life was duality. She thought she'd found her other half, but it turned out that he was one of her many halves. She could see things in him that she didn't find kind or good. They irritated her. Stung her. She could see the greater person he might be, but he didn't want that. Only she wanted that.

"You can't love me for something I might become, Marina," he had said.

That was something she'd discovered. You could love a person so hard they became unknown to you.

Two hundred miles. One hundred miles. Fifty miles. Twenty miles. Ten miles. Until there was only one more mile.

His team came ahead and told Marina that Ulay had found the best place to meet, a little farther on, so he'd wait for her there. As always, she had to take more steps, go the extra mile, to meet him. Up and up and up she went, step after step. And she thought how much she hated him for making her walk this much farther. Could he not have trusted that there was a perfectly photogenic spot wherever they naturally met?

Here she was, walking toward him like a bride, but she was no bride and he no groom. She breathed and let it go. Let it go, Marina. There is a river below and the land and the sky is reminding you that everything is changing every moment of every day and you and your feelings are nothing in this.

And there he was, in his blue coat, his blue pants. A blue dragon to her red one. He on one tower, she on the other. She felt her body quiver with the last thread of energy it cost her to take these final steps. Down, down she went, to the bridge. Down, down he went, to the bridge. Moving toward each other. Red dragon, blue dragon.

The sun was sinking. The land was golden, the sky was amethyst, the river mercury. The past was behind them. She sobbed then. Something dry and raw that welled up. He was there, ahead of her, his face, his beloved face, and he was smiling, and she wanted to hold him, to be held. Instead, she reached out her hand and they touched fingers for a moment. Skin-to-skin one last time, in that way. And then he gave her the briefest, most perfunctory hug.

It was, she thought, inexpressibly sad. This was goodbye. She saw—in his eyes, in his laughing, in his joking with the crew— that this was a performance for him. He was long gone. But it had been her heart.

37

LEVIN ABSORBED THE QUIET HUM of the atrium about him. There was a brooding light about Marina as the days went by, as if she was incubating another creature inside her.

"Do you think she'll make it?" a woman asked.

"I am certain," her male companion replied with a French accent. "But I am also certain that if this killed her, she would be unperturbed."

Levin agreed. Marina did not seem to be the least bit scared of death. Would Lydia have preferred to die? The thought struck him like a blow. Maybe she would have preferred to die. Maybe she had planned on death. Maybe there had been several scenarios and when she signed the legal papers, she had never really imagined anything being necessary other than her will.

Perhaps she hadn't only given him his freedom because it was the best thing to do for him. Maybe she hadn't wanted to face this either. Perhaps she had imagined she could run away from herself, cut herself off from all she had lost. Cut herself off from him, the one person who loved her more than anyone else. Perhaps she wasn't being brave on her own out there in the Hamptons. Perhaps she was frightened. Perhaps, for once in her life, Lydia was out of her depth. Perhaps she really needed him, but had no way of letting him know. Hal was right. He did have choices. But maybe Lydia didn't. She'd signed over her choices. She'd insisted that she could do it on her own.

He thought of all the times she'd never called a plumber because she could fix the pipe. For a girl with an impressive trust fund, she wanted to be the one to design the new kitchen in their Columbus apartment and source all the fittings. She had repaired tiles in the bathroom. She had replaced lighting and wallpapered walls. In her work she employed endless professionals, but in her own life, she had been ruthlessly independent.

What had she needed him for? The warm body in the bed? The familiar voice on the end of the phone when she rang from Buenos Aires or Madrid? Someone to complete the picture when she and Alice went out in public? School functions. Openings and award ceremonies. Sex?

No, it was much more than that. He wasn't going to dismiss twenty-four years. "You are my music," she had said as he played piano when she came home from work.

And she had been his. Kissing Lydia had resonated in every cell in his body. But somehow they had stopped kissing like that. Sometimes he was afraid of this confident woman he'd married. Sometimes he felt too small for her. There had been times, making love, when he had thought that if he kissed her, really kissed her, he'd disappear entirely.

Did she fantasize about other men when they made love? He was too afraid to ask. Had she been faithful to him? He didn't know. Despite all the traveling, she always came home to him and wanted him.

Had he been unfaithful to her? Yes—twice. Years ago on a skiing trip to Aspen with Tom after he'd sniffed God knew what up his nose. It embarrassed him to think about it, all over and done in seconds. He couldn't remember her face, only the brickwork under his fingers as he clung to the wall in a dark corner of the garden. Another time, a man he'd only just met had given him a blow job. It was an LA party that time, another night of powdered lubricant and a dark bathroom. He had been so young. He'd refused drugs after that. Never told Lydia about either event. Hidden it away and hoped he didn't get Alzheimer's and start confessing it one day.

He missed the warm languor of Lydia's mouth and her tongue winding and weaving into and around him. He missed looking into her eyes and seeing her smile. He missed them finding together the place where flesh became heat and release. And soul, he thought, though he had never liked the word. What sounded religious, but wasn't, was that he'd had faith in their marriage. He had never imagined the simple commitment to love Lydia would become so complicated.

If two people were holding on to a rock face and one of them lost faith, wasn't it up to the other person to tell them everything was going to be all right? Maybe Lydia was on a rock face in the Hamptons. She had told him to climb the rope. Climb, Arky, climb! She wanted him to save himself. And he had. He had climbed up. But she was still down there. Maybe she was waiting for him. Maybe she was waiting for him to come back and haul her up. Or at least be there to say goodbye when she fell. Maybe she'd been holding on all this time, wondering when he'd put his head over the cliff and say, 'I'm here. I'm back with help.'

38

IN THE DARKNESS, DANICA ABRAMOVIĆ perused the retrospective, observing the list of implements from the performance in Naples in 1972. *Gun. Bullet. Blue paint. Comb. Bell. Whip. Pocket knife. Bandage. White paint. Scissors. Bread. Wine. Honey. Shoes. Chair. Metal spear. Box of razor blades. Coat. Sheet of white paper. Hat. Pen.*

Seventy-two items in all.

Feather. Polaroid camera. Drinking glass. Mirror. Flowers. Matches.

And the instructions: *There are 72 objects on the table that one can use on me as desired.*

When she had first heard of it, this shocking thing her daughter had done, giving the audience this opportunity to harm her, Danica had been devastated.

"It's too much. Why would you do this?" she had asked Marina.

"I have to understand."

"Understand what? Enough that already you nearly die inside the star, nearly burn to death here in Belgrade, but now you must nearly get yourself killed in Italy as well?"

"I had to do it."

"You gave them knives, a loaded gun?"

"I didn't load the gun. The bullet was separate. They had to make the choice to put the bullet in the chamber."

"*Hold a gun to my head! Pull the trigger. Let's see what will happen?*" Danica had been shouting by then.

"No." Marina had almost whispered it. Her head down.

"That is not art! It is not art!" Danica had shouted.

A lot of mothers have daughters they did not understand. How many times Danica had come upon her colleagues discussing the latest thing Marina had done. The talk died as she entered the room.

Once Marina had said, "The fear frees me. You taught me that." And she had put her head on Danica's shoulder like a normal daughter and they had laughed.

But there was a war inside Marina. Later Danica had asked her, "Why make more violence, when there is enough coming in the world without you laying a table with such weapons?"

"You see the people in the pictures," Marina had said. "Every one of them was forced to think. They were drawn into the actions of the group—like soldiers. You know all about that."

"You take orders. You comply."

"I gave them their orders. They did comply. They will not forget the room and who they were when they realized what they were capable of. There were men who came out of that room and knew themselves as vicious. Women who were sure they were not until they had the opportunity to urge the men on. And when it was over and I started to walk around, they ran away. They were embarrassed, frightened of me. Frightened of themselves. They can never pretend violence was something they would not participate in."

Danica had shaken her head. "It's not right, Marina. This life you are choosing. It shames me."

"They could have chosen bread, wine, oil," she said. "Honey, cake, flowers."

"Did you really think they would massage you, drink to your health?" Danica had sighed, sat down, rubbed her forehead. "Remember Rochefort, the French lawyer? 'I don't deny that my client was carrying a bomb. But this doesn't prove he was going to use it. After all, I myself always carry with me all I'd need to commit a rape.' How disappointed you would have been by a room full of pacifists."

And then Marina had surprised her. She said, "I never thought they might kill me."

"But . . ."

"I understand that now."

And then she had left Belgrade to be with that German. Danica could never accept a German.

And in the end it hadn't worked out. They had done that walk in China. Some sort of grand romantic gesture. She understood that too. Three thousand miles was barely enough to let someone go. She would have done anything for Vojo. Even killed him if it meant he would love her forever. And whether anyone else knew it, she knew that was what Marina had done. She had made that man hers forever. What other woman would ever live up to her? What other woman would walk three thousand miles for him?

Danica sniffed in the quiet way ghosts do.

39

WHEN ARNOLD KEEBLE EXPRESSED HIS interest in sitting with Marina Abramović, he had been invited to join the VIPs in the greenroom for the 10:30 start. Ushered into the atrium at 10:25, Keeble was surprised at the intensity of the crowd in the foyer below. A tornado of voices was issuing up the stairs. He could hear someone with a repetitive, irritating laugh and overexcited conversation banging on the white walls. The actor James Franco was with him. They had been introduced in the greenroom. He admired Franco—particularly his new book of short stories—and told him so. Franco seemed pleased. He had offered Keeble the first sitting. Keeble wondered, as he sat down, if Marina would give any indication of recognizing him.

For a moment her dark eyes observed him as if he was a fresh canvas, then she blinked and her gaze settled. It felt like a spotlight had hit him. *Life specimen Arnold Keeble.* At first it was just the hard chair, the intense white of her dress, her face that seemed to emanate light as if Rembrandt had painted her. But then he felt the lens of her mind asking him a question. He was imagining it. It was part of this game of sitting. This game of mirrors. Still, it niggled at him. She was mute, and yet everything about her was loud. What did she want from him? The scale of the square had expanded so the noise of the crowd felt far away, almost as if he and Marina were underwater.

He thought of his wife, Isobel, and the coldness that had grown between them since he'd refused to have children. They had agreed, before he married her, there would be no children. It was typical of women to change their minds. But he wouldn't. There had been scenes. She had tried all sorts of tricks. He'd rather admired her determination to bring a little Keeble into the world. But not enough to allow it to happen. He had taken himself off for a vasectomy and told her about it afterward. He had wondered if she might leave him, but had guessed she wouldn't. He'd guessed right. She preferred him to see her suffering. The clothes she needed to buy, the jewelery, the vacations he owed her now that she would never have a baby.

It wasn't the childlessness that he questioned—even Marina had chosen that. It was significance. What had significance? When he woke in the night, he didn't want to reach for Isobel. Of late, he wanted to reach for Healayas Breen. That had disconcerted him.

He didn't like this train of thought. He wanted to think that Healayas was just another affair. No different to discovering a new vineyard or vintage. A new artist. A new motorbike. Their relationship didn't matter. It was art direction. He had an exquisite mistress. He had curated his life to be a gallery of careful perfection.

He felt a tear run down his cheek. He blinked and felt confused. Had he been sad? Then he dropped his head, stood up and, putting two hands to his face, rubbed his eyes and cheeks as he returned to where James Franco was standing with the security guard.

When Keeble checked the Flickr feed the next night, he saw he had sat for eight minutes. The photograph captured the moment when that single tear had reached the light on his cheekbone. He would have to answer for it. Had he been moved by the performance? Yes, he could say. I found it moving but also impenetrable. Isobel would surmise that he had regrets, when she saw the picture. But he didn't. Regrets would involve thinking about the past. A decade of therapy had taught him that thinking about the past was an expensive hobby.

What exactly had he been thinking? He regarded the photograph, the thick wave of hair, the fine block of nose, the way he held his chin, the uncertainty in his eyes. That was the bit he didn't recognize. He had liked to think he was never going to get past being a self-indulgent prick, because that was how he'd got to where he was. No one, not a child, not the many pleasures of Healayas Breen, not eight minutes with Marina Abramović, not even Isobel leaving him, was going to change that.

In the hallway of his apartment he stopped and sat down on a bench. Here he could look out over the bonsai garden and, beyond it, the Hudson. He sat for some time until he nodded, as if agreeing with something unsaid, then turned and went into the bedroom.

PART SEVEN

*Be faithful to that which exists
within yourself.*

ANDRÉ GIDE

40

LIKE ALL ADULT HUMANS, MARINA Abramović's body was made of some forty-three kilograms of oxygen, most in dilution as water. She also had the regular allowance of hydrogen, carbon, nitrogen, and a kilo or so of calcium in her bones. After the main elements, things in the human body get a little smaller. Around seven hundred and fifty milligrams of phosphorous, one hundred and forty grams of potassium, ninety-five grams of chlorine, a little magnesium, a little less zinc. There was also silver, gold, lead, copper, tellurium, zirconium, lithium, mercury, and manganese. Even a milligram or so of uranium. The human body is an incantation of earth, air, and water.

Through the tinted windows of the car, she watches New York go about its 9 a.m. business. Two girls in high heels are each carrying a large flowering pot plant like something from a French movie. Three men in skinny jeans and dark glasses are looking like an advertisement for *Vanity Fair*. For a moment I hear her consider that the real is literally unbearable. Traffic lights and crowds. Scaffolding where this building and that is being restored, repainted. New apartments advertised on giant billboards. New fragrances and movies and television shows. New everything every moment of the day. American luxury, so tantalizing, so tempting, and so treacherous.

Marina loves luxury as much as anyone. She loves fabrics and food. Simple is the hardest thing to achieve. She thinks of Klaus Biesenbach, who invited her to create this show at MoMA. Marina and Klaus were lovers years ago. He still loves her and she him, the way some people manage to do love in all its forms. He is one of the great curators. He has made this possible. You might imagine he has a house filled with art but he doesn't. He lives in the simplest apartment in the world. An ultimate Manhattan view with blank walls and not a painting or sculpture anywhere. Why would he need them when he spends every day in one of the most wonderful galleries in the world? Why indeed.

When Marina was sixteen, Danica employed an art tutor. He was very short, in a red coat, with a dark beard. He was the latest in a long line of people employed to make the young Marina into something Danica could be proud of. First it was a pianist, then a linguist. Later a historian, and then, as a last resort, an artist. Perhaps the little man understood this about a certain type of mother. So once the door was closed, and he was alone with the young Marina, he did not bring out paper and pencils. He unrolled a small canvas that he pinned to the floor. Then he squeezed red, yellow, and blue paint onto the canvas. He scraped the colors this way and that, until it was all a brown smear. From a glass jar he took grit and gravel and poured this onto the painting, again scraping and smearing. He took a small pair of scissors and clipped his nails, the hair on his head, and all of this went onto the canvas too.

"You want to be an artist," he said, "then it takes everything. Everything. You do the other. You get a job. You become a wife. A mother. You contribute to the machine. The machine is always seeking volunteers. But art is not a machine. It does not ask. You ask of it, in your unworthy way, if you might add a little thread. If you ever do add a thread, then that is something to be marveled at. I will never do that. I'm old enough to know that now. But you are still young enough. You have time to find it. Find what it is that lives inside you, and only you."

With this, he poured turpentine onto the painting. Striking a match, he picked up the painting and set it alight. It dripped and flared, and only when the flames licked his fingertips, did he let it float to the ground. It sputtered and smoked and the fire died.

He said, "Art will wake you up. Art will break your heart. There will be glorious days. If you want eternity, you must be fearless."

With that he gathered up his satchel and bowed his head briefly to her before closing the door behind him. Marina tacked the remnant of canvas onto the wall. It was as if she had been given the skin of a dragon. She pressed the charred flakes on the floor into her skin, where they left a dark powdery smear.

She watched the dragon skin through the autumn that followed, and the winter, and the spring and summer beyond. She observed as it aged and decayed. Art, she thought, could be something unimaginable.

She painted car crashes, portraits, and clouds, but they did not convey the unimaginable. She discovered Joseph Beuys, Yves Klein, and Zen Buddhism. Klein declared his paintings were the ashes of his art and she wondered if the little man had paid him a visit too. She read Helena Blavatsky, who said there was no religion higher than truth. But was there an art higher than truth? What was the most truthful art? She wanted to know what came before art, what was underneath art. She wanted to understand infinity.

She longed to harness the subtle bodies Blavatsky described. But it was hard to know how to leave her body. It seemed that other people visited more often than she left. There was a self that watched her parents fighting from a vantage point above the kitchen sink. There was a woman who appeared in the darkness and sang her back to sleep after her mother had forced her awake yet again, haranguing the young Marina to smooth the sheets and blankets on the bed, insisting that even in sleep Marina must have a soldier's eye for order and be ready for anything. There was an old woman in a white dress who sat beside the bed when the migraines came with every period, and put her cool hand upon the teenage Marina's brow.

The car pulls in to the curb and Marina's assistant, Davide, comes around to open the door for her. She is unbelievably tired. She has lost more than seven kilos. Sixty-eight days are behind her and seven ahead. Klaus is there to welcome her.

"I would like to lie on grass," she says to Davide in the green-room. "Tonight, once we are finished."

He nods and smiles.

"I want to lie and watch leaves."

"Then it shall be so."

"And we will do the invitation list for the party? Can you talk to Dieter? I cannot wait for a party. It will be so good to laugh."

She will make it now. Seven days is nothing. Surely.

41

IT WAS DAY SEVENTY-FOUR AND the atrium was crowded. Everyone recognized the actors. First it had been Alan Rickman, elegant and focused in a myopic kind of way. Now Miranda Richardson stepped from the middle of a huddle of MoMA staff and waited at the entrance to the square. The whisper of her name went around the atrium like a cave echo.

"She's tiny!"

"She looks great!"

She was dressed very simply in pale pants, a white wrap, her hair back in a ponytail. She had perfect cheekbones and looked to have aged carefully with no obvious work. The guard bent his head and spoke into her ear. She nodded and smiled at him. Marina sat at the table with her head bowed. The room had filled. People flocked to the white line, sitting, standing. Levin had never seen so many people. He felt giddy with fatigue; grimy, unshaved, and stiff from the night he had just spent on the pavement outside MoMA with forty-three other people desperate to sit with Marina on the second-last day of *The Artist Is Present*.

The guard nodded and Miranda Richardson moved to the empty wooden chair. The crowd hushed. Cameras clicked, flashes blinked.

"No photographs," a guard said loudly.

A man on the opposite side of the square openly ignored the guard and continued to aim his baby Minolta. People clandestinely positioned their phones in their hands and clicked away.

Marina raised her head, opened her eyes, and gazed at the actress. A flicker, perhaps only imagined, passed across Marina's face. The room swelled with an inaudible sigh. The city beyond vibrated with its eight million people, but there for a moment within the square everything was still.

For ten minutes Marina and the actress gazed unwaveringly into each other's eyes, then the actress bowed her head, stood up, and walked back across the square. The guard scooped up her soft brown sandals and handed them to her.

Next the woman accompanying the actress crossed the floor and sat. Marina opened her eyes and looked up again. The room shifted about. There were seven people ahead of Levin.

Healayas had been beside him for much of the night. He had told her his plan to camp out and she said she couldn't miss the chance to interview the people who were willing to sleep on concrete in order to participate in an art event.

"But not me," said Levin. "If you don't mind."

"Of course not, if you don't want to be interviewed," she said. "I'll just keep you company."

Still, he had been surprised and delighted when she had arrived at 9 p.m. and thrown her duffle bag and an air mattress down next to him, explaining to the boy next to Levin that she was a journalist and she wasn't jumping the queue or planning on sitting. She was just here doing her job. The boy looked so struck by her beauty, Levin thought Healayas could have told him anything and he'd have agreed.

Levin inflated the mattress for her as Healayas worked her

way along the line. He couldn't quite believe the madness of what he was doing. All his life he had avoided camping.

Healayas had told him to buy an air mattress, but he'd thought it would be overkill. By midnight he regretted acutely that he'd only brought his Pilates mat. For twenty bucks at Kmart he could have been comfortable. He could have cried at his own inadequacies that seemed, under the rigid overlit sky, to be countless.

"You can't be afraid of stars. How did I not know that?" Healayas had laughed as the chill crept into their coats and hats and they huddled against the wall in their respective sleeping bags.

"It's not something I can help."

"Well, be afraid of the sea. Or cars. Something that can kill you—but not something so beautiful, Arky."

"It's just emptiness. In fact, it's the past rushing at us. Everything out there, other than the sun, died years ago."

"That's kind of depressing. How do you get around such miserable thoughts?"

He had laughed. "Music."

"Is that enough?"

"Probably not."

Around them the conversation grew subdued. They settled down and waited for sleep to speed the hours to dawn.

At some point Healayas rolled over and looked at Levin on his pathetic layer of rubber. She grinned at him. He gazed back.

"Come. You look so alone there. Come cuddle me."

And he had. He had held Healayas Breen, and later she had held him, on an air mattress outside MoMA, spooning together like two children at a sleepover, while the city carried on around them.

Levin dreamed of Lydia. They were both laid out on funeral biers and elaborately clothed in traditional garments for the dead. They were being carried by a crowd of anonymous mourners into a funeral home. But they weren't dead. He had woken her, ran with her from the funeral home and across the street into a cafe, where he had kissed her passionately. When he woke he remembered a fight they'd had.

"What you're dissatisfied with has to be about you, Arky," Lydia had said to him.

"Well, fine, seeing your life is always going so well."

"Are you serious? Have you noticed something about my life?"

"I've noticed lots of things."

"But not the fact that . . . fuck, Arky, you are so blind."

"I do notice . . . but I'm the last person you help. It's always Alice first, then your clients, your girlfriends. I mean, when the fuck is it going to be about me?"

"It is about you, sweetheart. It's always about you. Everything is done for you, and you don't even notice. But I can't keep doing it. It's not my responsibility. I am pretty busy over here in my own life. Sorry if my being fulfilled in my life confronts you. So sorry if I don't have time to provide your fulfillment as well."

"Fuck you. If it's so desperate here, why don't you leave? You and Alice, just go."

"Oh, that's right, so everyone will feel sorry for you?"

With Alice gone there had been much less to fight about. But still he felt ashamed. She had been so ill and he had taken her positivity for buoyancy, not bravery.

When he woke again, morning had arrived and people were going for coffee and pie runs. A great cheer went up when the hot dog seller arrived opposite at 7 a.m. He and Healayas drank coffee and ate bacon, egg, and cheese sandwiches he brought back from a cafe on Sixth. They laughed at their night together and curled up again for a while longer as the morning brightened.

Then finally, at 9:30 a.m., they'd been allowed into the lobby of the gallery. And at 10:30, in an orderly single file, they were carefully conducted by security guards up the stairs to the familiar sight of Marina Abramović in her white dress with her head bowed, waiting on her chair. The night folk had been joined by new arrivals and there were now over a hundred people snaked back around the gallery, all waiting to sit. The famous people were over and done with by 10:50 and when they had departed everyone else, one by one, began to cross the floor to take their place opposite the artist.

"What if someone decides to sit the whole day?" Levin asked Healayas.

"There would be a riot. Don't worry, you'll get your turn. I know it."

Throughout the morning Healayas moved through the atrium, recording more interviews. When the person ahead of Levin finally went to sit with Marina, Healayas came back and stood beside him.

"Any advice?" he asked her.

"Count to ten as you walk toward her," she said.

"We're here from London," said some people behind Levin. "We didn't realize the queue would be so long. What time did you get here?"

"Five thirty," he said. "I mean last night. The gallery closed and we all walked outside and made a line."

"Wow," they replied. "You mean you waited outside all night?"

"Slept on the street." Levin grinned. "Hard core."

Levin considered how he would look on the live cam. He thought about Pillow-Marina and how he had thanked her yesterday afternoon before he'd dismantled her, putting her parts back on the couch and into the spare bedroom.

He thought about Lydia. Would she recognize him if she were to see him on the live feed? Would it compute? It pained him to think of it.

And then the person in front of him vacated the chair. The guard tapped him on the shoulder.

"It is time," he said. "Maintain eye contact, do not speak. When you have finished drop your eyes. Walk away."

Levin was crossing the square and counting to ten. He was taking a seat. The chair was fixed to the floor. He hadn't known this until now, but that's why everyone sat the way they did. He could not move the chair. Abramović had her eyes closed, her head lowered. He breathed. He could feel the prickling of fatigue and the same frequency of nerves that he had before the orchestra played his music for the first time.

He was acutely aware of people talking all around him. He closed his eyes and then he opened them, met Marina's gaze, and everything stopped.

42

LYDIA FIORENTINO, LEVIN'S LYDIA, SWAM in the night sky and she had no edges. She moved slowly, languorously, and the moon was her guide. The night embraced her and she was a tiny light in a great sea of lights.

Later she was no longer afloat on stars and sea. She was held, carried, washed. She had no words. She had no sound. She was amorphous, diaphanous, pixelated. She was a confluence of atoms released at the moment the universe began. She was a tender mottled sky drawn across the dawn. An ocean of clouds above the sand dunes. The days were a single strike on a triangle. The nights were voyages. She was the dove in Max Ernst's forest. She was Miro's star watching over the woman and bird. She was Man Ray's *Pisces* lying in the shallows and a silver fish at first light. She was a rose from Dorothea Tanning's table. She was the gold in a Turner and the green in a Seurat. She was gone from somewhere and there was only a faint remembering of things past. A flash of an eye, a fabric, a voice, a name. She must come back. But where was back? There was only here. Nothing was everything. She had no form.

She was the flower in the egg in the hand beside the pool with Narcissus. Ah, it went, and was lost, these four seasons.

She awaited the angel of uncertainty. Tight clouds stood watch on the horizon.

She was washed in rain. A shower of warmth above or below the fog. She was returned to a cocoon of white. Light played beyond her eyes. There was a taste in her mouth. And another. Good. Good, they said to her. That's very good, Lydia.

There was an arm and another, a leg and another. They were moved by people who came by day and night. There were voices and faces telling her things. They said over and over, Lydia, Lydia, Lydia. They moved the hand, the foot.

They wrapped her in blankets and light burned against her eyelids. She had no name for the warm thing and the bright surfaces that changed through the day. She had no words at all. Words were structures that she glimpsed before they fled again. *Sun*—it came to her and was gone. *Ocean*. And then the great void of everything returned and she floated. Weightless, form-less, speechless, timeless.

But time did pass. Weeks and months.

At some point she was aware of a young woman but she had no words. She liked the place with no words and no feelings. It was simplicity. There was a gentleness lulling her through light and dark and all the colors and textures in between.

Flavors washed over her tongue, sweet, soft, bright, dense. She tasted and with the taste came pictures. Faces returned to her and patterns, carpets, smells that made her think of rooms and people. Vanilla. It came back as if someone had typed the word on her mind and she read it to herself, sounding it out with some inner voice.

There was no outer voice. She was a silent observer of the room and its visitors. She was a recipient of sound. She was an inhabitant. She was a watcher and she was observed.

Shadows and sunlight moved in particles across the glass. She was the silence of mist coming in from the sea. She was the forming and unforming of clouds, paint stroke after paint stroke brushing the sky. She was the hush of waves on the heartbeat of the coast and every moment was new and new and new again.

Now there was flavor on her tongue. Now she swallowed. Now she woke. Now she saw birds leaping into the sky. Now she saw the sea discolored and rippled, the sand darkened. Now there was music. Music? Was that music? Yes. Yes.

Music swirled her through fragments and the road of memories coiled, rising up, wanting to whisper a name, make a sound, a sound, but no words for that were allowed inside her.

She dreamed her body was laid out, her feet in Manhattan and her head resting in the Great Lakes. She stretched herself farther up into Canada, south to Boston and Washington. She pushed her hands and fingers across into the Midwest, slipping them up into the grooves of the Rockies, stretched her toes all the way down to Florida. Her other arm reached all the way to the gray-pebbled beaches of Portugal. Her body continued to slip and stretch out around the world. Her skin swam into coastlines and over mountains. She gazed out into the void of darkness and she wanted to step off the world and slip away into starlight. She was sure that was the way home.

Home, she thought. Home. The words in her mind had been drained and emptied. A noise lived within her and like her it had no voice. Like her it could not move. It could not reach out and speak to the people who came to the room. Together she and the loneliness watched the light and the dark and all the colors in between that the sea and the sky made for her each day and she understood that something was waiting. Something was waiting and the stars could not have her back yet.

On the table by the window, letters and postcards accumulated. The nursing staff set them out so that Lydia could see them. They understood it was a strange case. It was Ms. Fiorentino's explicit wishes, spelled out in court documents, to be left alone save for her daughter and a few select girlfriends who came regularly. But it was hard, seeing it. It was hard to see anyone in the state she was in. She gave no indication of hearing or seeing anything at all. Her physiotherapy indicated that her body was, for the time being, able to maintain some strength. But it was probably only a matter of time before she had another stroke or her kidneys gave out. It was a horrible condition and people didn't last very long once it had gone this far.

They had seen worse, and they had seen better. This wasn't a place from which many people got to go home. But every now and again there was a sort of miracle. Sometimes the stroke victims regained movement. Sometimes the coma people woke up.

The staff read aloud to Lydia the letters that came every week from someone called Yolanda.

Dear Mrs. Fiorentino,

I hope you are feeling better every day. This week I made for Mr. Levin a lamb casserole and the frittata he always likes because the weather is warmer. Rigby is enjoying the couch by the piano and prefers to eat at the moment only tinned sardines. The lemon tree is showing signs of liking life out on the balcony.

And always every letter concluded with the same few lines.

I restocked with the usual items and everything is ready for when you are well enough to come home.

We all miss you very much and keep you in our prayers.

Yolanda

43

AND SO, AT LAST, THESE two people meet in person on two chairs opposite each other. Marina Abramović and Arky Levin. I am assigned to stand beside them—memoirist, intuit, animus, good spirit, genius, whim that I am. House elf to the artists of paint, music, body, voice, form, word. I have acquired the habit of never saying too much. And the trick of dropping in, rapping on the door of their minds in the moment before waking, in the moment of solitude staring out a window, in a cafe where everything for a moment stops, under a tree watching sunlight, when life is a set of dominos falling into place or a single moment of revelation about what comes next.

Of course, it can be years between moments. Mostly people say no. They say no, I don't want to get out of bed. No, I don't want to work that hard. No, today I don't have time. No, I'm not listening right now. People say no so often, and then they wonder why they feel so desperate. Desperation does not especially interest me. Being available, paintbrush in hand, pen, keyboard, clay, stage, strings at the ready, is much more attractive. And sometimes I just need to wake things up.

Do you see now the difficulty of my task? All that they are is stored up loud and insistent inside them. But what does it take to be an artist? They have to listen. But do they listen? Most people are filled up with a lifetime of noise and distraction that's hard to get past. At least that's how it feels.

Levin was listening now. He was pinned to the chair. Pinned to Marina's face. She was more formidable than he had imagined. Her eyes were moist ebony. He had imagined those eyes looking at him morning after morning, but they were deeper, she was farther away and so much closer too. Was she seeing him? What was she seeing? From the crowd there was a percussive undertone that might have been breathing or heartbeats. Levin's own pulse was slippery. Above him the atrium soared into the sunlight. He thought of Leonard Cohen.

> And the skylight is like skin for a drum I'll never mend
> And all the rain falls down amen,
> On the works of last year's man.

He saw himself standing in the *Kawa* forest. Marina walked beside him on the bank of a river. She laughed at something as if they were old friends. There were ferns crusted with the finest layer of snow and an arc of birds, long-necked and pale, passing overhead. There were trees with trunks wet and red and glistening and sun falling down like rain between the branches. He saw light falling as if it was rain. He saw every particle of life.

There is nothing to be afraid of, she said to him. *We have walked this way before.* He saw two sets of footprints in the snow ahead. He heard a calling bird. He saw the moon arcing between the trees, a sliver of moon in a blue sky, and she said, *We are all these things. We are no different from earth. We are no different from time. We are rock and leaf and bird, earth-born and earth-fed and earth-returned when we die. For forty thousand years we have been eating and living and burying ourselves on this one sphere of earth. See how we know the pattern of things, if we only watch.*

He saw Marina standing on the edge of a sand dune in another place where the sky was magenta and the earth was pink. Then they were in another place where two moons rose above a midnight sea, and they walked the shoreline. He knew he was going home.

But not yet, she said. *Not yet. You have forgotten something very important.*

He felt a sense of utter loneliness as if he had never lived in a world with anyone else. He wanted to hold Marina's hand but she was a ghost and she was Lydia.

Was there a secret tally somewhere in every marriage for each kiss, each orgasm, each Sunday morning? He saw the counter ticking over and coming to a halt. He saw Lydia's eyelashes, so very pale without mascara. He looked at her eyes and they were still the green of the sea thirty yards out.

"Lydia?" he said.

He saw her in a white room. He saw her watching the sea. He saw the sunlight that fell on the floor. He saw her lift her hand. She reached for a pencil. It fell.

He bent down to pick it up for her.

"Lydia?" he said again.

She did not turn her face. He opened her fingers very gently and placed the pencil in her hand. There was a notebook on her lap. He leaned down and smelled her hair.

"Can we go home now?" he asked. "I think it's time we went home."

Marina leaned toward him and he was speared with pain. He felt as if her face was that of an ancient woman, and now a boy, and now a girl, a monk, a nun. Now it was a bird, and now a fish, and now a tree and now it was a crystal, filled with power and understanding. Again it became human, but it was a face both eternal and temporal, dead and alive, calm and terrifying.

It is not about comfort, he heard her say, as if she had spoken the words right into his head. *It is not about convenient. It is not about forgetting. It is about remembering. It is about commitment. Only you can do it. And you must be fearless.*

When he left the square he hardly trusted himself to walk. Healayas watched him go and did not disturb him. She knew how deconstructed it was possible to feel after the experience of Marina.

Downstairs in the lobby, Levin looked at his watch. He found a quiet spot by the rear doors and dialed the number of Paul Wharton at his law firm. Wharton would not be in until tomorrow morning, he was told. Levin made an appointment. After that he called Alice. He remembered Healayas, and texted her, but she had to stay in New York for the final day of *The Artist Is Present*. Then he rang Hal.

"Do you think we could take a drive?" he asked.

44

AND SO WE ARRIVE AT day seventy-five. The final convergence. The floodlights are on. Marco Anelli watches Marina Abramović emerge from the greenroom and cross the square. He watches Davide arrange her white dress about the chair. He sees Marina's body submit to the chair this one last time. They are all smiling, but he does not want to think about it being the last day. He cannot afford to lose concentration.

He settles his camera and tripod at the top of the square and takes a single photograph of Marina as she stares at him down the long lens. The security team take their respective places.

One of the guards raises two fingers to indicate two minutes to go. The live feed clicks on. Viewers in Chicago, in Minneapolis, Montreal, and Mexico, in Cape Town and Cairo, Sydney and Salzburg, in Helsinki, Istanbul, and Iceland begin watching.

The gallery, the noise, the time, the people, the fatigue, the weather, the concrete beneath his feet, the white walls, the face of Marina, all of it had become like waves on the beach. Marco has lived so close to it he no longer hears it. Now sometimes in the atrium, when his thoughts arrive, they sound so loud it feels as if his mind is shouting.

He goes along the line collecting permission slips as if it was any other day. He focuses the lens on each face and watches for the moment when intensity spills from the eyes. He settles into the space and the light and the performance.

He has moved past himself. The pain that had been vivid in his legs and lower back, and his neck and shoulders, after almost three months on his feet every day, bending over his camera, standing on concrete, has left him. He feels light, almost transparent. He has survived the show. When he'd agreed to do it, he'd never thought of it as an act of survival. He had wanted to do it with all his heart. And now it is almost over. It reminds him of a question he was asked a few days before by one of the guards. "When you get to heaven, what would you like God to say to you?" "Not now!" he had joked. But today he just wants God to say, "Well done."

He had not expected the emotion that crowds the atrium, the joy that is in so many eyes and faces. It is as if some new idea of life has occurred to them. If I die today, Marco thinks, then it will be too soon.

45

AFTER DANICA ABRAMOVIĆ'S FUNERAL IN Belgrade, Marina had gone to her mother's apartment to begin the work of cleaning out her mother's things. In the bedroom she had found clothes ordered by color—beige suits, then blue suits, summer coats and winter coats. Light-colored shoes, dark-colored shoes.

The bed had a pale green counterpane. The bedside lamp that was never turned off in the night was finally off. In the drawer there was still a loaded gun. All her life Marina had known her mother's war stories. Her father had told them often. On the battlefield, as strangers, her mother gave her father a transfusion of her own blood when there was no other way to save his life. She had begun a degree in medicine six months before the Nazi invasion in 1941. Vojo had survived and, when he had recovered, he had ridden back into battle. The war had gone on.

A year later, still fighting, Vojo came across a group of sick partisans fleeing oncoming German soldiers. He lifted back the blanket to discover the woman, Danica, who had given him her blood. She was dying from typhus. He lifted her onto his white horse and rode with her to safety.

Danica never talked about the war. She sat in silence as Vojo told stories of waiting in snow for the Germans to ride past the explosives he and his men had buried in the roots of trees. How he was shot twelve times in the back and was saved by the thickness of his coat. The time an axe handle flew all the way across a river and nearly cut off his hand. The time he had to eat his own dead horse and later lost his mustache in the heat of an explosion.

But while cleaning out her mother's apartment, Marina came across a trunk under the bed she had never seen before. Marina spread the contents on the green counterpane. There were scrapbooks full of articles about her shows. But under the scrapbooks was a leather wallet containing documents signed by Josip Broz Tito, president of Yugoslavia. They noted that her mother had fought in seven Partisan battles against the Nazis. They awarded her mother the highest medal for bravery. In 1944, while she had been leading a convoy of trucks filled with wounded soldiers to a nearby hospital, they had come under intense fire. The fuel tanks were targeted. Everywhere there was fire and explosions. Chaos ensued. But Danica Rosic carried thirty soldiers, men and women, some half-conscious, some with terrible injuries, on her back and in her arms. Hauling them through the snow, somehow avoiding bullets and grenades, she brought each one of them to safety.

46

AT HOME, JANE MILLER WATCHED Marina Abramović on the webcam.

"Today is the day," she kept thinking. "Today is the day."

And she ignored the washing she'd done for her daughter that needed bringing in, and the ants that were invading a light switch on the wall, and the emails she needed to reply to, and watched. She understood that her fate and Marina's were somehow linked. When Marina stood up, Jane too must stand up. There had been this time of mourning and the mourning would live forever in her. Karl was as much a piece of her as her liver or pancreas. Grief was as tangible as rain. Millions of people were suffering from it at any one time. It'll pass, people said, but it didn't really.

Grief was a threshold thing that lived at the heart of the inevitable. She sensed that when Marina stood up, she, Jane, would take her place one step back from the inevitable. She would walk across Spain. She would carry her grief and her love and her observations of a life of fifty-five years. Here at home her children and their children would be among their own inevitabilities. And maybe this was art, she thought, having spent years trying to define it and pin it to the line like a shirt on a windy day. *There you are, art!* You capture moments at the heart of life. A boy waiting for the eggs to poach. A crowd listening to music in a park or walking in the rain or bathing in the Seine. Liberty leading the people and the guns of the firing squad raised against the men at the wall. The bloom of water lilies and the anguish of a scream, the red square that lived in every heart, a rhythm of color across a wheat field, stars wheeling through a night sky.

She was watching Marina Abramović in her white dress on this final day of her enduring love. For hadn't it been that for Abramović? An act of love that said, This is all I have been, this is what I have become in traveling the places of my soul and my nation, my family and my ancestral blood. This is what I have learned. It is all about connection. If we do it with the merest amount of intention and candor and fearlessness, this is the biggest love we can feel. It's more than love but we don't have a bigger word. It was Kant's thing, Jane thought. The thing that is, but is also inexplicable, until you see that it just is.

She knew once she would have tried to call it God, but that had caused so many problems in the world, trying to say what God was or is. She thought there ought to be another word and she decided she had a few hundred miles to think on that in Spain under a wide sky on a pilgrimage. And she laughed aloud, because to ruminate on the name of the thought that was God on a long walk seemed fitting. She and Karl would go a long way on that together.

She continued to gaze at the woman in the white dress. She sat and watched in honor of this woman sitting. She watched as the final hours of *The Artist Is Present* passed by, sitter after sitter in a gaze with the woman across the table. Jane felt she had witnessed a thing of inexplicable beauty among humans who had been drawn to this art and had found the reflection of a great mystery. What are we? How should we live?

47

MARINA ABRAMOVIĆ HAD BEEN SITTING on that chair for seven hundred and thirty-six hours, since March 9. Today she looked radiant. The buzz of the crowd was intense. Film crews angled for the best shot. Cameras flashed.

All day elation had been growing in Brittika too, tickling her ribs, feathering the skin on her arms, her scalp. A text came through from Jane in Georgia: *Bravo Marina! Such an achievement. I'm leaving for Madrid Sept 1. Carpe diem! My family think I'm crazy. I have surprised them. Nothing compared to what you did! My, oh my. But I feel I understand. Let's meet again. Will email you. Bravo you too!*

Brittika read the text and smiled. She adjusted the black wig she had worn to disguise her from the security guards who would almost certainly have thrown her out if they'd spotted her back in the gallery. They had made that very clear. But they had also been kind, after their initial anger. The police had not been called. There would be no charges. They had seemed to accept the complexity of the situation.

Today, without her pink hair, her colored contacts, and her makeup, she looked to all intents and purposes like any other Chinese girl. In short, she was invisible. She felt the press of the crowd about her. The atrium was packed. The balconies above were packed. She didn't really know why she had needed to do what she did. She had never been drawn to exhibitionism. But after all this time studying Marina, she had wanted to show her that she had given everything. And that everything was okay.

It turned out that she wasn't really that special. She had been naked for a few seconds, but really she was just one of more than fifteen hundred people who had sat in the chair opposite Marina over the past three months. She was one of the eight hundred and fifty thousand people who had come to see *The Artist Is Present*.

There were now photos of her across the internet snapped by people on their phones. It had been too fast for Marco, or perhaps he'd chosen not to include it. Her nudity would not be officially captured in the Abramović archives. She hadn't meant to disrupt the show. Or Marina. She hadn't even known she could do it until she did. It had happened so fast. But she didn't regret it. The pictures would be lost in the next million nude photos being uploaded today and another million tomorrow. Perhaps the photos would haunt her at university when she returned, but the ones she had seen made her look delighted. Maybe her parents would hear about it, or see it for themselves, and she knew they would be disappointed. Even angry. And she would face that when she went home too.

This wasn't her fifteen minutes of fame. She knew that. There would be better moments. But it had been the most honest, uncontrived thing she'd ever done. It had felt like she had birthed herself at last.

Suddenly, there across the room, was the butcher in the red gingham shirt, only today's shirt was blue gingham. He looked at her then looked away. Then he looked back, and she saw recognition light his eyes. In a few minutes he had moved through the crowd to stand beside her.

"Almost didn't recognize you with your clothes on," he said. And she laughed.

48

MARINA WAS AWARE OF THE white dress, the weight of the boots on her feet, the tiny shutter of her eyelids, the noise growing within the atrium. She sensed the tightness of the crowd. She heard cameras and whispers and escalators humming in the distance. Floodlights had turned the atrium into a stage. The white walls rose around her. She was aware of the skylight high above her and the clouds and sky and sun falling toward Europe and a window on Makedonska Street where a woman sat stroking the forehead of a girl with a migraine so severe it blinded her. Who had she been, that woman? The one who came when the migraines struck? She had worn a white dress. It was only now Marina understood that all her life she had been walking toward herself. The future and the past were present.

She was almost out of time. The barest thoughts came and went. Fragments of her manifesto.

An artist must make time for a long period of solitude.
An artist should avoid going to the studio every day.
An artist should not treat his schedule as a bank employee does.
An artist should decide the minimum personal possessions they should have.

An artist should have more and more of less and less.
An artist should have friends that lift their spirit.
An artist has to learn to forgive.

Her stories had traveled the world. They were fixed in time like the photograph that showed her once-small breasts and slender thirty-year-old body in a gallery in Naples, cut and bleeding from a crowd.

The body of work it had taken to reach this day swelled in her mind like a wind behind her. The letters, photographs, films, stage plays, interviews, tapes, sketches. The bureaucracy, submissions, applications, proposals, budgets, faxes, emails, phone calls, meetings, paperwork, visas and flights, floor plans, sketches, trains, maps, hotels, car rentals. Negotiations, gallerists, administrators, government officials, police, occupational health and safety officers, security, curators, agents, photographers, minders.

So many people. So much paper. So much intensity and laughter. So many bruises. Scars and wounds and faces she would never see again. A way to spend a life. She could feel the beat of her heart, the swish of blood through her veins. And then it wasn't blood but rain. She was standing in the rain in Serbia rubbing her naked breasts and singing Balkan songs with the women of her country. She was on the Great Wall with a thread of river far below. Sunlight flared against the red earth. The path was going up and on before her. Her legs ached. Her feet ached. Her heart ached for something she could not find.

Here was a snake around her shoulders. There were crystals on her feet. A scorpion on her face. A snake. Tears. Onions burning her mouth and throat and eyes. She could hear herself saying, "I want to go away, somewhere so far that nothing matters anymore. I want to understand and see clearly what is behind all this. I want to not want anymore."

Here was the doorway where she stood with Ulay, looking into his eyes while people pushed between them. Then she was on a chair, dizzy and losing all control of herself as the drugs for schizophrenia and then catatonia took hold of her.

A skeleton lay on her and she breathed and the bones rose and fell as rib cages did every day in the living. Now she was staring up at *The House with the Ocean View*. Dieter and all the staff had gone home and there was only the wooden bed, the wooden chair, the metronome and the silence and herself, eating her own madness, chewing away on the collective insanity of the world through the long hungry night.

Here were the children in Laos holding replica AK-47s. Here were *Eight Lessons on Happiness with a Happy End*. Seven Laotian girls between pink sheets accompanied by their machine guns.

Here was an arrow poised to pierce her heart and Ulay holding the bow. Here was the van driving round and round and round for sixteen hours while her voice over the loudspeaker slowly broke down. There was the woman who fell in love with a man who had the same birthday as hers: November 30.

Here was the flesh of her stomach and the star that must be cut into it with the razor blade, again and again and again. Here was the child fed on her mother's discipline and the pain that came if she failed.

Here was the child who went with her grandmother each day into the incense and colored light that poured through the high windows of the cathedral. Here was the child who watched her grandmother light the candles at dusk in the apartment, making shadows that danced down the hallway to bed.

Here was the woman who was once a girl and will yet be dead. Here is Marina Abramović, who knows something of what life can be—a series of moments, blades and snakes, honey and wine, urgency and delay, patience and generosity, forgiveness and despair and a hundred ways to say I love you. Here was Antony Hegarty singing, "*Hope there's someone who will take care of me, when I die, when I go. Hope there's someone who will set my heart free, nice to hold when I'm tired . . .*"

This is it, she thought. I am dying. I am living. They are both entirely the same.

It was easy to gain strength from chaos because it had about it the abyss—always so tantalizing—as the heroin addicts knew. But the journey to the abyss was short-lived. The harder road was to draw strength and not power. To gain footing not in the wild uncertainty of immortality but the abiding knowing of mortality.

The days had been fields of faces, bright, unique, vivid, strange. There was no greater solitude, and no greater connection, than being within the performance with the audience holding her in its gaze. She had expected it to be an energy exchange. A simple thing. But it hadn't been simple. Every face was a song that carried her like love or pain into nothingness. Every face told countless lives and memories and parts of humanity she had never glimpsed, not through all the years of seeking. Here was the truth of people writ mysterious in every line and angle and eye. The taste of their lifetimes faded on her tongue as they each stood to go.

Until at last there was Klaus. Dear Klaus. He was her cue. After Klaus it was the end. It was day seventy-five and there was only one thing to do. Still, she took in his eyes, the sense of no time and all time and the infinite words of silence. She loved him. She loved everyone in the room. She loved everyone alive and everyone who had ever lived to bring them all to this time, all the millennia that had gone before and the millennia of people yet to come. She felt enormous.

Klaus dropped his head. He stood.

Don't go, not yet! It is too soon, she thought.

But Klaus was walking away.

Suddenly she sensed her mother high on the balcony looking down at her. She heard her voice as if Danica was right beside her.

"You must step away from the fields and forests, from the voices and tears, Marina," she said. "I wave you a farewell. You must slip back into the skin of yourself. And I go on. I will see you when you are ready. But not too soon. That place you have in the country, spend time there. Take a new lover. This is your great work. You have added a thread to the great tapestry of art. This is what they will write about. So rest now. Be happy. You're not getting any younger. And believe me, you are dead a long time."

Marina didn't want it to end. She wanted to stay in this place. She didn't want to surrender to the wild wind of life. But it was time.

She dropped her head and for a moment pure grief struck through her. She must let it go, this room, this story, this work. It was over. She must relinquish this atrium where she had lived from winter until almost summer. She must give up the faces that had shown her a mystery that had no explanation. But how to stand? How to rise and meet this room?

She felt her legs trembling. Would she stumble? She was the sadhu walking from the cave. She lifted her head and opened her eyes. She summoned the strength in her legs and back. She felt the floor beneath her feet. She breathed in once and then again. A rush of cold burned through her.

Then she was standing. Her arms were outstretched. She felt the welcome of the crowd swelling inside her. Cameras were flashing. Applause was rising up into the atrium. It was pure cacophony, a study in simple, unbridled delight.

Klaus was beside her. Davide too. Francesca. Marco. Dieter. Everyone was clapping, crying, and cheering. The square had become a great circle of people. They were calling her name. They were calling to her. She was burning with return. She was inbound, flying home, white with light, bright, bright, brighter. She was laughing and crying and every face she looked into was doing the same.

49

AND SO WE COME TO the part that might break your heart. Certainly, I cannot bear such moments, because there are days beyond this even I cannot see, and they are not always good or easy days. Yet this is also art. The things that sear a heart. Make of it what you will, and hold on to it, as the days beyond appear and there is no turning back. A human life is short and yet filled with moments of wonder and convergence.

Lydia Fiorentino is seated in a wheelchair by the window. Her hair is drawn up away from her face. She is wearing a white kimono embroidered with gold butterflies. The room is warm and quiet. She is staring out to the silvered evening sea. The hue of sunset is beginning to mark the sky from west to east.

"I'm here," Levin said as he sat down beside her. He took her hand.

"Hello, my darling," he said. "I'm here. It's Arky."

She blinked.

"Lydia. Sweetheart. I'm so sorry. I didn't understand. I've been in a sort of hell."

She continued to stare at the sea and her hand was limp in his, her skin cool.

"I have missed you so much. I want you to know I do understand. You were right. I have no way to take care of you. I don't have a part of me that can do it. But I want to try. It isn't home without you. It isn't my life without you. There is no one but you who matters to me."

She gave no indication of hearing or seeing him.

"This is our moment. One of us needs care. Both of us need care. I'm here. I'm not ready. But there isn't time to be ready."

Her face was the face of night. Tranquil, vivid, startlingly empty. Her gaze was unfocused. Carefully, he angled her chair to face him.

In this fragile world there is so much to despair of. When certainty can be so frightening, uncertainty can be a form of protest, a sort of passive resistance. Levin gazed into her face. In that moment she was the whole world and all women and one woman and his wife, and he was her husband and all men and one man in the whole world.

There was the murmur of the facility about them. The distant breath of waves. And her face was as pale as moonlight. But he had come.

Levin did not know who he would become with Lydia to care for. There were questions that terrified his sense of order. His deepest sense of how life should be lived. *Ought* to be lived. But *should* and *ought* were words for certainty. What words belonged to uncertainty? Today, he thought. Today is uncertain. Now. Now required something. I feel . . . I feel could be the most uncertain of beginnings. It was what happened when he waited for an arpeggio, a melody . . . as if all creative ideas were simply feelings waiting to be plucked from some flowering sky. He understood with vivid clarity that the best ideas came from a place with a sign on the door saying I don't know.

I don't know . . . that's what made things happen. His thoughts abhorred a vacuum but his heart responded to the blank canvas. Every song, every painting, every book, every idea that changed the world—all these things came from the unknowable and beautiful void.

And then, as if a conductor had indicated the beginning of a symphony, Lydia shifted her eyes and gazed back at him. She continued to hold his gaze and now there was intensity in her eyes as if she was reaching out, pulling herself up, drawing herself in. Perhaps it was a trick of electricity running through her brain. But he would take it.

IN GRATITUDE

TO MARINA ABRAMOVIĆ, TO WHOM this book is dedicated. Thank you for your remarkable life and for your trust in allowing me to represent you in fiction.

To David Walsh, for so generously providing me with a studio at the Museum of Old and New Art (MONA) in Tasmania.

To Marco Anelli and Davide Balliano, who also agreed to be represented in fiction.

To Sean Kelly of the Sean Kelly Gallery.

To Guiliano Argenziano for endless support and kindness.

To my father, Kevin; my mother, Dawn; my sister, Melinda; and my many friends who consider art and literature to be of such vital intent. In particular: Caroline Lawrence, Harrison Young, Delia Nichols, Genevieve de Couvreur, Barbie Kjar, Natasha Cica, Brigita Ozolins, Christine Neely, Katherine Scholes, Roger Scholes, Caroline Flood, Mary Dwyer, Amy Currant, Brett Torossi, Cath Maddox, Jane Armstrong, Ross Honeywill, Greer Honeywill, Peter Adams, and Tania Price.

To Simon Kenway, Cameron Robbins, Felice Arena.

To Mary Lijnzaad and John Kaldor.

Also Beth Gutcheon, Martine Gerard, Milton and Denyse Kapelus, Hugh and Elisabeth Hough, Hank Stewart, Jimmy Stone, and Fernando Koatz.

In loving memory of Wendy Weil, Neil Lawrence, and Mark Clemens.

To Gaby Naher, Jane Palfreyman, and Elisabeth Scharlatt.

To the wonderful teams at Allen & Unwin in Australia and Alqonquin in the United States.

To Madonna Duffy and Christin Rohr.

To Varuna and the Eleanor Dark Foundation.

To Danielle Wood, Liz Caswell, and Kate Richards.

To everyone who deliberately or accidentally offered enthusiasm at just the right time.

And most importantly, to my children Alex, Byron, and Belle—three more artists for the world.

AUTHOR'S NOTE

THIS BOOK IS A STRANGE hybrid of fact and fiction. All of the characters are completely fictional with several notable exceptions.

Ms. Marina Abramović gave me permission to include her as herself. I have drawn extensively from interviews and performances given in the years leading up to her 2010 performance at MoMA. This does not mean that the thoughts I have attributed to the character of Marina Abramović at any time in this book are a true reflection of any event in history, or how the real Marina Abramović thinks or feels. That is the risk the novelist takes, bringing to life what we can only imagine. In allowing me complete creative freedom, Ms. Abramović again demonstrated her unremitting courage.

Also, with permission, the photographer Marco Anelli appears as himself as does Ms. Abramović's assistant, Davide Balliano. Any thoughts or acts attributed to either of these people are completely fictional. Also referenced is Klaus Biesenbach, the curator of *The Artist Is Present* and director of MoMA.

The character Carlos is based on Paco Blancas who sat with Marina twenty-one times.

I am indebted to James Westcott for his biography *The Life and Death of Marina Abramović*. Also to Chrissy Isles, Klaus

Biesenbach, Sean Kelly, and other curators, art historians, and commentators who have contributed to the review and analysis of Ms. Abramović's work.

The event that was *The Artist Is Present and Retrospective* at MoMA took place from March 9 to May 31, 2010. Fifteen hundred and fifty-four people sat with Ms. Abramović over 736 hours, and more than 850,000 people observed from the sidelines. Marco Anelli's book *Portraits in the Presence of Marina Abramović* is a complete record of all those who sat.

This novel is in part a gift to them all.

Further reading:

MoMA, *Marina Abramović: The Artist Is Present*
Marco Anelli, *Portraits in the Presence of Marina*
Thomas McEvilley, *Art, Love, Friendship: Marina Abramović and Ulay Together & Apart*
James Westcott, *When Marina Abramović Dies*
Marina Abramović, *The Bibliography*
Kristine Stiles, Klaus Biesenbach, Chrissie Iles, *Marina Abramović*
Marina Abramović, *Walk Through Walls*

QUESTIONS FOR DISCUSSION

1. *The Museum of Modern Love* is inspired by Marina Abramović's performance piece *The Artist Is Present*. How has reading the novel influenced your ideas about art—and in particular performance art?

2. Jane Miller is drawn to return again and again through her precious days in New York to the Museum of Modern Art (MoMA). She finds it helps her process her grief. How has grief affected your life?

3. The novel is a hybrid of fact and fiction. Discuss how the story moves between the real and the imagined.

4. We meet Arky Levin at a dark hour of his marriage. How has he contributed to the situation in which he finds himself?

5. What do you think Lydia's motivations are in distancing herself from Arky? What would you do in her shoes?

6. All the characters in the novel are affected by *The Artist Is Present*. What impact do you think art can have on individuals and on society as a whole?

7. Has the book encouraged or inspired you to look more deeply into the work of Marina Abramović? What have you discovered?

8. The presence of Danica Abramović presides, ghost-like, over the event at MoMA. Discuss Marina's relationship with her mother and how Danica's mothering affected Marina. How does your mother still have a presence in your life? How may she have influenced choices you have made?

9. The book is also a study in commitment—commitment to marriage, to family, and to love but also to creativity. Discuss commitments you have made (or would like to make) to living your life as fully as you can. Do you set aside time for creative pursuits or other hobbies? Have you done so even when there are conflicting pressures?

10. Eye contact is a normal part of life, but extended eye contact—*the gaze*—is intimate and revealing. Try it with a friend or loved one. See what happens. Share your experience.

11. Have you discovered other Australian writers?

HEATHER ROSE was born in Australia in 1964. Her novels have been shortlisted or have won awards for literary fiction, crime fiction, and children's fantasy. In 2017, *The Museum of Modern Love*, her seventh novel, won the Christina Stead Prize and the Stella Prize. It is her first novel for adults to be published in the United States. Heather lives by the sea on the island of Tasmania.